I0819008

THE MONUMENTS OF PARIS

ALSO BY VIOLAINE HUISMAN

The Book of Mother

THE MONUMENTS OF PARIS

A Novel

Violaine Huisman

PENGUIN PRESS
NEW YORK
2026

PENGUIN PRESS
An imprint of Penguin Random House LLC
1745 Broadway, New York, NY 10019
penguinrandomhouse.com

Image on page 122 courtesy of the author.

Designed by Amanda Dewey

LIBRARY OF CONGRESS CATALOGING-IN-PUBLICATION DATA
Names: Huisman, Violaine, 1979– author
Title: The monuments of Paris : a novel / Violaine Huisman.
Other titles: Monuments de Paris. English
Description: New York : Penguin Press, 2026. | "A version of this work previously appeared in French under the title Les monuments de Paris"—Title page verso.
Identifiers: LCCN 2025037578 (print) | LCCN 2025037579 (ebook) | ISBN 9780593833766 hardcover | ISBN 9780593833773 ebook
Subjects: LCSH: Paris (France)—Fiction | LCGFT: Fiction | Novels
Classification: LCC PQ2708.U37 M6613 2026 (print) | LCC PQ2708.U37 (ebook)
LC record available at https://lccn.loc.gov/2025037578
LC ebook record available at https://lccn.loc.gov/2025037579

Originally published in French, as *Les monuments de Paris*, by Editions Gallimard, Paris.

Printed in the United States of America
1st Printing

The authorized representative in the EU for product safety and compliance is Penguin Random House Ireland, Morrison Chambers, 32 Nassau Street, Dublin D02 YH68, Ireland, https://eu-contact.penguin.ie.

For the girls

THE MONUMENTS OF PARIS

I

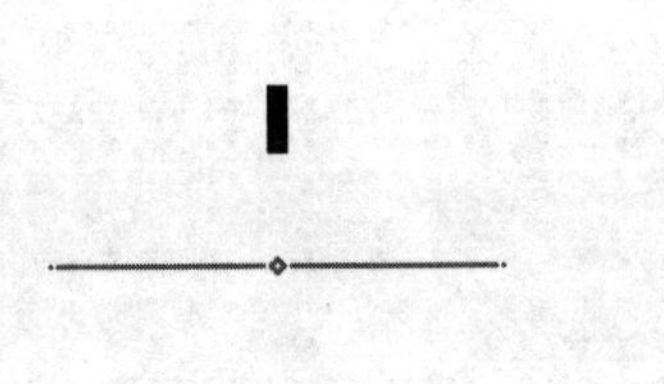

To see you collapsed in front of the TV in the middle of the afternoon breaks my heart. I mute the sound. Silence. The glow of the screen colors the air as if the light has filtered through a chapel's stained glass. Late afternoon sun from the window to your left forms a halo around your white hair. On the shelves behind you, a vast expanse of brown leather-bound books, gilt titles shimmering on their spines. I push your wheelchair aside to clear a path to you. I sit on an ottoman beside your mechanized recliner and take your hand. You raise my wrist to your lips, cover my arm in kisses. "How sweet of you, my beloved darling, to visit your decrepit old father. Your ancient papa, a poor old fool." "Hush, come now." I smooth back your hair. I brush away crumbs from your unevenly shaven cheeks. I lower my surgical mask to kiss your neck. I hold back tears. How I will miss your scent. Now the room smells of pharmaceuticals and piss. You welcome my embrace with a kind of calm acceptance that the Greeks might have called *ataraxia*—a word you taught me.

I moved back to France to be near you as you neared death. You often lamented the distance between us over the two decades I spent in America. We talked regularly, you called me late at night, until you stopped being able to use the phone. You still have your beautiful head of hair, and your temples still carry the smell of the little round plastic brushes you used to smooth it. You bought them in elegant old-fashioned pharmacies, along with your signature bottle of Schoum, a lime-green digestive tonic I never saw anyone else drink; extra-strong Ricqlès peppermint spray; eau de cologne Impériale; and an array of other novelties that you simply couldn't live without. These scents permeated your skin; your scarves and overcoats; the dashing suits you used to wear, linen or cashmere, dark gray, navy, or camel, with Dior ties and matching pocket squares. Now the suits are stored away—forever, most likely, but I prefer to think that they are waiting for you, as I so often did.

You fall asleep mid-sentence. I enjoy watching you at rest. The way you hold your head remains as dignified as ever, I decide, despite the stains on your sweater, the diaper protruding a little from your sweatpants. You keep your legs crossed as you did in your reading chair, in your office, a gentleman's pose, but now there are elastic bands around your bony shins, your enormous, bandaged feet stick out. Your feet are covered in scabs, sores, and cuts that won't heal, won't ever heal again. Your left foot looks like a Cubist sculpture underneath its dressing, your toes crooked, the big one entirely black. That monstrous toe was already terrifying to me as a child—a nail the size of a baby tooth clinging to its flesh.

As I hold your hand, I couldn't care less that you remember nothing—not my age, not my children, not my mother's suicide. The war is pretty much all you remember, so when you resurface from sleep, I ask you one more time to tell me about the Nazi invasion, the exodus, your family's destitution under Vichy. From your recliner or your sick bed, you bring me, again and again, aboard the *Massilia* in June 1940. I follow you each time onto the deck as though it were a stage. And at the conclusion of each performance, I hear, in your rapid heartbeat, the audience applauding—a protracted curtain call, a refusal to let the drama end. May it never end.

My father was a man of another generation, one might have said to excuse his misogyny or his pedantry, a man whose success supposedly justified his arrogance, whose affability could turn suddenly to rage, whose excessive, baroque, and unbridled displays of affection betrayed his eccentricity or explained, in part, the devotion he inspired in spite of his impossible temper. I was his baby girl—"Number eight" was how he referred to me in public. In private, he called me "Little angel." In addition to me and my sister, Elsa, two years my elder, my father had six other children, from three different women, spread over thirty years.

In the spring of 2020, I told my daughters, who had been in "remote school" for months, that we would be moving to France to be near their ancient grandfather. George and Sissi were born in New York and thought of English as their mother tongue. They called my father "Doggy," a nickname passed down across generations, its origin obscure, and which they hadn't questioned until their formerly commanding Doggy found himself diminished, dependent, and so the term of endearment became disturbing, shameful. It didn't help that my father and his wife also owned a very barky and incontinent Yorkshire. Over four decades of marriage, they had owned a series of Yorkies, each impossible to tell apart from the next. They had no children, but they always had a dog, who Doggy called his dog-child.

"And why is Doggy's dog named *Loup*?" Sissi asked me, as she tried to condone my father's odd nickname. Good question, my beloved darling. We must have some kind of compulsion to mix up names and species in our family. I recognize in my little girl's puzzled look the confusion I felt as a child when trying to figure out our family tree and my place in it, to separate out myth from reality in our genealogy. I, too, still struggle to understand, and I keep myself from telling her. "Sissi, *mon amour*," I reply, "didn't you name your bunny rabbit *Wawa*, like a puppy's bark in French? Well then."

A nurse from the French welfare system comes several times a day to change your dressings. Your wife wants to keep you home, a decision for which we, your children, are grateful. Another private nurse helps you travel from your bed to the living room in a wheelchair at mealtimes or when you have visitors. You thank her with pompous courtesy, then implore us to fire her. What in the world does this woman want from you? You beg to be left in peace. Why can't she let you enjoy your daughter's visit? You break down in tears of rage and humiliation. What is this talk of changing you? Have we all lost our minds? You insist that you and I must dine out, that you will take me to a restaurant. I try to mollify you. Instead of stating the obvious fact that you're in no condition to leave the house, I remind you that public spaces are closed until further notice. You have always preferred eating out. At lunch and dinner, on vacation, and in Paris. Soon, your wife will bring you a tray with a bland meal that I will help you ingest in child-sized bites. This role reversal reverses time, past and future collide, interpenetrate, dissolve.

My girls love hearing stories about you. Fanciful adventures where Doggy goes on epic quests—such as shopping for dinner, skipping the customary restaurant. We call this story "Doggy Goes to Market." And here we have Doggy on his way to the bakery. (You are always already old in these stories, but charmingly so, without shit or suffering.) Doggy has a chair waiting for him by the shop entrance—*his* chair, Monsieur Huisman's chair. Doggy sits, cane in hand, and greets Madame the Baker, whom he has known for a very long time—yes, a *very* long time, longer than his little angel has been alive! "*Bonjour madame*, *bonjour mesdemoiselles*, how are you this morning?" says Doggy to the young ladies who work there, a twinkle in his eye, before calling out his order from his seat: "My dear lady, I should like, if you please, six croissants, eight pains au chocolate, and, let us see, four raisin rolls, and give me"—here, I tap on his shoulder. "Papa, slow down, who's this all for?" "Well, everyone!" "Everyone who? There are only three of us: Elsa, your wife, and me. With your diabetes, you can't have any of this. Nobody's going to eat it all!" "Of course we will, everybody will, these are exceptional *viennoiseries*! Where was I? Oh, I see your *pâtisseries* look especially fine today. Let me get this tart here"—he points with his cane—"and what is it, may I ask? Apricots! It looks like it's encrusted with emeralds. Ah, pistachios! Marvelous! And that superb Black Forest cake, did your husband make it? Congratulate him for me. What a fine fellow he is, and so talented. And a sample of éclairs, yes two, no three, of each, yes, chocolate and coffee, and a box of your fabulous sugar cookies, world famous really, and . . ." (What do you think, girls? Do you think he's ordered enough? No, you're right, it's never enough for Doggy.) "Papa, this is really too much! We're never going to eat it all, please stop!" (Do you think he listens? Of course not.) When we finally leave the shop, I'm balancing six boxes of cakes, one on top of the other, four bags of pastries are dangling from my wrist, and I have three baguettes wedged under my arm. Next stop: the butcher! (Can you guess what happens there? It is never enough . . .)

When we arrived in France, I asked the girls if they wanted to visit Doggy with me. "Oh yes," they'd replied, "we'd love to!" I thought they laid it on a little thick. On our last visit, when the pandemic was still a distant nightmare, my father had asked George ten times who she was. "You're asking me again? I've told you, lots of times! I'm George! George! Your granddaughter!" Doggy had burst into laughter. "Of course, my beautiful George. I'd be just as indignant if I were you. How awful to have to put up with such a senile old fool." (You'd raised her wrist to your lips, covered her arm in kisses.) "Little angel!" (*Little* little angel.) "My, my, growing old is no fun . . ." The three of us had laughed it off, embraced. I'd taken my beloved father's hand in mine, his knotty, bluish hand, his fingernails yellow and striated like dandelions before they go to seed. "It's okay, Papa, you're allowed to forget a few things after a lifetime of remembering so much."

"Maman," George had said with great seriousness, sensing my doubt. "I swear I'm happy to see Doggy. Even if he has no idea who I am."

Through me, George inherited my father's eyes: large, obsidian, perpetually on the verge of tears, whether of joy or sadness, always registering the emotional weather. Whenever they were together, I watched my father marvel at George's face—which is easy to mistake for mine at her age—and as I watched George consider his withered face in turn, the scene would organize itself into a kind of painterly composition, a relay of gazes that transcended time. And in such moments, my father's sickroom was transformed, however briefly, into a sanctuary, a place where love or care might find expression beyond words.

When awake and lucid, you talk ceaselessly about your past—a past that precedes me. You stroll through a version of Paris I know only through your eyes. You're not making conversation; you're delivering a monologue, except when you suddenly call on me to supply a word or name that escapes you. I must help you recover it in order to keep you going. "Not *watertight*, but you know—*impermeable* is not it, Christ—*hermetic*, that's it, yes! The stem of a fruit—I mean the technical term—a *peduncle*!" Phalanstery, paleontologist, rodomontade. You embellish reality with abandon, but your vocabulary, your ornate lexicon, will tolerate no approximation. Your intimate cartography of the city has its unique set of references, a network of associations, which only your immediate family can follow or repair. "Come on, you know, Place de la Madeleine, the Art Deco restaurant, lobster salad . . . Yes: Lucas Carton! That's it." Helping you find the missing word has been one of my favorite games since childhood. You still speak with authority, in professorial tones: You are perpetually giving a lecture in a grand hall of the Sorbonne—even now, from a mechanical bed, facing death. You recite poems, soliloquies, passages from political speeches. A motet of names issues from your mouth, names of old scholars, long-forgotten luminaires and statesmen, for whom so many Parisian streets were named. Yes, streets, not people, are summoned for me by this litany of names: In the portrait gallery your reminiscence conjures, I see—instead of faces—the famous white and blue plaques that mark the street corners, the intersections, of our respective youths.

My father had lived his entire life within a two-mile radius of the Eiffel Tower. As a young boy, he had grown up in the Élysée Palace, where his father had served as secretary of state under Paul Doumer. And *Paul Doumer* became the name of an avenue in the sixteenth arrondissement that originated Place du Trocadéro, or more precisely by the Palais de Chaillot, whose construction my father's father had later overseen. On the opposite corner was the Carette tearoom, between Avenue Kléber and Avenue Poincaré: "Raymond Poincaré," said my father, "not to be confused with his cousin Henri Poincaré—eminent mathematician, member of the Academy of Sciences and the Académie française, author of *Science and Hypothesis*, greatly admired by Albert Einstein, etc. etc.—also a member of the Académie française, president of France from 1913 to 1920, three times prime minister, whose alliance with Russia made him rather unpopular, he was decried as a bit of a warmonger—*Si vis pacem, para bellum!*—and he gave that notorious speech: A diminished France, a something France, wait, how did it go again? A diminished France, a France exposed, something something, would no longer be France! To which Clemenceau replied: War is too important to be left to generals! Anyway, the First World War, which everyone thought would be over within weeks, lasted four years, more than a million and a half dead, a quarter of the men of that generation slaughtered, Papa's generation. But Papa had been spared because he served in the air force—which wasn't yet called the air force, but *aeronautics*—not as a pilot, he served on the ground, as a technical observer. That's why he refused the medal of the Legion of Honor: He protested that he didn't deserve it. What a fool!"

When I was a child, my father always stopped at Carette on our way out of town for the weekend or holidays, so we would have snacks to eat on the train. And on such train trips, eating our sandwiches, I would unfailingly receive these monologues—at once mesmerizing and utterly baffling—his personal history mixing with that of the Republic. Fast-food chains had not yet penetrated the French market, and regardless, Carette, my father believed, was the only place in the world to offer acceptable sandwiches, finger-sized rectangles of crustless white bread individually wrapped in wax paper stamped with the store's iconic logo. And so for me, the names of my father's heroes, Paul Doumer among them, are forever associated with Carette, with the flavor of the Parisian sandwich par excellence: the *jambon-beurre.* Not just any buttered baguette with ham, this was a sandwich with pretensions to an *entremet.* While I ate, I would hear my father's thunderous voice, somewhere between the Petit Palais and the Pont Alexandre III, braiding personal anecdotes with official history. This was an old habit. Apparently, my father, at the age of three, had walked into his father's office in the Élysée Palace and asked out of the blue: "Say, Papa, what news from Pierre Laval?"

A family favorite, this story brought my father great joy; he retold it constantly. Sure, it was amusing to imagine a precocious toddler asking for news of a politician. But as my father repeated the story over the years, a different meaning surfaced: a child compelled to question his father on state affairs to get his attention. I could relate to that. But what was perhaps most curious to me about this anecdote was the name *Pierre Laval*. He who had no street named after him, wasn't he the monster who had sold Jewish women and children to the Nazis? Wasn't he the one, who, together with Maréchal Pétain, had organized the Vélodrome d'Hiver roundup? Weren't we—my father, my grandfather, myself—Jewish?

"But Pierre Laval started out on the Left!" my father would explain. "Like Benito Mussolini, for that matter," he'd add, nibbling his sandwich. "The ham isn't bad, but the best one is the egg salad, I don't know how they make that mayonnaise, it's incredible. As for Laval, it never occurred to any of us that he would become such a dirtbag! One can never overestimate French anti-Semitism though . . . Papa used to say about one of his army buddies from the Great War that he had forty centuries of Christian hypocrisy and bourgeois avarice buoying him." I would ask again: "But aren't we ourselves Jewish?" "Of course we're Jewish. Obviously, but that's beside the point. The question is who's asking! And Pierre Laval was absolutely on the Left. He'd taken up almost every role in government: Minister of Justice, of Labor. That's when he passed the social welfare law—he was absolutely a Leftist! He later became Minister of Foreign Affairs, of Economy. And then, voilà, his deflationary policies proved catastrophic, it was a disastrous decision in the midst of a recession, the stock market crashed, etc., the Front Populaire was elected, to my father's delight . . . So, isn't the egg salad marvelous? I usually hate crudités, but I must say this little cucumber sandwich is divine."

In the presidential palace, you launched paper planes out of the tall windows overlooking the gardens, from where you watched the changing of the National Guard. Madame Paul Doumer, who had lost all four sons in the war, pampered you as one of her own and organized a surprise party for your third birthday. A few days after that magical celebration, you dropped a letter opener—the one you used to cut a fly into your pajama bottoms—from the balcony of your bedroom window. The dagger fell a hair's breadth from the president's head as he passed below. And then you were caught peeing on the Doumers' hydrangea hedge. Your father gave you a real earful! Almost a century later, you still feel responsible for having unintentionally foreshadowed the assassination of Paul Doumer. You grew up in a literal palace, surrounded by statesmen, while your grandmother—on your father's side—liked to remind you that she was descended from mere common folk. "We common folk," her sentences often began. Nonsense! you would roar. We were almost royalty! Then came the war. Then your father lost your home, his social standing, his livelihood, his titles, your nationality, and ultimately even your name. You all lived in hiding, under an alias, to escape the roundups. That you are not about to forget. Even as I come in and out of focus, even as fact and fiction blur, the memory of that collapse remains unalterable, the ultimate raft of the real.

My father was among the last living witnesses to this collective tragedy. His family survived, but the persecution he had suffered as a child had, of course, shaped him. It was often evoked, rightly or wrongly, as justification for his extravagance, as if his past could explain or excuse his present. But soon enough, his stories—and stories like his—would only remain through artifacts and archives. The indignities he was subjected to under the Vichy regime would no longer live on in his feverish, animated, if contradictory accounts; they would be fixed, but breathless, bloodless. And so as long as my father lived, I wanted to hear him describe it again, this historical cataclysm—describe it as he lived it, as he relived it in the telling, in the unverifiable chaos of intimate experience, a truth beyond mere facts.

Calamity taught you the need to appreciate life and enjoy it to the fullest, to excess. You abhorred moderation even more than you detested waste. One must choose the lesser of two evils, you often said. You burned through money. Stale cakes were always being thrown away. A mixture of largesse and hoarding: One had to be very careful when opening the refrigerator door, an avalanche of expired yogurts and rotten leftovers crashing down behind a month-old cup of coffee. You sought quantity in all things. In the most prosperous years of your career, you boasted that your entry in the *Who's Who* was longer than General de Gaulle's. When people expressed amazement at your array of medals, you answered, with only a touch of self-mockery, that while you might not have deserved them all, at least you had asked for them. "Most people wait to be given an award," you explained. "That's ridiculous! Those who don't ask don't get—or get very little. I took great pains to ask, and in exchange I got quite a few of the things I asked for." Your children—and my children—wondered about the red rosette on your jacket lapel. "What does it get you?" we asked. "Nothing, my poor little darling. Absolutely nothing. Except flatter the vanity of old men like me. Or rather, it does do one thing: Once you attain the rank of Grand Officer of the Legion of Honor—a red rosette on a gold and silver plate—no common police officer can summon you to the station; the commissioner of police himself must come and arrest you at home." I was unclear how such a privilege might be useful for you. One can't get arrested for gluttony or compulsive shopping. Whereas my mother did get stopped for speeding, for shoplifting. Maman had no medals and called yours baubles. She swore like a sailor and blithely insulted the cops who wrote her up. But you were an upstanding citizen; you spoke to officers of the law the same way you spoke to shopkeepers, with exemplary courtesy that bore witness to the perfect education you had received, despite your one grand misfortune: that you were a Jewish boy in 1940.

At restaurants, when you couldn't finish the twelve dishes you'd ordered, you knocked back a healthy swig of Hepatoum straight from the bottle and asked for the leftovers to be boxed up to go. You howled at the suggestion of skipping dessert. One couldn't end a meal without at least a little chocolate! We were always the last to leave. Patrons could never be importuned in these palaces of fine dining, and there you lingered into the night, holding forth, holding court, addressing no one in particular. Overcome with boredom, my sister and I would start rolling breadcrumbs to flick across the table. You chuckled when one landed on your lap. "That's a very silly game," you'd say. If you asked us to cut it out, your voice carried so little conviction that Elsa took your recriminations for encouragement. She siphoned a little of the Château Margaux to add to her witch's brew in a crystal glass, along with sugar, salt, and mustard. "Try it, Papa!" "Oh là là, that's very naughty," you'd say distractedly as you went on analyzing the importance of play in human development, the symbolic castration in the diachrony of infantile experience described by eminent French psychoanalyst Françoise Dolto (who gave her name to a street in the thirteenth arrondissement). We knew we had at least another hour to kill when you moved on to the *Massilia*: the *Massilia* being the name of the ship your family had boarded in June 1940 and whose journey proved far more catastrophic than the *Titanic*'s, not least of all because no one had heard of it, no one ever spoke of it, and posterity had failed to maintain any record of it, except for the walls of every fancy restaurant in Paris, across which your voice seemed to echo for the rest of time. Elsa would grab me by the hand then and drag me downstairs to the phone booth by the bathroom stalls. She devised a game where I was to place random calls to strangers she found in the book, using additional volumes of the Yellow Pages as a footstool so I could reach the dial pad. You knew we were up to no good, but you couldn't have cared less. Doggy did not discipline.

Anecdotes of our prank calls enjoy pride of place among the tales and legends of Doggy. When I recount them to my girls, they squeal with excitement at imagining their beloved aunt being so naughty. Tata Elsa hasn't changed. Only the context has. Indeed, when Tata Elsa and I were their age, there were enclosed spaces for calling people known as phone booths; there were books listing the numbers of every person who owned a phone line, known as phone books, or *bottins* in French. Sébastien Bottin also has a street named after him in Paris—a narrow cul-de-sac near the Seine. Eventually, Rue Bottin becomes the Rue Gaston-Gallimard, for the founder of the prestigious eponymous publishing house. It was in that discrete town house at number 5 that I signed the contracts for my novels, including this one. "Little angel, Gallimard!" you cried when I shared the news. "Gallimard! How extraordinary! There's nothing more distinguished! It's Mount Olympus!" You wished you could have published novels at Gallimard, or that you'd been an editor there, or both, because you wished you could have done it all.

You were fifty when I was born. You were rich and famous, celebrated or loathed for your flamboyance, for your contradictions. You were somehow both a dandy and a serious intellectual; a libertine, you thought of yourself as a dedicated socialist; you considered yourself a dedicated family man (father of eight from four different mothers, thrice divorced, a relentless womanizer). To describe your profession, you coined the term *academic-businessman*, meaning you were both a philosophy professor and the owner of a flourishing chain of private schools, focusing on test prep, on shortcuts. Both an entrepreneur and a teacher, but also an author, an editor, a television producer. In my eyes, you were invincible, omnipotent, too big and too great. I would try to reach my arms around your belly—I stretched and stretched and tightened my grip—but I could never get my fingers to touch. You were fat with other stories from other households, other worlds—stories that preceded or excluded me.

Now, out of modesty, I pull down your sweater to cover your navel. It is a cashmere turtleneck, felted through many hot cycles in the wash. You have always been sensitive to cold, but today you complain of being chilled to the bone. "Aren't you freezing in that little camisole?" I would have called it a tank top, but I tell you I've been walking fast, I was in a hurry to get to you. (Your room is sweltering.) I can see life withdrawing down the veins in your arm, their ridges blue like the folds of the mask I set down on your bedside table, next to your dentures. I kiss your sunken cheeks, I slip my hands under your back to sit you up. I blow on your collarbones to warm you with my breath. You did that to me when I was little, as I snuggled into the pleats of your overcoat. The smell of your toothless mouth makes me a little ill. Your protruding ribs fill me with dread.

My father first married at nineteen to a girl his age, an orphan whose parents had not returned from camps four years before. Since my father was young and penniless, his parents advised him to wait until he was more established to start a family. He didn't listen. My father had completed his studies brilliantly and early and was just starting out as a literature professor before turning to philosophy. He supplemented his meager income by giving private lessons, first to a few students chosen from among the worst in his class and then, once his tutoring proved successful, to hordes of deadbeats whom he promised to help get their high school degree—a promise that he never failed to keep and that made him so legendary among the slouchers that the line to his top-floor walk-up on Rue d'Assas, with its wonderful view of the Luxembourg Gardens, extended down the street. In short order, my father and his young wife had four children one after the other; they named their offspring in alphabetical order: A for Arnaud, B for Bruno, C . . . Until my father had a fling with a secretary from the baccalaureate test prep school he'd opened in the meantime. "Just a little fling!" my father comforted his wife. But D was the product of this indiscretion. (No, I'm wrong. I just checked the chronology. E was born before D; the alphabet of my father's affairs is difficult to track. In any case, my father would ultimately drop the alphabet and move on to numbers.)

He explained (even though I certainly didn't ask) that he and his first wife, both virgins on their wedding night, had agreed to seek elsewhere the sexual pleasure they were unable to find with each other. A certain openness was in the air. One generation earlier, Léon Blum, leader of the Front Populaire, had published a popular book called *Marriage*, an indispensable addition to any serious personal library at the time. Nearly forty years before women won the right to vote, Blum had championed not only gender equality of a sort, but also the importance of waiving the bride's virginity requirement. My father, like his father before him, was sympathetic.

Women must be allowed desire, be emboldened to seek pleasure, be given the right to act and not just submit. Girls must have the same autonomy over their bodies as boys and learn to enjoy sex every bit as much. At least in theory—in practice, my father preferred his women, if not submissive, then at the very least accommodating. His supposed feminism did not extend to a recognition of equality; it was less about equal rights and more about privileges granted to the weak. A bountiful lord, he was benevolent enough to recognize a woman's right to sexual pleasure. He did indeed encourage his wife to fool around. At a loss as to how to go about it, she sought out one of her husband's best friends. Papa didn't hold it against her. On the contrary, he insisted on hearing every last detail: "I was a good sport about it!" I stop him when he starts telling me about the mistresses he shared with my mother, their propensity for cross-dressing, S&M, threesomes. It doesn't occur to him that his stories are inappropriate (to put it mildly). He forgets that I am his daughter, that he is my father; his speech is addressed to an imaginary interlocutor whose only role is to listen.

After divorcing his first wife, Papa remarried in church to please the mother of the second. Number six was born. In the meantime, his career had taken off. He was full of new ideas and wasted no time turning them into successful enterprises. He had founded a chain of public relations schools in the early 1960s, a pioneer in the emergent sector. His schools trained the press agents of the future, male and female alike, at a time when women were just entering the workforce. He sold his Rolls during the students' uprising of May 1968, tired of finding his tires slashed and windows broken. His second marriage didn't last. At the height of his success, he met my mother and promptly fathered two more girls: Elsa and me.

Catherine, our *maman*, was almost twenty years younger than Papa and knew nothing about anything that mattered to him. She was ignorant and déclassé, but her beauty made up for her meager education a hundredfold—no, a thousandfold! She was breathtakingly beautiful and as extreme in her appetites as he was. The stunning Catherine was a perfect match for his extravagance: "A real whack job!" said Papa in jest, only it was true.

The medical establishment gave our mother's eccentricity a decidedly less playful diagnosis. Maman was clinically bipolar. Maman was mentally ill. And watching her struggle to keep up with Papa set Elsa and me apart from our other siblings: Our childhood was mainly articulated around our mother's breakdowns. She was hospitalized for all of my sixth-grade school year, very much against her will, and very much against her daughters'. Her breakdown had turned into a psychotic episode, in which she spiraled into a depression so deep that she nearly killed herself and her two beloved girls. After that, she remained perpetually at risk of descending into madness, of being taken away. And so protecting Maman from excess—excess of feeling, excessive behavior, excessive demands—became our most urgent concern. Meaning that Papa's dangerous influence on Maman became for us a matter of life or death.

Papa married a fourth time after Maman asked for a divorce. She was the one who slammed the door on him, he explained, after he had asked her to tolerate "a meaningless little fling." In our mother's retelling, that affair had been even more humiliating than the last, and she was through, she couldn't take it anymore, she had to save herself. Maman had also attempted to remarry after her separation with Papa, a disastrous episode that ended with her yearlong institutionalization. By the time she got out of the mental hospital, I was eleven and Elsa was thirteen. Papa had set up a new life—is it useful to mention here that Papa's fourth wife was initially a friend of our mother's?—and Maman, heavily medicated, alarmingly sedated, attempted to rebuild hers as a single stay-at-home mom. Papa had remained close to all the women in his life, all of his exes. That and the fact that Elsa and I were school-age children made it easy to justify his attachment to our mother despite their separation. It was harder to explain why he stopped by our apartment every single night. Our parents didn't have a shared custody arrangement. Papa took us in on random weekends, for winter and summer vacation. The rest of the year he saw us as he pleased, meaning daily. Our home was his, too, not only because he paid for it but also because he showed every sign of belonging in it. We were his other home. Maman was his other wife, who, as his ex, could also lay claim to having held the title first. Our parents' relationship was ambiguous, to say the least. Judging by the passion with which they hurled insults at—or clung feverishly to—the other, their romance was hardly settled history. Only advanced old age, my father said, had allowed him to free himself from the cruel and unpredictable master that was his libido. He described his innumerable infidelities playfully, with only a dash of contrition. He seemed to feel that the intensity of his desire was sufficient justification for his exploits; how could he have suppressed such a need for conquest? Certainly his desire for Maman had never fully exhausted itself, and in spite of their separation, passion—and especially jealousy—continued to govern their relations. None of this was playful for her. My mother became a prisoner in the apartment he rented for us, financially and emotionally dependent on the father of her children, the man she loved despite herself.

As soon as I finished high school, as soon as I could leave home, I didn't just move out, I put an ocean between myself and my parents. I spent a summer in New York for an internship and then decided to stay. It was hard for Elsa. We were each other's anchor, our most solid base, along with an unsinkable barge of childhood friends. She understood that I needed to leave, she said, and in a way that she couldn't express out loud, I knew she was also relieved: I had always been more troubled, more confused. It was unclear what I was going to do with my life. What if she had to take care of me, too, into adulthood? Elsa excelled in school, she had studied law, and she was on track to build a successful career, which she did, with extraordinary success. I moved to New York at nineteen with no such grand plan when I found a job in a small independent press; I started earning a living at twenty, a modest living to be sure, even so. My exile allowed me to break free, to break away from my family history, its ghosts, and its untenable weight. (Or so I liked to think.)

After trying out different positions in publishing, I eventually transitioned to the performing arts and ended up organizing festivals and cultural events. I wrote my first novel while working freelance as a curator and translating authors I admired into French. I had the professional life I had dreamed of and a stable, loving family—"His name is Tom, Papa, remember? Of course you've met him, many times; you've taken us out to dinner on countless occasions. You went into raptures watching him change George's diaper when you visited us in New York for her birth. 'He can do that? How extraordinary! What an extraordinary man you have found, *ma chérie*!'"

You often berated me for not marrying him—"A lovely man! Charming and sweet and clearly madly in love with you!" you reminded me at every meal, including one night at dinner in a fine restaurant, where you solemnly offered him my hand. *He* hadn't asked for it, not out loud, not explicitly, not that night in any case. I looked at you aghast. You gave him your blessing, you declared emphatically, unprompted. Tom smiled politely and thanked you in his best French, which you asked me to translate. He told you that he would be thrilled to one day marry me. "But that is, of course, up to your daughter." You turned to me in shock. "My daughter!" you cried. "My daughter must be crazy! Come on, why would you refuse to marry such a wonderful, handsome, kind, and intelligent boy? So charming, so generous, and obviously madly in love with you!"

Well, Papa, I did get married. When I tell you at your bedside between nurse visits, you scowl: "You mean you didn't invite me to your wedding? That's not very nice, shunning your poor old father. I would have given a good speech!" There is no doubt about that. The one you gave at Elsa's wedding, bent over your cane—your last public speaking performance—set off gales of laughter among the assembly. Elsa and her wife's guests were stunned to hear this distinguished old man tell smutty jokes about his own daughter. But Tom and I had no wedding. I was married at Brooklyn Borough Hall, a few days before the lockdown. We figured it would be easier for us to move to France with a wedding certificate. And in fact it was: Without a whole stack of duly authenticated documents, we wouldn't have been able to come to you.

My husband, my children, and I spent the lockdown—what we would later call the "first lockdown," in spring 2020—in Upstate New York in a cabin that friends had lent us. My girls' school "holiday" in March eventually became "remote schooling" that lasted through June. I often thought of how you described the 1939–40 school year, which you spent in Brittany following your summer vacation, a period history books called the Phony War. You were not yet in mortal danger, but you were already living in fear. I spent our first week of lockdown making our borrowed cabin as functional as possible without being able to change its layout: There was a bathroom with a child-sized claw-foot tub off the kitchen—the kitchen that served as the study, the living room, the exercise room, the washroom, and the one communal room where I prepared meals, cleaned, and homeschooled the children before sending them to bathe. My professional identity had vanished as quickly as the virus had spread. Projects were cancelled one after the other, and the translation I had been hired to work on was delayed indefinitely, which was just as well, as it proved impossible to do anything but attend to housework.

Tom is a journalist. After filing his articles, he washed the dishes, checking Twitter on his phone. (He's a modern man who shares domestic chores—yes, I know, Papa, the very concept is alien to you.) Generous amounts of alcohol helped me sleep at night after wiping down the table. I didn't attempt to read. I put a pillow over my head to block out the blue light from Tom's iPhone. He would distractedly massage my neck with one hand while with the other he'd scroll, tracking in real time the end of the world.

Eight days after we moved into the cabin in the woods, I began to be plagued by the unspeakable idea that I should never have had children. Becoming a mother, building a traditional family, the whole thing was a travesty, a trap set by the patriarchy. I could have dedicated my life to other things, writing among them. Housework and child care were no longer inevitable plights of the female condition, I had simply made poor choices; I had lost sight of my deeper calling out of conventionalism, self-deception; I had only myself to blame for being so stupid and conformist; and worst of all, I had brought innocent children onto a dying planet. Suicide often occurred to me, but my mother had killed herself and I couldn't do that to my girls. I had brought them into the broken world and couldn't just leave them there as my mother had, but it was simply too hard. I would never make it. I was choking, COVID or no COVID, and no amount of oxygen would be enough to keep me alive if I couldn't find a way to escape for even a few minutes a day so as not to sink into madness. I spent weeks on end in this state, an incessant and toxic interior monologue itemizing reasons to despair, while I carried out my maternal duties, no one suspecting that I was a step away from breaking down or fleeing. Or maybe they did suspect: Once, in the middle of the night, I felt George, then seven, patting my body in the dark, confirming my presence.

At the end of our street, Store Road, the shop that had given the street its name was still open. The shelves were coated in dust. Next to a vacant lot and a trailer park, the store supplied the neighborhood with beer, soda, cigarettes, and lottery tickets. The region is famous for its rock cliffs, the Shawangunks. "Picture a cross between Fontainebleau and the Alps," I told you on the phone. "My husband loves climbing"—"Ah an alpinist!" you exclaimed. "Yes, kind of," I said. "But COVID has shut down the parks; even the mountains are inaccessible."

One day on a short afternoon walk with the girls, I came across an abandoned shipping container in a field next to the trailer park. I announced, insanely, that I was going to set up a room in it, a room of my own, that I'd move into it just for a few days, just to clear my head. The next morning, white flakes whirled in the air like dandelion seeds. Half a foot of snow fell that day. I gave up on my plan.

I scolded myself, I tried to calm myself, I told myself the reasonable things: The height of a pandemic isn't a time to review life choices, to make life changes. You can't just leave your family in the midst of a global crisis, I told myself over and over while I imagined disappearing into the forest, while I scanned the horizon for some way out.

"Pick up your feet, girls! Can't you see me trying to sweep? And how many times do I have to remind you to leave your muddy boots at the door?" I cleaned the floor three times a day with desperate zeal, judging by the clear water in the bucket as I hand-wrung the gray strings of the mop. Indeed, I took up mopping as a practice. It was the closest thing to writing I experienced in those days: committing myself with irrational fervor to a process, developing a ritual, a method—from the left-hand corner to the door on the right in horizontal sweeps, damp streaks tracing my progress. Yes, it resembled writing—applying myself to a grueling task the importance or necessity of which is mostly lost on others. The girls made me bouquets of daisies, pansies, and hellebores; we made herbariums, books of hours.

When I wasn't scrubbing the kitchen linoleum, I emailed the French consulate for instructions on what to do to move back to my native country. The information I received was incoherent, inconsistent, and contradicted by Reddit and what I learned from better-informed friends. Officially I was told that I would have to wait until the pandemic was over or less of an emergency; I'd have to wait until the offices reopened at some time yet to be determined; I'd have to wait for an unpredictable date in a future to which you might no longer belong. In June, I drove to the French Consulate in Washington, DC, and begged and cried at the gate until somebody helped me.

We returned briefly to Brooklyn to box up our apartment as we prepared to rent it out. We told the girls to leave their toys: "You'll be happy to see them when we're back," I said, with no idea when that would be; the toys might well be relics from another life by the time they saw them again. I promised them that their aunt in France would give them lots of new ones. ("Elsa has taken over from you as gift-giver in chief, Papa!") Their clothes would no longer fit them by the time their new school began, and as it was now summer, all they needed were a few dresses and a couple pairs of pajamas. (The school would be bilingual because my girls, though fluent in French, are English-speakers first and foremost; I've birthed two little Americans, with singsong accents and soggy *r*s.) We left for France with one suitcase each.

We moved to a village near Fontainebleau. The first time I tell you—and then every time I remind you—where we have relocated, your eyes widen from the depths of your mechanical bed. You prop yourself on one elbow, disheveled, your toothless mouth so dry you have trouble forming words. "But that's a provincial nowhere—that's a dump!" you exclaim. Yes, Papa, it's nowhere. We moved into a vacation home whose owners were willing to rent it on a yearly lease. I chose a place that had a school—a real school, not a "remote" one—that I felt met my girls' needs, and in any case, wherever we were, we'd all been grounded, all public life and space had disappeared, so why not favor the country?

From Fontainebleau, I take an outdated clunky regional train to see you, always empty at the times of my commute. Upholstered seats of threadbare green velvet and the pleated curtains of synthetic wool add to the sense of time travel. The clack of the wheels, the gentle rocking of the carriage, the unfurling countryside the color of raw tobacco—melancholy set in motion. You were a loving father after your fashion; I was, I am, a devoted daughter. I can't allow the imprint of your kisses to disappear. Even as a child I longed for the time—a time I also feared—when I would be grown and you would be old and we could speak openly: You would stop with your tirades and your sweeping arguments and your quotations and your witticisms and look me in the eye and tell me something true, something heartfelt and honest. Through the reflection of my face in the train window I see a forest bared of its leaves, a diorama of nature in mourning. I am suddenly surprised and frightened by the sight of my surgical mask. I do not have a surgeon's poise; I would never have the courage to sever myself from you. The blue of my mask merges with that of the sky. I see my own eyes reflected in the glass—obsidian orbs like yours, like my girls'.

Two years before the pandemic, a sore developed on your foot. You couldn't put weight on it. It grew difficult for you to get around. Once immobilized, your muscles atrophied and walking became a perilous and then an impossible exercise. You were hospitalized, first at the Georges Pompidou European Hospital, on the left bank of the Seine, across the bridge from your home. This marked the onset of the terminal phase of your illness.

That Christmas I'd come to Paris with Tom and the girls, whom their aunt had showered with presents. Before our flight back to Brooklyn, the Christmas gifts stuffed into two extra suitcases, I wanted to visit you one last time. We all went up to your hospital room. I showed the girls the great big boo-boo on your foot. They were very impressed. They hugged you affectionately. Your eyes shone brightly as you squeezed their plump little arms, dispensing little kisses down to their wrists. Tom offered to take them to the nearest playground to give us a moment alone, to give the girls some fresh air before the long journey. I was getting up to leave when Tom called and said not to panic. They were in the emergency room on the second floor. Only a few minutes after admiring the big bandage on your foot, George had broken her leg on the playground. With a plaster cast from the top of her thigh to her toes, her dressing was considerably more impressive than Doggy's.

Eventually, we made it back across the ocean, and you made it back across the Seine. (In France, home care is provided by the state—"What a great country this is," I kept saying with amazement, having grown used to the United States.) Until the pandemic, I continued to visit you as often as my publisher or my projects brought me to Paris, imagining each time it could be the last, the last time I would lift your dry hand to my lips, breathe in the scent of your hair.

I named my daughter George—after your father, her great-grandfather, our famous forebear who died twenty years before I was born. You were so instantly taken with my choice that the decision seemed preordained. It seemed there must have been some sort of ancestral injunction, that somehow, somewhere it had been written that I would become a mother and name my child George, no matter the child's gender. You expressed no surprise. You found it marvelous; you were moved, deeply moved; you approved completely. The truth is, it was partly your choice: You had given me and all your children, boys and girls alike, George as a middle name. Gender fluidity was not yet in fashion when my daughter was born, and even less so in France than in New York. I had often been told that the name was highly unusual for a girl, if not troubling. But you found it charming. Your radical permissiveness contrasted with your patriarchal pose. Yet in approving my choice, you were also giving me claim to the history we shared. You were allowing me to make it my own.

Elsa called me on FaceTime in the early months of the pandemic every time she went to visit you. You couldn't understand what you were looking at. "No, she's really there! Well, she's live. She can see you, too," Elsa tried to explain to you, pointing to the little rectangle in the upper right corner of the screen. You weren't so much amazed as perplexed. At ninety-one, age had carved deep furrows into your face that the sleek surface of the iPhone made all the more vivid. "Yes, it's me, Papa *chéri*!" I said, unsure I could convince you. I glanced at my girls beside me at the kitchen table; they were wearing headphones, busy with Zoom school, while you, Papa, still talked of sending telegrams. I measured the distance that separated you from my girls by the fact that you had never *touched* a screen.

The now antiquated telephone was our favored mode of conversation, our magic trick of connection, for decades. Your voice could reach me at any point night or day—and it often still does in dreams. I much preferred it when you called me, and the truth is, I was *terrified* of calling you: Interrupting your day meant running the risk of rejection. You always answered the phone immediately in a thundering voice filled with alarm—for only an emergency would warrant such a disturbance! In the seventies and eighties, you had a car phone, an unheard-of novelty at the time. You were the only person I knew to own one, and you made avid use of it, despite the crackling and frequent interruptions, especially in tunnels, which you entered shouting, "Cutting off! Tunnel! Tunnel!" (When I think of driving beneath the Pont de l'Alma, it's not Princess Di's death that comes to mind, but your ridiculous antics.) "Nothing bad has happened, Papa *chéri*," one had to explain immediately when one dared to call you at random. You always expected the worst, and the worst having occurred often enough in your life, you assumed any unexpected call might announce a fatal accident or the outbreak of war. But once I explained there was no catastrophe, that I was simply calling to check in, your priorities returned: "This is a very bad time!" you'd yell, your anger so sudden, bizarre, disproportionate, that it *almost* seemed like you were joking. My call might be blocking a more important one, or you might be in the middle of a meeting (but you always answered), or you simply weren't in the mood. You lost your temper the way some people blow their nose: messily, cartoonishly. You were the perfect embodiment of the French expression *soupe au lait*, literally "milk soup": "Imagine milk boiling over," I tell the girls, both to warn and comfort them. They find it very funny, picturing Doggy as a messy pot of boiled milk. I simply never got used to it. The minute you raised your voice, I was on the verge of tears, I was four again, I wanted to disappear, to never have been born. I learned early on that begging you to calm down only stoked your fury. Better to end the call as quickly as possible. Eventually, I knew, you'd call back with no memory of your anger. I would have liked to be your one exception, the one person you were always happy to hear from, your little angel at all times, but I had to wait for the right time to hear you declare your love. And so I waited.

I, too, answered my father's calls instantly, and on the rare occasions when I failed to respond immediately, Papa, who had missed the transition from answering machines to voicemail and still believed calls could be screened, left a message that began with a series of urgent injunctions to pick up: "Hello, hello, *petit ange*, it's Papa, it's your papa who loves you, pick up the phone please—damn, what are you doing?—my darling little angel, it's Papa trying to reach you, *allo*?" Then the message devolved into a stream of consciousness: He jumped from one topic to another, asked if I had enough to eat, proper clothes to wear, is my coat warm enough, did I need new shoes, one always needs more pretty shoes, offered to send me money for new ones, told me about his day, digressed into a historical anecdote, the Élysée, Pierre Laval, briefly recalled his initial reason for calling, it's urgent, but not too urgent, reminded me not to forget to call him back, and concluded with a litany of farewells: "I love you, bye-bye, *petit ange*, I love you, goodbye, *ma chérie*, I love you, I love you, Papa loves you, bye-bye, I love you, farewell."

He often called me in the middle of the night in France, knowing that it was six hours earlier on my side of the ocean. He was an incurable insomniac. I'd slip away from my own dinner guests to take his call. When I explained as I got up from the table that it was my father calling from Paris, I was naturally excused—it must have been an emergency for my father to call so late, for me to leave the table instantly to take it. No, nothing important, nothing bad. Papa would walk me through his busy week or the reshuffling of the government of the Third Republic; he would ask about the weather until his yawns began, indicating he was preparing to attempt sleep. But talking about the weather was no trivial matter: We discussed it with great earnestness. After all, what could be more pertinent to our presence in the world? It both measured the distance between us and briefly bridged it.

Yes, he always asked about my shoes, my clothes. Papa had always worried about my wardrobe, he loved playing dress up, he loved dressing me. Shopping, like eating in elegant restaurants, was one of my father's defining activities; shops and restaurants, not domestic interiors, were where we spent our time together. And as much as I disliked these shopping expeditions, I submitted with a smile. There was no limit to what he would buy me—or rather, there was a lower limit; no matter my protests, he would always purchase more. And more. I still own many of the outfits he gave me, outfits I dutifully wore to our lunches or dinners so he could trot out his favorite joke: "A man of taste must have given you that ravishing blouse!" As a child and even more so as a teenager, I wanted less, I wanted nothing. I pleaded: Please, nothing. Not even that adorable little dress that he pointed out in the window, insisting it would flatter me. I gave in, I always gave in, under the outraged look of the sales clerk: What kind of brat seems on the verge of tears because her father is so generous? But I didn't want that kind of generosity; I wanted his love to be immaterial, I wanted it to be pure. I wanted to prove to him how disinterested I was, to exist outside the web of transactional relations he wove around himself. But it was hopeless.

Pleasing him was the condition of his affection, so I strove to keep Papa happy, whatever the cost.

Maman had warned me often enough: "You'll never beat your father at his own game!" My father would stop seeing me if I didn't bend to his demands. I had reason to believe she was not wrong. Papa set a telling example with my older brother and sisters, who were less gifted than Elsa and me at flattering his pride, at dutifully swooning in his presence. So I swooned in the pretty heels he bought me, I carried the matching leather handbag, I wore the elegant dress that he considered neither too sexy nor too demure, just the right amount of je ne sais quoi. I would appear to his specifications, or he would disappear.

You were not one to forget dates, so the first time you forgot to wish me a happy birthday, I took it to heart and I knew it marked the end of an era, the beginning of your senescence. For the previous fifteen years, you'd come to New York to celebrate the day in person. You spent a week at The Plaza overlooking the park. The fact that I lived miles away didn't matter; the circumstances of my everyday life were inconsequential. You couldn't possibly come to dinner at my place or even set foot in my then apartment, which, by your standards, was a dump. In any case, you preferred restaurants, and luckily New York had a great many of them. Throughout your stay, I served as your secretary and interpreter, while maintaining my role as model daughter. You spoke the language of Shakespeare with a posh British accent and excessive politesse, using idioms that hadn't been heard since Waterloo. "Speak not of it!" you declared when the bellboy attempted to thank you for his tip. *May I*, *Shall you*, or *Would you be so kind* preceded each of your requests to the concierge, which surprised him less than your bewilderment at his reply. For while you spoke English eloquently, you understood it not at all, and in that sense, these exchanges in New York exemplified the asymmetrical nature of all your discourse. I had to be ready to step in to avert every catastrophe: the late arrival of a limo driver, a restaurant not to your liking, the lack of French newspapers at the local news stand. But on every May 8, I would receive delivery of an extravagant bouquet of thirty-one red roses (roses could only be given in uneven numbers) along with a potted, lavish, many-stemmed orchid. Then I would join you for dinner at whatever restaurant boasted the most Michelin stars at the time.

I had imagined that everything would change once I became a mother, that I would no longer allow myself to be swept up by your demands or be so desperate to please you. I would give priority to my children. My little George was six weeks old the last time you came to New York. She joined us for lunch and dinner (at restaurants, of course) each day. You were neither surprised nor shocked that I nursed her at the table, or that I continued to breastfeed until she was two and a half. (Such nursing was considered scandalous in France, let alone in public.) You were eighty-five when Sissi was born; you weren't able to make the trip to meet her, so I brought her to you. We celebrated Christmas together at a restaurant a couple of blocks from the Élysée; George was the age you had been when you had lived there. I nursed Sissi as I had her sister, and you cherished watching her fall asleep at my breast as the evening drew on, despite the barely concealed shock of the waiters. You said it was so wonderful, that nothing could be better than dozing on a mother's chest, that I was right to nurse her for as long as she wanted to nurse and as much as she wanted. I shouldn't deny the little angel, you said, and you covered her forehead with kisses, your hand in mine, while she sighed in contentment above my open blouse. Who knows what you see when you look at my girls? I can feel your heart swell, if not with pride, then with a sort of piety. The word may be excessive given your atheism, but you did seem awed—perhaps because in such moments you occupied several temporalities at once, seeing your past in her eyes but also a future beyond your death. Your face took on a look I associate with certain religious paintings. And you would, for a minute or two, fall uncharacteristically silent.

The span of life that we shared, you and I, was uneventful compared to the tragedies that preceded it. You lived what you considered your best years—those of your pharaonic projects and endless romantic entanglements—before I was born. I am convinced that my mother was the woman you loved most, but that love was already in shambles by the time I could see it. Maman has not vanished entirely from your consciousness. When I mention her, you can still discern her silhouette through the shadows of your memories. "Ah, she was magnificent, Catherine! Breathtakingly beautiful." Her splendor fascinated you. You could never quite believe that you had laid claim to a woman so sublime, that she had given you two daughters as beautiful as she was. "They have their father's intelligence and their mother's beauty," you said again and again. You never understood why that statement offended her. You somehow thought of this as a compliment: She had the looks, you had the brains; she had intuition, you had erudition. You shared an overpowering desire for each other, for life itself, or maybe what you shared was an overpowering desire for overpowering desire. Your love was incompatible with domestic life and daily hassles. Perhaps you lied to yourselves, believing that you could have it all—the tumult of passion and the stability of family—but in reality, your children ended up as the collateral damage from your cataclysmic passions. You raised us with scant consideration for our day-to-day needs but also with affection to spare—perhaps too much affection. We were somehow at once neglected and smothered with kisses.

Not so long ago you would have asked after Maman. You remained connected right up to her death—toxically but intimately connected. The last time you asked, I told you Maman killed herself. "That was more than ten years ago, Papa." Saying it out loud, sharing it again, made us both experience its reality anew, a pain beyond description. "That she never met my daughters, her granddaughters, continues to break my heart every day," I added. You looked upset. You stayed quiet for a while, searching in the distance for something to say. I hoped you would spare me an explanation. You said that my mother had always been very troubled. Yes, Papa *chéri*, I know. You regretted not having loved her as she deserved; you regretted you were unable to help her. I know that, too. Your sadness and regret are at once genuine and maddeningly self-exculpatory. You acknowledge the tragedy, but with a fatalism that absolves you: That's just how she was! That's just how I am! That's just how things are!

My father published his first book at twenty-five, a short treatise on aesthetics—that fugitive realm at the crossroads of science, criticism, and history (his definition). It was published in the *Que Sais-Je?* series, of which he had entire shelves full in his library. My copy must have once been part of a set that my father had bought from a bookstall on one of his sprees along the banks of the Seine, across from the Académie française, to which he desperately wished to be elected. Its price, 40 francs, is penciled on the cover page. The book opens with a *citation choc*—a flashy quote—a tactic that Papa deployed in all of his writing and lectures, a tactic he recommended to his students in another book published that same year, *L'Art de la dissertation*. This quote is from Hegel, whose dialectic—thesis, antithesis, synthesis—was also, my father insisted, the universal key to securing a decent grade on any subject, a blueprint answer to any problem: An essay should either be structured Yes-No-Yes or No-Yes-No (Example: Does God exist? Descartes: Yes; Nietzsche: No; Kant: Yes). If you had a drop of Hegel and a *citation choc*, you were good to go. In two paragraphs, the introduction to his *L'Esthétique* quotes Socrates, Montaigne,

Kant, and Étienne Souriau, his professor at the Sorbonne, who had most likely been responsible for securing his publishing contract. A little later, he cites his own father, Georges Huisman, in a footnote: "The last Director-General of the Beaux-Arts administration of the Third Republic was the first to acquire works from new painters for the national museums," it says, "commissioning Matisse, Braque, Picasso, etc."

This, the very first entry in my father's sprawling bibliography—he wrote or cowrote or ghostwrote or edited almost a hundred books—appeared three years before my grandfather Georges died in 1954. Aesthetics, still an experimental area of philosophy at the time, was my father's specialty; he was determined to make it a serious realm of study. He promoted the need to establish a faculty of aesthetics. He had his own agenda to that end: He saw himself as heir to Étienne Souriau's chair; he pictured himself becoming, if not a great philosopher, a public intellectual, a professor at the Collège de France, then at the very least a member of the coterie to which his own father had belonged. Entering the Académie française would have been perfect. Papa at that point had already fathered three children, taught in four different schools, given private lessons at all hours, labored nights on a dozen books simultaneously, and by dawn would be hard at work on the next project; whatever it was, it needed to be launched immediately. Aesthetics would remain his prime focus even though he had no interest in art. My father never took me to a museum or to the opera; I never heard him describe any powerful aesthetic experiences, unless descriptions of female beauty count; he suspected me of putting on airs when he heard me tell of my passion for dance, experimental theater, or the work of

Marcel Proust. Restaurants, not museums, were his temples of the spirit.

I resented my father for favoring success over thought, spectacle over study, but he had already had a mother who had chastised him relentlessly, faulting him for his intellectual laziness and his taste for luxury—two sins that, to her, represented the worst possible insult to her late husband's memory. And honoring his father's memory was a duty that his mother had drummed into my father assiduously. As far back as I could remember, I had heard my father talk of writing his memoirs with the principal aim of reclaiming the reputation of a great man who had been robbed of everything by the Vichy regime, a hero whose name had been lost to posterity through sheer iniquity, a name that should have been given to a street. And so my father was always just about to get down to work on the book that would redeem his father, or he announced that it was high time to get down to work (it was always almost time); he had finally found someone suitable to take dictation; he was on the right track; he had a good thirty pages; he had hours and hours of recordings, all he had to do was transcribe them and he would do that tomorrow, always tomorrow. Although my grandfather had also authored many books, he, too, had always postponed writing his own story. Only Bonne-Maman, Papa's mother, had gotten down to it; she completed a manuscript about her late husband, Georges, shortly before her death at the age of ninety-seven.

Papa's greatest publishing success came barely two years after his first book, in the form of a textbook, a philosophy primer, which in 1956 seemed to his fellow professors not only absurd but also in very poor taste, with the exception of his coauthor, André Vergez, a celebrity in my mind who I was shocked to discover had no other claim to fame than the *Vergez & Huisman*, as their publication came to be known. The book was reissued so many times that, forty years later, in a philosophy class at a prestigious Paris *lycée*, my teacher couldn't resist making a joke about it: "Have any of you ever noticed," he said, hands in his pockets, pacing back and forth before his desk, "that clowns always come in pairs—the sad clown and the merry clown, Laurel and Hardy? The same is true with literature and philosophy textbooks: just look at *Vergez & Huisman*!" It was mandatory for scholars to sneer at that reductive, lowbrow manual, which simplified everything and explained nothing. Papa's famous textbook spelled the end of his career as a serious intellectual. He would never again be anything but an object of ridicule among academic circles. Somehow he had failed and succeeded at once: *Vergez & Huisman* sold more than five million copies. The craze for primers turned out to be durable. Making the best of it, my father moved on to a series of study guides for high school students, the ABCs of the Baccalaureate, small spiral-bound notebooks that he designed in such a way so students could tear out pages as crib sheets, which would also make them unsellable on the used-book market. That was clever. It was the work not of a scholar but of a resourceful businessman. His efforts were met with the scorn of his university colleagues, but his success meant he could ignore them.

My father would have been so proud to see his portrait in *Le Monde*. As I read his obituary, I was overcome with sorrow at the thought of the joy that death had robbed him of. We, his children, all agreed that the article was exemplary, irreproachable—it was beyond perfect. His life was encapsulated in a newspaper article that somehow managed to impose order on the chaos of my memories and prove that I had not been making it up. Roger-Pol Droit, a highly respected journalist writing for a highly distinguished publication, described Papa as:

> a genius of communications, both a scholar and a businessman, a professor of philosophy and of public relations, unique and in a class of his own, whose many endeavors left their own particular mark on the second half of the last century . . . A jack-of-all-trades, he was able to juggle a variety of businesses that are generally considered to be incompatible, with the felicitous combination of guilelessness and generosity that made him a personality worthy of Balzac.
>
> A great gourmet, a great ladies man, a great man about town, a great naif, he sometimes seemed ahead of his time and at others outdated, perpetually out of sync. Earning and spending profligately, apparently tireless in his quest for titles and recognition, in his relations with those he loved he could also be extraordinarily affectionate and sensitive.

Yes, it was word-perfect. In the 1960s and 1970s, as the article noted in its lede, every high school student in France knew my father's name, but his celebrity had earned him more derision than praise. He had even been the subject of a television biopic, in which he was portrayed as a social-climbing dilettante, a capitalist showboat, a heinous character. As he lay sleeping fitfully in his mechanical bed, I streamed the movie on my laptop.

To a question about his vanity, he replied: "I do not consider myself one of the great philosophers of my time. That would be absurd! But I am certainly France's best known . . ." As if the words weren't damning enough, there is the person uttering them: his manic, rapid-fire delivery and the snobbery of his affected, mannered speech; he is wearing a trench coat indoors, sprawled in his armchair in his magnificent office on the fourth floor of his PR school, just off the Champs-Élysées, where the little desk plaque reads, in English, "Smile! The boss is happy." The producers made sure to provide French subtitles.

What kind of jerk lets himself be filmed barking orders from his car phone? All of his students (the presenter said off-camera in this scene) refused to speak on the record. His own mother lamented, on camera, his choices, his gall, his extravagance. Somehow this is my father, at exactly the age I am now—that is, eight years before my birth. I do not know this man. If our successive selves are deposited as sediments within us, like geological strata, if that intolerable buffoon was still somewhere inside him when he became my father, at least he eventually ceded his place to a less self-serious, a less affected, and a warmer (if no less extravagant and mercurial) iteration of himself.

Papa's father was also forty-two when he moved to the Élysée as secretary of state to the presidency of the Republic. That was Maman's age when she was institutionalized after her psychotic break, when I was ten. That is the age she remains when I picture her in memory. As I reach the age that Maman will always be in my heart, I look down as I braid my girls' hair and see her hands, and something rips in my chest. "Do you know what my mother would have said if I'd whined like you?" I say to my tender-headed girls. They are far less eager to hear stories about my mother than about Doggy. I sometimes tell them about how Maman drove up onto the sidewalks of Paris when the streets were clogged with traffic, but I don't mention the day she deliberately drove headlong into a stream of cars on the Champs-Élysées, Elsa in the front seat and me in the back, nearly killing us all. "What a weird grandma!" they reply in English. There's something uncanny about the idea that Maman could have been a grandma when she didn't speak a word of English. "You're right, girls, my mother was weird, but she would have made you laugh," I say, even as I think that I never would have entrusted—not even for an hour—my daughters to her care.

The last scene in the documentary takes place at the Tour d'Argent, the famous restaurant where my father liked to celebrate important events. This is the first time, the only time, in the film that you see him listening, not just blathering. He is attending intently to his dinner guests—the major intellectuals of the time—as they answer questions from the producer in the midst of a profusion of plates and glasses of all shapes and sizes, their cheeks clearly aglow (despite the black-and-white film) from the fine fare. There are pretty young women seated randomly among them, beaming vacantly. This man, my father, is unquestionably an arrogant jerk, there is no doubt about it, and yet Papa suddenly declares, with a casualness that has the poignancy of truth, how insignificant he feels in the face of any kind of posterity. No, nothing will remain of his work. He prefers not to think about death. No, really, he couldn't care less about posterity. Everything he's done will disappear into the void.

C*itation choc*: "To philosophize is to learn to die." Papa often remarked that he felt profoundly unworthy of his profession under those terms. He couldn't even prepare himself to sleep. As a remedy for his insomnia, in addition to an arsenal of pills, he simply chose not to go to bed. In the dead of night, Papa spent hours reading, writing, or organizing his library. Perched on a rolling ladder, he ordered his stacks of books into rows with maniacal zeal, aligning the volumes one by one with exacting precision. He arranged them not in alphabetical order, nor by subject, but by height and color, and thus often by series. His enormous library showcased the pale yellow covers of Fayard, the off-white of Gallimard, the vermilion of old Flammarion, the cyan blue of Librairie Félix Alcan. He didn't care if there were duplicates so long as they were visually harmonious. And as Papa mostly bought his books in bulk in the green stalls by the Seine, they were sometimes still wrapped in transparent plastic that he hadn't bothered to remove. His library was an aesthetic composition, a color field painting. It was his way of organizing the real, of ordering memory. He built a cathedral of words in chromatic patterns, abstracted narratives in panels of stained glass. Its scale was overwhelming. It was his guiding passion to acquire all things in vast quantities, and Papa had outdone himself with books.

When I was a child, his library was also his office. Elsa and I weren't banned from the room, but we weren't welcome either. He preferred it private, off-limits. Under no circumstances could you touch his books. A request to borrow something—there were rarities among his volumes that had long been out of print—was met with categorical refusal. "Absolutely not! You'll leave a hole!" His response was all the more puzzling because Papa otherwise never said no to anything. He would spontaneously hand me his scarf if I commented on it; he would give us anything we asked for—along with so much we didn't. Except for his books. He was happy to buy us a new copy, but lending was out of the question. There were public libraries for that purpose! He was not especially attached to any particular volume; it was the whole that he cherished. He loved his collection of books as he had arranged it, in the exact order in which he had organized it. Making a hole—that is, taking a book down from the shelf, leaving a gap in a row—was to open a wound.

Later in life, Papa moved his library to a separate apartment in order to prevent his dog-child, his *Loup*, from pissing on the lower shelves, and because his wife could not live with that mountain of musty old books. Papa was not so sorry to have an excuse to leave the house to attend to his library (and establish a love nest): a vast two-bedroom apartment on the third floor of a fine Haussmannian building with floor-to-ceiling bookshelves built against every wall, around every window, along the hallway, even in the kitchen, even in the bathroom, above the toilet. It was furnished with the sofas from when we lived together with Maman—sofas upholstered in royal blue velvet with worn armrests, sagging springs, and cushions that shimmered with dust as the sun shone through the vertical blinds. I spent long afternoons there after he was no longer around to stop me from touching his books. At night, a single floor lamp illuminated the room like a ghost light in the theater—the lamp that remains lit onstage when the house is dark and empty. I shook out the cushions of the couch and found riding crops slipped behind the seat backs—sexual accoutrements, no doubt, hidden and then forgotten. I returned them and tried to forget them myself.

"I can't say I find much interest in what goes on in the world," you tell me soberly after I read you the day's headlines. The news bores and numbs you, the tally of the COVID dead. The few novels you keep by your bed—you and your wife have slept in separate rooms for as long as you've been married—stand in a messy pile. I ask you about the distant past to keep you awake. You were eight or nine when you started collecting books. The *Classiques Larousse*, purple postcard-sized paperbacks. You had noticed them in the window of your local bookstore, where you often admired the stacks. The series was new at the time and consisted of only a few titles, and you were eager to collect the full set. You acquired them with the pocket money you received for every good grade you earned. That was surely the only time in your life you ever tried to save! War was brewing, and you'd acquired the entire collection by the time it broke out. "Of course, they've been out of print for ages now," you say. "Gorgeous little books." You lost them all during the war, along with the collection of Dinky Toys you had to leave behind during the exodus from Paris; the trunk of the car was too full because your father had decided to bring along his mistress, and you had to make room for her luggage. Choute, Duchess of Montmoreau, née de Troguindy. You never called her anything but Choute—the feminine form of *chou*, a common term of endearment for little kids or loved ones. Elsa, my closest friends, and I all call each other *Chouchou*—a redoubling of *chou*, similar to the redundancy of "sweetie pie." What initially started as teenage sarcasm stuck forever. I also cannot remember you addressing me with my first name. I was only ever *petit ange*, *amour adorée*, *chérie mignonne*. Or you wouldn't call me. When one importuned you, one ceased to even have a name. That Choute was only ever referred to as Choute didn't seem so uncanny; I didn't make anything of it. And having read Proust, that an aristocrat be known to the world by her nickname—like the Baron de Charlus, known as Mémé—seemed fitting.

You told me the exodus story a hundred, a thousand times: Choute was always its star. Choute owned a Siamese cat that you held on your lap in the car. The cat wailed throughout that interminable journey from the Château de Chaumont—where your father had moved the Beaux-Arts administration—to Bordeaux, where the government had regrouped in haste as the Germans descended upon Paris. It was in Bordeaux that you boarded the *Massilia*, along with Jean Zay, Édouard Daladier, Georges Mandel, Pierre Mendès-France—all familiar street names by the time of my Parisian childhood. *Massilia* was also the ancient name for Marseille, where you would end up after your return to France.

You recall those nights in Bordeaux as you awaited your fateful escape to North Africa. You recall those two years in Marseille, 1940 to 1942, until your father was arrested. He was lucky; the chief warden of the prison on Rue de l'Évêché turned out to be a decent guy and let him go, but it had become too dangerous for the family to live out in the open, the free zone had been shut down, and Jews were being tracked down relentlessly. You remember the frigid Marseille winters—heavy snowfall in the Mediterranean. It was as though the historical upheaval was so profound that it had scrambled even the weather. You remember the mistral, the biting northern wind, on your walk along the waterfront to the Lycée Thiers, and the bad blood between your parents. Your poor mother had finally come to see, in the midst of the exodus, that your father had brazenly cheated on her for months! Choute had had to decamp as soon as you reached Bordeaux because Maman was livid with rage, you say. "And then one fine day, in Marseille, Papa vanished: He had gone to Choute. Never had I seen my poor mother cry like that. She cried all day, all night; she cried and cried until her body ran out of tears. Her husband had abandoned her and her children in the middle of a war. And then, after weeks or maybe months," my father would claim, "Papa appeared in my room, in that dingy little apartment that my mother had furnished with mismatched hand-me-downs. In the middle of the night, he materialized at the foot of my bed and said, 'I'm leaving for good with Choute, and I'm taking you with me. Your mother will stay with your brothers, you come along.' It took all the might of my eleven years, and a courage I didn't know I had in me—I was up against a towering man, very impressive with his deep, grave voice, the former secretary of state to the presidency of the Republic, the directeur des Beaux-Arts—to say no. No, Papa. Do what you will, but I'm not leaving Maman. Abandon us if that's your wish. I'm staying with my mother."

You tell me this story again from your bed, your hand in mine. It is part of our new ritual. The endless succession of restaurant meals has given way to a choreography of medical care. Tears roll down your sunken cheeks, catch in the white stubble. Your eyes are at once clouded with age and shining with timeless emotion; they are at once focused and distant; they are transfixed by memory. "No," you repeat once more. "I told him no! I will not leave Maman!" You listened to your parents negotiate all night long through the paper-thin wall of your bedroom in that crummy Marseille apartment. By morning, it had been decided that your father would stay with the family. Choute was never spoken of again. The matter was closed. You had kept your family together.

You tell me this as I sit in your sprawling apartment in the sixteenth arrondissement, stroking your arm, thinking of the father who left Elsa and me every night. You were going home to your new wife, or you had business to attend to, or you had another rendezvous. And if your wife called our apartment, we were to tell her you were running late, that you'd had a bite with us—just make something up, you said, anything. And we did—we'd cover for you with the woman you'd left us for. You stopped by after we had come home from school, at homework time, yet despite your famous tutoring skills, I always refused your help in Latin, philosophy, French. I'd rather have failed than resort to your tricks, which stood for all the deceit, all the ruses. You lounged about our rooms, you played the family man, you stretched out on the living room sofa—a half hour, an hour, more or less the amount of time that I now spend at your bedside before I require a break. You left money for Maman, you paid her bills, you settled her debts. The two of you argued. More often than not, you left after a fight. "Your mother is truly insufferable," you'd say as we walked you to the door. "She's completely nuts, totally irresponsible, this woman is mad!" You left us with the madwoman. And Maman was always much worse after your visits. She would turn to alcohol and pills. She fainted often. We'd revive her with smelling salts, or white vinegar, as she had instructed us; when we couldn't rouse her, we called the fire department. In the fall or spring—the weather had its own cycles, independent of hers—she'd check herself into a clinic, to the madhouse where you so often said she belonged. When she was hospitalized, you continued to visit us just the same. There was less shouting as we walked you to the door. You asked if we were sure we didn't need anything. We were two teenage girls living without a parent. "No, nothing," we replied, "thank you, Papa. Yes, very sure, nothing." What we needed was not on offer.

If I had gone down on my knees and begged you, Papa *chéri*, if I had threatened never to see you again, would you have stayed? Was there anything I could have done? Would shame or a bad conscience have jolted you? I'm a grown-up now, I have children of my own, and it's all ancient history. Yet as I sit here watching you so late in life cry over your own father's betrayal, I wonder once more: Could I have made you stay? Could I have compelled you to take care of Maman?

In 1984, I was five. You and Maman separated, and you published your landmark two-volume *Dictionnaire des philosophes*. Bernard Pivot invited you to appear on his famous TV show *Apostrophes*—an honor that had not yet been extended to you. A coup! A huge deal. France's star presenter encouraged you to discuss your work as a serious writer, surrounded by highly reputable philosophers; it was a sort of anointment. You smiled for the camera, you were so proud. I recognize the poses and verbal ticks of that man on the screen: no swagger there; I see you trying to make a good impression. Pivot quoted from an article by Roger-Pol Droit to introduce you. No one could accuse him of trying to flatter you: "Huisman. The name alone often provokes hostile reactions. The public persona—and he is one!—doesn't always have good press. A man of business and public relations, as enamored of publicity as he is of reasoning, is for many the face of '*choc* philosophy' . . . In attaching his name to this dictionary, he appears to have moved on to '*chic* philosophy.'" "That's a very good line!" you replied in earnest. "It doesn't bother me at all, it's quite true I've done a lot of things in my life!" *Chic* and *choc*—you certainly couldn't argue. You weren't there to bite the hand that fed you; all press was good press. You took what you were offered, you took everything without fail, if also without discernment. Watching you smile broadly for the camera, I am suddenly reminded of your old teeth, your real ones. Before they all fell out, your teeth were mostly rotten, brown not from tobacco—you were never a smoker, although you bought cartons of cigarettes for your friends, lovers, or daughters—but from your astonishing lack of oral hygiene. You freshened your breath with great blasts of Ricqlès spray, but I'm not sure you ever brushed your teeth. You also never stepped into a shower, but rather you'd steep yourself in very hot water and wait for the woman in your life to scrub your back in the tub. There was something disturbing about your odd sense of grooming, and yet you always smelled good. When I bury my face in the hollow of your neck, I recall how much I loved to linger there as a child.

"Of all the honors he has received, and of all the books he has written, it is certainly the *Dictionnaire des philosophes* that will remain the most durably associated with his name," wrote Roger-Pol Droit in conclusion to my father's obituary. "Whatever the fault-finders may say, the flamboyant Huisman has served philosophy well." Your dictionary was not only a highpoint of your career but also a major event in our country's intellectual landscape. The most eminent scholars had agreed to participate; it listed thirty-five hundred philosophers from around the world, including Africa, Asia, and Oceania. It was a remarkable and broadly inclusive overview. When Pivot criticized its flaws or the unevenness of its selection, you laughed openly. You didn't take offense; you confessed your errors and missteps. Some contemporary philosophers even wrote their own entries. "What a funny idea!" Pivot exclaimed. "Not at all," you responded graciously. "There's nothing strange or heretical about it. Didn't René Descartes write his own life story in *Meditations*? What about Montaigne?" Michel Foucault, in his own entry, distinguished between the author function and the author person, a distinction still controversial at a time when the term *autofiction* had just been coined. You might have gone deeper into the intellectual innovations, the new philosophical vocabularies that you were helping to introduce; you might have become a spokesperson for a school of thought, you had the insight and eloquence, but you were not interested in ideas; you were interested in money, attention, the next big thing.

Papa was content to play the role of popularizer. His work was less about writing than about compiling, making lists. The originality of his style was most evident in his speeches—at our family gatherings or in the countless award ceremonies and other official occasions over which he presided. He was an exceptional orator. He could make his audience laugh to the point of tears, as he did at Elsa's wedding, or move them to tears from his sudden pathos. I mostly found him bombastic, a verdict with which Maman vehemently agreed. She went on and on about how his eloquence was bullshit, about the vacuity of his supposed erudition, having herself been treated as a supreme moron by Papa and his entourage because of her lack of education. What they called culture was just a form of self-importance, a way to make you feel stupid, but it had no substance. I heard her, but I heard him, too. I felt that Maman had indeed identified a hole in his bag of tricks. Papa may have loved Descartes, but he wasn't interested in self-doubt in any form. He claimed authoritatively that his father had messed up, that he should have followed de Gaulle to London, but this wasn't about principle—it was just his way of retrospectively siding with the victor. He was a master of equivocation: You have to know how to pick your battles and keep your powder dry, that there's good and bad in everything, and that in the end nothing is simple, but money makes everything simpler. He had a sweeping argument for any occasion, he studded his speeches with authoritative quotes, but he himself had no interest in self-reflection. It was the successful life, not the examined one, that was worth living.

Despite his supposed lack of interest in posterity, my father ultimately decided that his memoirs must be published for his eightieth birthday. And finally admitting that he was never going to write them himself, he fell back on the idea of a commissioned biography, which he assigned to an old colleague in broadcasting. My father had been screening candidates for this august task for years. He'd approached a slew of young women about the prospect; they'd all fled. There were some deserving writers who'd been open to the idea until they realized they would not be allowed to express a point of view, only parrot one. Then there was a sportswriter who had authored a number of biographies of world-renowned athletes, which was particularly perplexing given that Papa's only interest in sports was its dress codes—the whites of a tennis player, the jockey's jodhpur and helmet, the cyclist's cap—but Papa took to him nonetheless. After recording hundreds of hours of conversation, the writer had submitted a few pages to my father, which were then forwarded to me, along with a handwritten note: "What do you think?" signed "Your Papa who loves you." I don't remember the specific nature of the pages, just how horrifyingly embarrassing they were. Faced with his family's consternation, Papa reluctantly rejected this version, which he himself had rather enjoyed—it had rhythm, it moved along nicely. In the end, *Une faim si dévorante—An All-Consuming Hunger*—the title chosen by the broadcaster Papa eventually contracted—was even more painful than the previous attempts. While everyone agreed that the book was appalling, it was the cruelty with which it portrayed my mother that revolted me most. Maman did not deserve such scorn.

Georges would have had to live a year longer than the oldest person on Earth to have met his great-granddaughter, his namesake. From his birth to that of my little George, France had experienced the Dreyfus affair; two world wars; the invention of the telephone, plastic, and movies; the development of nuclear power; the commercialization of air travel; the widespread installation of electricity, gas, and plumbing; the creation of machines automating domestic and agricultural tasks; and an increase in leisure time that gave rise to a variety of activities to counter the monotony of manual labor. Culture was democratized, as was entertainment; education made spectacular advances. France had the *Trente Glorieuses*, the thirty prosperous years that followed the Second World War, during which you made your fortune. And as technological progress accelerated at a dizzying pace, people began to feel as if they were in a permanent race against the clock, despite all the time supposedly freed up by modernity's dazzling achievements. It has become impossible to imagine the world your parents experienced: a world without phones, without light switches, with limited access to water, without planes. You brought your father back to life for me in countless stories, perennial tributes to his glory and his unjustly scorned memory. But however majestic and monumental his portrait may have been, it remained spectral, shifting—a history based on anecdote, full of gaps.

The actual canvas that long hung in your office off the Champs-Élysées depicted your father at a gallery opening, in his official duty as directeur des Beaux-Arts, just before his downfall. He is in the foreground, in profile. Taller than his companions, he is wearing an elegant pin-striped suit and polka-dot bow tie, a cigarette dangling from his lips. The women in the background of the painting seem to regard him admiringly; all eyes on Georges Huisman. There is no mistaking how important he is, how charismatic; and yet it all seems, as in your stories, a little overstated, a little overblown, bordering on the cartoonish, the unreal. When you sold your schools and vacated your offices, I asked if I could have the painting. Nobody else claimed it. Expedited to New York by cargo, it traveled the way one used to. And as Georges' oversized likeness was sailing across the Atlantic to my home in Brooklyn, I learned that my grandfather had in fact made the same journey sixty years earlier. I learned this from a literary agent I happened to meet at a party in New York; he told me his first wife had been the daughter of the French artist who had painted Georges' portrait before the war. In gratitude for my grandfather's patronage, the then young couple had felt duty bound to greet him upon his arrival, to welcome him to America, as I was soon to welcome his portrait.

When I hung the painting in my living room, I saw the hero of a story in which I could almost—almost—give myself a part, maybe more of a cameo. (I was reminded of the provincial dukes who make appearances in old paintings but are otherwise overtaken by oblivion;

they are less memorialized than made into symbols of the fleetingness of memory.) The canvas, in its florid, gilded ornamental frame, clashed with the rest of the decor and took up an inordinate, ridiculous amount of space on our wall. The portrait dominated the room like an aristocrat of old, yet Georges was no more royalty than I was. Georges, with an *s*, was born in 1889, the year the Eiffel Tower was inaugurated. He was a hieratic and inescapable figure in our family history; he was our national monument, our patriarch of contradictions.

Bonne-Maman had been a widow for more than twenty years by the time I was born. Her identity was folded into her devotion to her late husband. The memoirs she wrote in her nineties amounted to a hagiography of Georges Huisman. Tirelessly enumerating his great deeds, she portrayed him as a legendary hero akin to those in the children's book they'd written together, *Contes et légendes du Moyen Âge français, Tales and Legends of the French Middle Ages*, the only book my father had kept with him during the war. I found an inscribed copy in the attic of the Huisman family home in Valmondois; Bonne-Maman had dedicated it to "her darling little boy." The best known of these tales, reprinted in numerous anthologies, was titled "Lavish Folly."

I was sixteen when Bonne-Maman passed away. I can't say I mourned her. She had never displayed any tenderness toward me whatsoever. Perhaps she'd had enough of playing grandma by the time I was born, and being my mother's daughter didn't help my case. Her son had gotten mixed up with a slut—Bonne-Maman did not mince words—a woman too crazy to even play the role of trophy wife! I suspect Bonne-Maman faulted my mother for making my father even more scattered, for making his follies even more lavish. And accumulating wealth was nothing to be proud of. Worse yet, being in business and wallowing in luxury was an embarrassment to their kin. Georges had never sought medals or honors. He had accepted them reluctantly and only when absolutely necessary: a veteran of the Great War, he had served in the Air Force as a technical observer on the ground. He had not taken the same risks as his fellow pilots and so he declined the medal he had been granted, for he operated according to a moral code higher than any military honor. As directeur des Beaux-Arts, he had refused to be inducted into the Académie, even though it would have been quite appropriate. He was afraid of being co-opted by the artists among its members and wanted to preserve his neutrality to support contemporary avant-garde art, antithetical to academic conformism. ("How stupid was that?" Papa exclaimed.) Georges had been a pure product of meritocracy, the son of a naturalized French citizen, a salesman, who could neither read nor write, and a schoolteacher, who believed fervently in the virtues of higher education. And yet, according to my father, this wasn't moral rigor; it was stupidity, an excess of obedience bordering on servility. When he was told to board the *Massilia*, he had simply complied—he should have rebelled, followed de Gaulle to London! "What a sucker! What good did his moral code do? Georges was left destitute, entrapped by corrupt politicians." My father, on the other hand, had mapped out his journey for himself.

After the premature deaths of Papa's two brothers, he and Bonne-Maman became the last custodians of Georges Huisman's legacy. His mother had drummed it into my father that it was his duty to keep the glorious memory of his father alive. But I found it difficult to grasp what message they were trying to convey. That

French fascists had robbed them of their identity? That Georges Huisman deserved to have a street named after him? That his fall into oblivion foreshadowed the erasure of the Holocaust from French national memory? His story had to be told over and over again, chanted like a prayer to a god we had stopped believing in two generations earlier. Papa and Bonne-Maman argued endlessly over trivial details, losing sight of the point they were trying to make. "No, you're wrong, it was a Tuesday! I know I'm right, it was the day we played bridge, and we played bridge on Tuesdays, and you weren't there in any case because you were at school, I remember it clearly, it was precisely three p.m. on Tuesday, March 23, 1942, when the Gestapo searched the apartment . . ." "No, Maman, you're plain wrong! It was a Thursday because I wasn't at school, I was there. How could I ever forget, it was a Thursday, I swear on my children's heads. Come on, why would I make it up?" Ultimately, their nit-picking overwhelmed the story they were trying to tell, robbed the anecdote of its tragic charge. No one dared tell them that the day of the week was less meaningful than the deportation they had narrowly escaped, the reality of which their bickering obscured.

Because her Georges had failed to document his exploits, failed to ensure that his name would endure, Bonne-Maman stepped in. At ninety-five, she was still very much of sound mind—far more than you, Papa. Almost four decades after her husband's death, she remembered the names of his war buddies and not only the chronology of events but also the most insignificant details: the classes he had taken in primary school, the books he had read, the names of his childhood friends, the songs he had danced to. She set it all down. You told Bonne-Maman that you had submitted her manuscript to a highly respected publisher, Les Éditions du Platane—a new house, you assured her, that's why she'd never heard of it—and that it had been accepted with great enthusiasm. Then you had her manuscript typeset, printed, bound, and—to further simulate legitimate publication—you'd hand-delivered copies to her neighborhood bookstore, the only one she was likely to visit. And then you presented her with false royalty statements to prove that her book was flying off the shelves!

A decade earlier, Bonne-Maman had asked you to use your connections to approach the administrators of the Cannes Film Festival and request that they officially acknowledge the role Georges Huisman had played in creating the event. For it was Georges, as directeur des Beaux-Arts, just before the war, who had come up with the idea for the festival. And no one remembered! He had been marginalized, his name had been erased. And he was so modest, Bonne-Maman lamented, and he had never written his memoirs—how could anyone know the truth of his importance? The story of Georges' unacknowledged founding of Cannes was told on a loop, devolving into arguments over, say, the exact day Louis Lumière arrived at the Cannes municipal casino, where the first festival was to be hosted. "August 22nd! You know perfectly well everyone would have been back in Paris by the 29th. Let me remind you, you were ten years old in 1939—how would you know?" "Maman! These dates are documented! I'm not just pulling it out of my hat!" Buoyed by increasingly passionate arguing, rocked by fantastical digressions and sub-digressions, the ship of the story capsized over a misattributed street name, righted itself, was ultimately sunk by some dispute over details. But all roads, all waterways, led to Cannes. Or to the

Massilia. For Cannes and exile were tragically linked: The opening of the first film festival was supposed to take place in September 1939.

You went to great lengths to get a plaque installed inside the Palais des Festivals, where the Cannes festival was held every year after the Second World War—a shiny golden plaque screwed to the wall outside the main screening room. You attended the festival religiously; it was a pilgrimage, and while your school was a sponsor of the event, and you had professional reasons for going, you mostly went to pay tribute to your father. "Was the plaque still there?" Bonne-Maman asked invariably upon your return. The implication being that it might have been removed for some nefarious reason by some depraved enemy. Then the daughters of Jean Zay, Georges Huisman's supervising minister at the time of the initial festival—the leadership of the Beaux-Arts reported to the Ministry of National Education—also wanted a plaque for *their* father. And so, for some time, there were two plaques in the Palais des Festivals attributing the paternity of the festival to two different statesmen in scrupulously identical language. Did someone note the confusion? The festival administrators decided one day to take down Georges Huisman's plaque and only keep Jean Zay's; then they figured it was easier to remove them both. No one who attended the star-studded event could care less which unjustly forgotten old Jew had launched the festival. Except you, Papa. You certainly cared a great deal.

For my father and his mother, the plaque not only acknowledged Georges' role in the founding of Cannes but also commemorated the abject injustice that had befallen them all. Their belongings had been returned to them after the war; nevertheless, they had lost everything. The plaque sought to redeem the irreparable, like hundreds of plaques across the city: plaques by boys' schools, former public bathhouses, Resistance hideouts, churches. The crimes of the Vichy government were etched into marble rectangles all over France.

But the story got murkier, messier, with each telling. I would attempt to confirm with my father that it was because Georges was a Jew that he never received his due credit as founder of Cannes. Yes, of course, absolutely, no doubt about it! But not only. Mostly it was because of that bastard Philippe Erlanger! A common schemer, an infamous turncoat. Once all eyewitnesses were dead and buried, Erlanger rewrote history, literally, and made it all about him! Suddenly he was the founder of the festival. Erlanger! Come now, how could such a pathetic loser, who had never been more than Georges' errand boy, have invented the Cannes Film Festival? It was laughable. Erlanger had managed to publish his memoirs. "A pack of lies! When there was no one left to contradict him. Shamelessly, in all impunity, he wrote about the flash of inspiration that came to him on the overnight train back to Paris from the 1938 Mostra di Venezia. The scoundrel! It was Papa who sent him to Venice!" my father would shout. "And just like that it supposedly came to him, on that night train from Italy, where the jury had awarded Best Foreign Film to Leni Riefenstahl's *Olympia* (Best Italian Film went to Goffredo Alessandrini's *Luciano Serra, Pilot*) in a textbook display of fascist propaganda, and it came to him—a lowly subordinate!—why not establish a rival festival on the French Riviera? Are you kidding me? The guy was a nothing, a mere scrivener. It was Papa who had appointed him! Erlanger was his secretary in 1938! He stayed in office until 1968, did very well for himself indeed." "And

Erlanger wasn't Jewish?" I asked. "Is that how he pulled it off?" "No, no," my father replied. "Erlanger was as Jewish as they come!" "What?" "Yes, of course he was a Jew, but that's irrelevant. He belonged to a wealthy French family, he had tons of money and connections, and he was a scoundrel, a turncoat."

Papa would fulminate against that buffoon, that inveterate liar, he would make him the prime perpetrator of his father's downfall. Erlanger had deliberately betrayed his father because, as they were leaving the Château de Chaumont during *l'Exode*, when millions of French fled the German invasion, Georges had refused to take him in his car. "There was Choute and her cat, there was no room for Erlanger. That was the start of it all, his plot against Papa!" (So it wasn't anti-Semitism, I was to understand, but a vengeful fellow Jew he'd failed to help escape because there wasn't room in the car with his mistress and her cat?) And now we were back on track, the story could start again: Choute, the exodus, the Élysée, Cannes, the *Massilia* . . .

And this meandering history was rendered all the more fantastical or dreamlike by the fact that, after his divorce from Maman, Papa and his new wife had moved into a modern (and hideous) building in the sixteenth arrondissement—on the Rue Erlanger. Of all the streets in Paris, my father lived on *Rue Erlanger*. A nondescript thoroughfare between Rue Molitor and Boulevard Exelmans (both marshals and *pairs de France*) where a surprising number of tragic events took place during the time my father lived there: a famous Israeli pop singer threw himself from a window; a Japanese student killed, carved up, and ate his girlfriend; a drunk killed ten people when she accidentally set fire to her building—all this florid horror on the same narrow stretch of pavement. My father was born in that arrondissement, his own father had grown up there, and both died within a half mile of that address. My father lived on Rue Erlanger longer than anywhere else in his life. I remember asking him as a child if there was any connection between the notorious *Philippe* Erlanger and the name of his street. I hesitated to ask, knowing that his response was likely to confuse me more. He stared at me, aghast. "Of course not!" The Erlanger of his street had been a German banker, absolutely no connection to Philippe Erlanger, who was related to the Camondo family, the son of a composer, tons of money and connections, a distinguished French family. "That bastard Erlanger! A despicable character, a turncoat, full of subterfuge!" The very antithesis of Georges, whose sole sin was his surfeit of integrity. Be that as it may, my father lived on Rue Erlanger.

And in that spacious, modern apartment on the Rue Erlanger, with its roof terrace overlooking the Haussmannian buildings on the far side of the Boulevard Exelmans, the walls were hung with photographs—of my father, of Elsa and me and his other children, of pictures taken in the various vacation homes Papa had inherited from his parents. But in these photographs, Maman never appeared. There had been no place for Maman in those houses, and her presence had been erased from the walls, from the family albums. She was the only one of my father's ex-wives, or even of his former lovers, who had never participated in any family events; she was invited neither to weddings nor to funerals. Papa loved getting the whole family together for the traditional Catholic holidays—Christmas, Epiphany, and Easter, which we celebrated like any good, self-respecting French family (despite my father's being "a little Jewish around the edges," as Maman had once put it). For his birthday, he would organize a great feast, with pyramids of assorted sandwiches and palettes of *petits fours*, followed by the mandatory group photo, taken by a professional hired for the occasion.

Maman was not invited, the explanation went, lest she make a scene. And Maman's outbursts, it must be said, were not for the faint of heart: Tables were overturned, glasses were shattered, there were screams and tears and drama worthy of telenovelas. As if Papa minded. No, the reason Maman was not invited was because Papa's wife, who had tolerated her husband's escapades, had imposed as a nonnegotiable clause to their marriage that her immediate predecessor and main rival would never set foot in their home, never share the same room as her, and that even Maman's name would not be uttered in her presence. Among my unrelenting grievances against my father was the fact that Elsa and I, throughout our childhood, had to call our mother in secret. We had to wait for Papa's wife to go shopping or have business elsewhere before we were could pick up the receiver on the Rue Erlanger and punch in Maman's number hastily, when no one was looking. We couldn't call from the antiquated phone on the pedestal table in the foyer at our family country house, and we could definitely not call from the car phone. At six, ten, or fourteen, we had to hide to hear our mother's manic, plaintive, haggard, or drunken voice. We weren't to talk about her at dinner. We weren't to talk about her ever.

After Maman killed herself, you broke the rule; you brought her up in your wife's presence. Remember, Papa? We were at a restaurant (always at a restaurant) where I had gone to meet you straight from the airport, I had left my suitcase at coat check, it was only a few months after her death. You started reminiscing about her wildest feats, your greatest embarrassments—as though I, who had so recently lost her, wasn't there beside you, trying to breathe. "Ah, Catherine, she was impossible! So beautiful, surreally beautiful, she was unbelievable, how we laughed the day she . . ." Your wife stormed out mid-sentence. (After all, Maman was not the only one to make scenes.) You asked me to go get your wife, to apologize on your behalf. You must have kissed my wrist. You sighed that life was very complicated, that the women in your life were so very complicated, that you were very sad about my *maman*, that you were very sad that I'd lost my *maman* in such tragic circumstances. "Go find my wife, please, my beloved darling little angel, oh là là, she must be very upset."

Maman's grievances against you far surpassed my own. She found you revolting, she less spoke than spat your name, and yet we were never allowed to disrespect you in her presence. She demanded that we obey you totally even if she would then punish us for our obedience. We loved you more, she'd say, because you were rich and powerful, because you took us places, because you bought us all sorts of junk. We were ingrates, we were mercenary little bitches. And yet once, I told Maman that I didn't want to spend the weekend with you, that I didn't want to see you, that I was on her side. She stared me down, blew her cigarette smoke in my face, and instructed me to get my sorry little ass to my father's before she taught me a lesson. Her story, your story—neither story was mine, and yet I couldn't escape them, I had to somehow make sense of myself through them. Maman never tired of harping on your mistreatment of her—it explained and justified everything—just as you never tired of telling us of your family's dispossession under Vichy—which also explained and justified everything. Resentment and repetition were your shared religion, gave order to your otherwise disordered lives. You both taught me by your words and deeds that there are things one simply cannot get over. Your interminable monologues, Papa, turned to the two years you spent in Marseille, a life of false papers and assumed names in Vaison-la-Romaine, and then a liberation that failed to liberate. While for Maman, the rupture, the war that never ended, was your breakup.

That summer of 2020, as we arrived from the United States, my father was carefully moved from Paris to Brittany, where he would spend one last summer. After I completed my quarantine, I traveled to see him in L'Arcouest, in the Côtes-d'Armor. The bay had been nicknamed the Sorbonne-Plage in the 1930s for the group of intellectuals it harbored, including my father's parents. They had established their summer quarters there among their friends, colleagues, and allies in the Front Populaire. In Jean Zay's posthumously published journal, which he kept in the prison at Riom following the *Massilia* affair, he recalled the joys of that picturesque landscape. As a child, Papa had been photographed there for an article in the prewar press; he is depicted beside his Georges, who is wearing a straw hat. They stand in their espalier garden of hydrangeas, hawthorn, and laurels. It was a profile for a popular cultural magazine, and Georges has the blissful and carefree look of a man on holiday. He spent that summer of 1939 organizing the Cannes festival that did not take place.

For generations, the entire family would gather in L'Arcouest.

Papa's first wife even bought a house there after their divorce. Their oldest daughter had married a descendant of the Sorbonne-Plage cohort; she, too, was a philosophy professor; she, too, spent her summers there. During king tides, when the beach stretched on for miles, we would all convene on the bay to dig clams, each of us armed with a three-pronged rake and a basket, each dressed in one of the navy-and-white striped sweaters Papa bought in bulk, and on which he had our names etched in velvet letters. Since his current wife didn't like entertaining, and since he preferred restaurants anyway, he took his children and grandchildren for lunch or dinner at Le Barbu, where his parents had once been regulars. (This hotel-restaurant across from the island of Bréhat, famous for its pink granite cliffs, was forever known to us as Le Barbu, no matter if its name had changed.) You could almost swim to the island, Papa said every time, but the currents were so strong that all who tried, even competitive athletes, had to be rescued before they drowned.

During that first summer of COVID, I found that Le Barbu had become a Best Western. My father was bed-ridden, but I went on a sort of pilgrimage to the restaurant during one of his naps. The dining room had been painted teal to match the enormous sign out front. The smell of plastic and disinfectant overwhelmed the briny scent of seafood platters I recalled from Papa's former tables. Outside the bay windows in PVC frames, the ever-changing colors of the wild, brooding ocean—now glittering cyan, now slate gray—contrasted with the drabness of the decor inside, all the history and particularity of the place reduced to globalized mediocrity.

Several summers before, I had set about recording my father with no particular intention other than preserving his memories, which had begun to waver, however slightly. I came up with a structure: Papa was to extemporize on each of his successive addresses in chronological order. He was sprawled in an armchair at his home in L'Arcouest, his legs crossed as usual, his reading glasses perched on the tip of his nose. And I can position myself perfectly into the scene, recall with eerie precision the setting of the voices as I tap the black arrow of the voice memo app on my cell phone. "Yes, my little angel, where were we?"

"You were on the *Massilia*, or just about to board the *Massilia*—in other words in Bordeaux, in June 1940, where you, your mother, your father, and your two brothers were staying in a great old mansion."

"Ah, yes, a very impressive town house that belonged to the departmental archivist-in-chief, who had been in the same year as my father at the École des Chartes, because when you graduate from the École des Chartes, you automatically become archivist-paleographer, and if you graduate in the top tier, you become a departmental archivist. You can do other things, you can work in the private sector, but typically, the top tier would head a departmental archive. That's not what my father did, even though he was most definitely in the top tier. Let me tell you, looking after stacks of old paper was not my idea of a good time! I could never for the life of me imagine doing anything like that! How dreadful."

"And so in this beautiful town house in Bordeaux . . ." Ensues a long digression on Bordeaux, capital of the Gironde department, digression on the hierarchy of departmental and regional archivists, digression on how the Nazi invasion of 1940 differed from the Prussian invasion of 1870, then detour through Chaumont, digression about Choute, digression on the previous year spent in Rennes, digression on his mother and father's feud.

"But there you are in Bordeaux."

"Yes, that's it, we are in Bordeaux, and in Bordeaux Papa has two options. There is one ship leaving from Bayonne heading to London, and another leaving from Bordeaux to Algiers, French territory, with an official travel order signed by the president of the Council, the Minister of Foreign Affairs, the Minister of War, a super-official travel order with four or five signatures. The document is totally aboveboard! The plan is to continue the fight from North Africa. And France has troops, officers, matériel; Americans have sent us tanks and planes, all sorts of stuff to keep fighting. And in principle, the last government of the Third Republic has decided to continue the war. Unfortunately, that government falls and Pierre Laval launches a *coup d'état*. Laval is the big linchpin in all this, very clever guy. He organizes the whole thing, he suppresses the Republic, establishes a dictatorial state, appoints Maréchal Pétain, and becomes prime minister. The Republic of Liberty, Equality, Fraternity is replaced by the French state—Work, Family, Fatherland—with its capital in Vichy. You see, Papa spoke Greek, Latin, and German. He didn't know a word of English. I'm convinced that the idea of going to England without having any English played a big role in his choice between Algiers and London. But we didn't end up in Algiers, of course, we ended up in Casablanca."

You see . . . *Of course* . . . My father's verbal tics implied that his meaning was obvious, that the narrative thread was clear, that only a fool would have to ask for clarification. But I couldn't ever see what I was supposed to see, couldn't grasp what was supposedly so clear. There was no causal chain in the events he was narrating; his memories were organized by emotion, not objective chronology. I'd heard him mention the word *Massilia* a hundred times in stories, but

I had to learn from other sources that the term denoted the steamship that his family boarded in the port of Verdon on the eve of the armistice, in June 1940. Georges, under official travel orders from Admiral Darlan, was to meet up with his administration in Algiers. But the ship was a trap, as the armistice was signed while they were at sea. Docking not in Algiers—Algeria was still France—but in Casablanca—Morocco was only a French protectorate—the parliamentarians on board, many of whom were Jewish, were accused of desertion.

"All lies, filthy slander!" cried Papa. He could not tell this story without reliving the indignation of the eleven-year-old boy he had been on that boat. Intimate and historical tragedies collided: Choute was no less important than Maréchal Pétain. The story of the *Massilia* left me swamped under a flood of names and anecdotes. Laval, Mandel, Zay. I did see that Georges Huisman, his father, was a hero who had been betrayed by fascist pigs. "Because he was a Jew?" I asked. "Because we are Jewish, right, Papa?" "Of course because he was a Jew! France is a deeply anti-Semitic country," said Papa in the eternal present tense. "But Erlanger was also a Jew," I confirmed. "Well, yes, but not a very Jewy Jew." For it's possible to be more or less of a Jew. In fact, there were plenty of Frenchmen who were hardly Jews at all: us, for instance! "Mendès-France was also a Jew, but that didn't do him any harm to speak of after the war. It was the collaborators who had reason to be worried when the purge began, what was called the purge . . ." "So why Georges?" I asked, yet again. "Because Papa was a man of the Third Republic," my father concluded. Oh. Surely I should have *seen*, surely it was obvious, *of course*, but I had no idea what this meant.

. . .

I returned to France with no intention of moving to Paris, where my father lived and where I grew up. I justified this to Elsa and my closest friends, who were waiting to finally welcome me back as a practical decision: I didn't want to bring two young children into a densely populated city at the height of a pandemic; I couldn't navigate the public schools' complicated districting policies or the lack of bilingual programs; the cost of living was too high. I could come up with any number of excuses, but the truth was that I just couldn't return to the center stage of my childhood. Paris was the historical headquarters of the emotional conflict between my parents, the epicenter of my divided loyalties to their respective influences and legacies. Paris was the ancestral home where I could be nothing but their daughter: the daughter of a crazy mother, a lavish folly of a father, and the granddaughter of a great if unjustly forgotten man. I had built a life for myself elsewhere because, in Paris, there was a cobblestone at every corner waiting to trip me up.

Anywhere but Paris, so long as I could get there easily enough to see my father. So why not a village in Seine-et-Oise? "A dump!" my father cried each time I reminded him where I was living. A dump if you say so, fine, but the girls were flourishing there. Tom covered the 2020 American election from the French countryside. The night the results came in, the noise of the joyful crowds in Brooklyn—we watched online—merged with the bleating of a flock of sheep from our neighbor's field. I was starting to consider things other than cooking and cleaning. I had accepted a new translation assignment. And I had begun a research project around my father and his father.

Now when I sat beside my father, prompts were no longer necessary to get him talking about Georges. My grandfather was the last standing monument among the rubble of my father's memory. Georges at the Élysée; Georges on the *Massilia*; Georges and Choute; Georges in Cannes; Georges dying; Georges and posterity. A hero in stained glass, like Gilbert le Mauvais under the ogives of Combray, Georges was at once vivid and two-dimensional. He didn't have the substance of a living being; he was forever frozen in a pose, painted by my father and my grandmother, luminous but spectral.

Papa's brothers were no longer around to fill out the picture: They had died before my birth, both by suicide. What could possibly have gone on in that family to set off such a trail of tragedies? My father's niece and nephew had both killed themselves, following their father. Papa's explanations were vague, contradictory, useless. In her memoir, Bonne-Maman—who also touched in passing on the suicide of her younger brother a few weeks before the Liberation—was as cryptic as Papa on the topic of these losses. It just so happened that there were a lot of premature and self-willed deaths in our family. Voilà. Papa had also lost two of his three sons, one in a car accident, the other in what was euphemistically referred to as an accident. Yes, our family knows tragedy, but one moves on! Papa and Bonne-Maman had kept on with their lives; mourning had not slowed them down, even if it murdered their sleep.

The last living person to have known Georges was my half-brother Bruno. He was just a young boy when our grandfather died, but his recollections of Georges were indelible, and, more importantly, he had preserved Georges' papers at the family country house outside Paris in the village of Valmondois, where Georges had once been mayor. Bruno had bought the house, a handsome turn-of-the-century property, from my father after Bonne-Maman's death. Bruno was in his forties at the time. A philosophy professor at a prestigious school in Paris, he would eventually run for mayor of Valmondois in his own right.

To celebrate Epiphany, Papa always gathered his phalanx of children in the dining room on Rue Erlanger. There would be a *galette des rois*, an immense puff pastry confection from Lenôtre. Following tradition, the youngest would hide under the table and designate who would be served next. Whoever received the slice with the little trinket hidden inside the cake became king or queen. I was always the one under the table. "And who's next?" Papa would bellow. And I'd call out the names of my elders, one by one. By the time I emerged, flakes of puff pastry were strewn all over the table like yellow French coins, like the contents of the piggy bank I had once broken open to help Maman after I'd heard her lament her poverty. We were made to perform for Papa. The scene had the air of classic literature—somewhere between *The Cherry Orchard* and *King Lear.*

It was at one of these gatherings—after the cake had been consumed—that Papa formally announced that he was selling Bonne-Maman's house to Bruno. Obviously, the sale was cheating the rest of us a little, he couldn't make his own son pay market price, and the home would no longer belong to all of us equally, but such was his wish, and he wished for us all to rejoice. I timidly joined in my elder sisters' protest: Over and above financial considerations, our brother was dispossessing us all of a repository of memory! Well, yes, yes, Papa answered wearily, putting an end to the argument. Please no fighting, he moaned, washing his hands of the conflict. The house belonged to Bruno, end of discussion. I would return to

Valmondois for my nieces' weddings; I would return for my father's funeral. Our dead rest in the little cemetery on the hill above the mayor's office.

Georges Huisman's archives—his paintings, books, and correspondence, or what was left of it after the war—were stored in the attic of the house at Valmondois. That our family inheritance had fallen to the eldest son was a fact I didn't have a say in; the youngest can hardly contest primogeniture from her hiding place under the table. And regardless, as Maman's daughter, I was never too sure of my legitimacy. Maman, who the most charitable pitied for her illness but whose existence everyone found quite inconvenient. Where, since I stood with and for my mother, did I stand in the Huisman family? And in the social functions we called reunions, where each of my half-siblings competed to outwit the other, to impress my father with their erudition, earning his approval, I felt not only younger but lesser.

When I returned to France during the pandemic, I'd been away for more than twenty years. I had built a career and started a family. I had published two books; I had told the story of my mother to the world. And while I didn't ask permission or expect praise from my family—a family that had shunned my mother—my books provided me a new status. I was now a writer, well reviewed; I was suddenly respected, listened to. Maman's voice ordered me to spit in their faces, but it was a relief when she stopped screaming in my ear and manipulating me from beyond the grave to wreak her vengeance on the world. For there were pockets of warmth in this family, too: Elsa and I had always been close to our nieces, Bruno's daughters. Papa was their grandfather, but we were the same age and had grown up together. They often spent weekends with us: long evenings in telephone booths in the basements of restaurants, plundering the candy buckets in the Valmondois bakery, our pockets bulging with coins Doggy had given us. Bruno had read my books generously and distributed them to his friends and colleagues. And he was thrilled to help me conduct research on Georges Huisman.

Maman," Sissi asks me in English, "how old were you when your maman was *morte*?" "Sissi, is it too much trouble to ask you to speak French? We've been living in France for six months. From the day you were born, I've never spoken to you in anything but French! Can you try a tiny bit harder?" "I speak French!" "Okay, *mon amour*, I knew it, I'm very proud of you. I'm listening." Sissi rephrases her question. I have to correct her grammar, but I must admit that French grammar can feel misanthropic. I was thirty when my mother died. She was sixty-two. "That's not very old," Sissi replies. Behind her frowning brow, her bright hazel eyes filled with mischief and sunbursts, I can see her calculating feverishly. "Doggy is much, much older than that." "Yes, *mon amour*. Doggy is ninety-one years old." "Ah, yes, he's very, very old! So is he going to die?" "Yes, he's going to die, my sweetheart." "And are you sad, Maman?" "Yes, I'm terribly sad, but it's also right for him to die, he's very tired, he's sick, he can't do much of anything anymore, it's time for him to go." "Are you crying, Maman?" "Sissi!" her sister shouts as she enters the room. "Why would you talk to Maman about Doggy dying? You know she'll cry." They leap into my arms. I am entitled to a double cuddle, one girl on each knee, their hair plastered across my face, their squabbling little arms held down in mine, kisses planted on my neck as they kick each other. "Are you quite finished brawling like a pair of *chiffonnières*?" "Like a pair of what? Are you quite finished crying, Maman?" That's the kind of respect I get from my daughters. "Don't bite! Just a little nibble here," Sissi pleads. "Gentle! Promise you'll be gentle!" When I was little, I would tell Maman to keep some for the next day, that she couldn't eat me all up in one go.

At an outdoor café one summer, between spoonfuls of chocolate ice cream, George, who was six at the time, asked me without warning why she had never met my mother. My first novel, in which I fictionalized my mother's life and channeled her voice, had come out a few months earlier. We had planned a family trip around a literary festival where I'd been invited. I had spent the day signing copies of my book in the banquet hall of the local township. Her question set my heart pounding. I looked at Tom, silently soliciting his support. We had somehow never finalized the version of the story we would offer our girls when they were old enough to ask. Tom took my hand. "My mother died, George. That's why you never met her." "But how? How did she die?" she asked. I had to decide, fast. With the steadiest voice I could summon, I said, "She chose to die." "Why?" George howled, her question dissolved into an agonized wail. "Why?" The violence of her reaction reverberated through my body. My fingers slipped from Tom's hand and tightened into a fist, but I remained calm—that is, I managed to sound calm: "Because she was sick, my sweetheart." "When you're sick you can get better," the child replied. "Yes, *mon amour*, yes, most of the time you can get better, that's true. Plenty of sick people get better. But my mother had a sickness that the doctors didn't know how to cure. And she suffered a great deal. So she chose to die. I'm so sorry. I'm sorry you never knew your grandmother, that you never got to meet my *maman*. I'm sorry this story makes you sad. I am so, so sorry." From my daughter's huge eyes, tears began to flow, forming rivulets in the chocolate ice cream she'd managed to get all over her face. She threw herself into my arms, smearing snot and tears and chocolate on my white dress. "Maman, you must have cried so much!" I'm sure that George spoke to me in English, yet I remember these words in French—my mother tongue, my father's—the only language either of my parents spoke.

Do you have an itinerary in mind, Monsieur Huisman?" "No, no, whichever way you think is best," my father would say to his driver. Then after a beat: "Well, if I were you, I'd take Avenue Pierre Ier-de-Serbie, that way you go past the Palais d'Iéna, the Palais de Tokyo, Chaillot, and then you head for Les Maréchaux, see, all the way to the Porte d'Auteuil. Otherwise, in a pinch, you could take Rue Franklin and Rue la Fontaine. Whatever you do, do not take Avenue Paul Doumer! Remember Avenue Mozart is one-way. Oh, and I'd like to make a quick stop at Carette."

Papa was chauffeured from his office to his home every day, with quick stops at the apartment we shared with Maman, or at his old mother's place while she was still alive, or at one of his mistresses', or at his favorite shops. His chauffeur, José, and he had driven these streets together countless times, yet Papa always negotiated his itinerary: "Where are you going, José? Avoid the river, it's always jammed this time of day!"

When Maman was committed to a mental hospital, it was José who drove Elsa and me to school every morning. In the afternoon, if the parking space in front of the school was taken, he waited for us by the street corner. I couldn't look him in the eye. I was ashamed, and ashamed of being ashamed, of José and his Portuguese accent, of being picked up from school in a chauffeured limo like a rich brat, but a rich brat whose father was too busy for her and whose mother was institutionalized. Papa had given us his room in the Rue Erlanger apartment, as he had always done on weekends when we slept at his place, but now our stay had been extended indefinitely. We were jolted out of bed every morning when José rang the doorbell. "You're going to be late, girls!" He urged us to grab a croissant from the mountain of pastries Papa had left for us in the kitchen. "It's bad to go to school on an empty stomach!" We were very late every morning, which was no different from the days when Maman had taken us, except that she, at least, drove the car up onto the sidewalk to speed things along. José drove cautiously, and we ended up very late indeed. He would give us a peck on the cheek at the gate, as if on behalf of our absent parents, and wait until we were inside. "See you tonight!" he called after us.

There should be a word in French for the exile who returns home. I often felt the need for it in the first months of my resettlement in France. German must have such a word. (My dictionary says *repatriate* can be used as a noun in English, but it doesn't capture the mixture of familiarity and alienation.) A sense of the *unheimlich* pervaded my days. I found myself overwhelmed by a deep, intolerable sense of disorientation. The condition was not merely symbolic or metaphorical; it manifested as a continuous physical loss of spatial awareness, an inability to orient myself. Running errands in my village became a nightmare. I would pass the same storefronts again and again in a kind of endless loop, awkwardly acknowledging the shopkeepers. I lived only a few blocks away, but the trick was remembering in which direction.

When I got off the train at the Gare de Lyon in Paris and plunged into its labyrinth of corridors, I had to choose between taking the yellow subway line to Franklin Roosevelt, the station for Papa's office, then changing to the green one, which crosses Paris from east to west like an arrow through the heart of the city, and connects my mother's parents' apartment, in the blue-collar suburb of Montreuil, to Papa's on Rue Erlanger, the two landmarks of my childhood—or I could emerge from the train station and cross the Pont d'Austerlitz to the Jardin des Plantes and get back underground and take the brown line. On that route, I would have to pass the Forensic Institute, the specific morgue unit that houses the dead by criminal cause—murder or suicide. That was where I had seen Maman for the last time, or Maman's corpse anyway. I knew these streets in my bones. I could visualize my location on the map with painful precision. I was the opposite of lost; I was in too many places at once, the city a frightening palimpsest. I would be crossing the Pont d'Austerlitz when suddenly, overwhelmed by the surge of signs, of histories, I no longer knew which side of the Seine I was approaching. The Right Bank, of course; Papa had always lived on the Right Bank. No, that couldn't be. The Right Bank had been uninhabitable for centuries because of its extensive swamps; that's why Lutetia had been built on the slopes of Montagne Sainte-Geneviève, on the Left Bank. That's why all the eminent schools of Paris, the Latin Quarter, Saint-Germain, the Sorbonne, and the Senate were on the Left Bank. That's why Saint Laurent, Rive Gauche. I had to stop halfway across the river, Notre-Dame in the background and a succession of bridges receding into the distance. On one side the morgue; on the other the Gare d'Austerlitz, where the Vichy regime had rounded up the Jews of France, starting with immigrants and political refugees, to be sent to Drancy and then to Auschwitz.

Like so many, the parents of Papa's first wife, Bruno's mother, had left from the Gare d'Austerlitz. She and Papa met toward the end of the war through neighbors, friends of the family. She was a year older than he; they were seventeen and sixteen, respectively. For several months, Papa joined her in the search for her parents at Hôtel Lutetia, the meeting grounds for deportees returning from camps all over Europe. They went every day, just in case. By August, they were forced to give up; the center was shut down, her parents were not coming home. In moments of extreme mental confusion, my mother would claim that her father had been exterminated in the gas chambers of Auschwitz, even though she was born two years after the camps were liberated. My mother in her mortuary chamber across the Seine.

I stand at the middle of the bridge, at a loss as to which side my subway line is on or which I am looking for. I have no idea which way to turn. I eventually take out my phone to look at the map. That is, to determine from the map which bank of the Seine the Jardin des Plantes is on. Ahead of me. Unless it is behind me. I begin to follow the little blue dot that crawls across the screen as I walk; I begin, in other words, to follow myself. No, I am heading in the wrong direction. I raise my eyes from the screen. I am indeed in front of number 55, Rue Erlanger, but I don't recognize the little ultramarine ceramic tiles around the building entrance. How is it possible that I have never once noticed them in thirty-five years? Their color is the same as, eerily identical to, the enameled street signs of

Paris. I have to walk down to the corner to check that I am in fact on the right street. Yes, Rue Erlanger. I return to my father's building and enter the security code. That I can remember: the letter *A*, the year of Papa's birth, and the postal code of Marseille.

When I returned to France as a "repatriate" and asked after the materials in the attic, Bruno explained to me that Georges Huisman's archives had been only partially cataloged. "We should bequeath them to a national collection, there are amazing documents in there!" He said "in there" like he was referring to a jungle, only partially explored. The archive was sprawling, unstructured. It was partially catalogued because, some years before, a brave woman had begun the Herculean task of sorting through it for her dissertation—sorting through the piles of boxes full of disparate correspondence, dog-eared business cards, photographs, notebooks. She was a doctoral candidate working on cultural politics between the wars. In the course of her research, she had decided to focus on our grandfather as a pivotal figure. Papa had often spoken of her: Béatrice Duval.

My image of Béatrice had always been vague. Initially I pictured her as young because she was still in school, but then Papa had mentioned that she'd taken up her studies later in life; I didn't have a clear sense of her age. And Papa hadn't said anything about her looks, which was surprising, because a woman to him was always necessarily embodied, her potential for seduction being her most notable quality. A woman was either old and ugly or a young pretty thing, but Béatrice was only "the doctoral candidate." Her focus was on Georges' years running the Beaux-Arts on Rue de Valois, what is now known as the Ministry of Culture. I knew that Papa had met with her many times in his office behind the Champs-Élysées, under Georges' portrait. Needless to say, he had often taken her to fancy restaurant lunches. She had consulted with him for years as her work dragged on; Papa would complain every once in a while about how she was taking so long to bang out her damn dissertation. (During the course of their conversations, Béatrice would later tell me, she developed a deep affection for my father—for the old man he was, and for the little boy he'd been.)

Bruno sent me Béatrice's contact and her thesis as an email attachment. I took notes as I read it and found myself often overwhelmed. Despite its academic structure, her writing was surprisingly intimate. The correspondence she chose to excerpt, the conclusions she drew from certain episodes of history, her interpretation of events felt laden with emotion, genuine affection. She had restored Georges to life half a century after his death. *Georges Huisman, Rue de Valois (1934–1940)*, her doctoral dissertation in art history, was submitted in 2014. Béatrice had hand-delivered a copy to my father, with a heartfelt dedication. Papa was still sound of mind at the time. He was perfectly capable of reading it. He never did; he never responded to Béatrice. She was wounded by his silence, not so much hurt as disappointed, she would tell me (but surely she was hurt). When he had failed to appear at the defense of her dissertation, she had convinced herself that some ill-timed illness or small emergency had kept him away. Otherwise, how could my father, so obsessed with his father's legacy, not have attended? (I didn't mention to Béatrice, when she told me of her surprise, that my father had failed to attend *any* event in my life—graduations, my mother's funeral—where his presence would have signaled support.)

After I read her dissertation, I called Béatrice and told her how much her work had moved me. She would be happy, she said, to help me with my own research regarding my grandfather in any way she could; she had read my books. I suggested that we go for a walk in the woods some weekend; Fontainebleau was gorgeous in the fall, it would be so nice if she wanted to come down. I could pick her up at the train station if she didn't drive. I would invite her for tea, but meeting indoors still wasn't recommended, and then there were my girls. Yes, she understood, she was also a mother. A walk in the woods would be lovely. She would come by car.

The woman stepping out of a dark blue Renault with Paris plates—a practical family car—is nothing like the person I'm expecting, not that I know what to expect. But it is the only car in the parking lot at the appointed hour: ten a.m., in front of the Barbizon tourist center. We planned to walk the loop made famous by the nineteenth-century landscape painters. The path is marked in yellow, the easiest trail in the walking track grading system, but extraordinarily scenic, at least according to the information leaflet: "The site as wild as when Corot painted its ancient stands of oak and rock formations." The woman has improbably long and curly ash-blonde hair that's backlit by the sun. She seems to have stepped out of some fairy tale. I can tell she is smiling broadly despite her mask because of the lines that form around her green eyes. Our outfits are startlingly similar, down to our leather boots, totally inappropriate for a forest hike. Our faded jeans are identical down to the topstitching. We each carry a tote on our shoulder—hers from a Paris museum—and each are wearing a dark-colored mid-length coat. The coincidence feels staged. I am caught off guard by her unquestionable beauty. How did Papa not describe her as ravishing?

No doubt because a woman cannot be both smart and beautiful in Papa's book. A pretty young thing cannot be an intellectual.

The leaflet is right—the trail is enchanting. We walk at a steady pace, side by side, our steps in sync, quickly giving up on trying to protect our leather boots from the mud. My most pressing question for Béatrice is about Choute, what she knows about her, if she can at least confirm her reality. I'm embarrassed to ask in a rush after a figure of familial, not historical importance, but I can't help it. "You know, the one person who can tell you about Choute is your father! A marquise by birth, she had married a duke and soon became his widow. She met Georges in L'Arcouest, among that cohort of intellectuals, artists, and scientists on the Bay of Launay. Rich aristocrats, she and her husband threw a lot of parties; they were renowned patrons of the arts." "But was she really at the Château de Chaumont with Georges?" "I don't know," Béatrice replies. "She was certainly at Chaillot; he refers to Choute several times in the journal he kept at Chaillot. You know, it was Georges who oversaw the construction of the Palais de Chaillot for the 1937 International Expo. Jacques Carlu, one of the great architects of his generation—he had worked in the United States and taught at MIT—was an old buddy of Georges, they had belonged to the same unit in WWI. Carlu coincidentally returned to France the year Georges was appointed directeur des Beaux-Arts. Carlu had also been director of the Fontainebleau art school, where he hired Georges to teach art history. It's an amazing place, housed in the Louis XV wing of the Château de Fontainebleau. Its archive is fabulous—there's a lot of Georges in there. I'd assumed that's why you moved your family to Fontainebleau?"

Georges was a handsome man, with piercing eyes so blue you

can tell their color even in black-and-white photographs. "A truly charismatic man," says Béatrice. "Laure Albin Guillot became something like his official house photographer, he created a position for her to start collecting and organizing photography and cinema archives. That was very forward thinking; cinema wasn't thought of as a real art, neither was photography, the notion of a cinematheque was very avant-garde. Georges had a deep passion for movies, and although his field of expertise was primarily architecture and painting, he loved all the arts. He believed in art's political impact, not only as a diplomatic tool—the first thing that comes to mind, obviously, is the Cannes Film Festival, but then there are so many other examples. All of this your father found naive, to put it kindly. 'What a fool!' your dad would shout—he got particularly worked up about that medal Georges refused after the war. Georges wanted to make culture accessible for all, he wanted to bring art into schools, into daily life, into the streets. He commissioned several murals from Fernand Léger, who became a true friend, a great friend." (I remembered, as Béatrice talked, the Léger high relief in Bonne-Maman's living room, which I always associated with the Egyptian friezes they taught us about in elementary school. Papa sold it, surely. Along with the Braque collage—a dove against a purple background—that hung over the kitchen table in my childhood apartment.)

The light is beginning to fade, filtering through the chestnuts and turning the path to gold at our feet. I think of Apollinaire—"The wind and the forest weeping / Their tears in autumn leaf by leaf / The leaves / Trampled." I ask Béatrice if Georges knew him. "It's possible. They moved in the same circles. It's all the same generation. They all fought in WWI together, or, if not together, at the same time. Through Léger, perhaps? Apollinaire has this line about Léger—a play on the meaning of his name, lightness and light colors."

I ask Béatrice about WWII, the war my father lived through. She tells me how so many artists immigrated clandestinely to New York from Marseille. Marseille, where Papa and his parents spent the first two years of the war, after the exodus, the armistice. But they didn't immigrate. They stayed. As I try to picture them in Marseille in my mind's eye, I see no one, I see an abstracted version of *la corniche*, an immense stretch of blue on the horizon, and I see the idea I have of an enormous boat, the *Massilia*. The passengers had to be ferried to the ship on little tenders, huddled together with their piles of luggage. It was an immense ocean liner, a little like the *Normandie*, Papa had said, an analogy that did nothing for me, so I imagined the *Titanic*, or the *Titanic* from the movies. My father was ten years old. His mother forced him to wear a life jacket, which looked totally ridiculous, consisting of a ring of enormous cylindrical floats that made his arms stick straight out. "Of course," Papa would roar each time he told me the story, "I took it off the moment I was out of her sight. It made me look like an absolute moron!"

"Why didn't they go to London instead of boarding the *Massilia*?" "I don't think we can fully grasp," says Béatrice, "what being Jewish meant for these men. The *Massilia* was supposed to dock in Algiers, which was still part of France, they were going to keep fighting. Leaving the country, fleeing to England, would have lent credence to all the anti-Semitic slander they had suffered—that they were cowards, traitors. The British had made Georges Mandel a clear offer of sanctuary, de Gaulle had personally tried to convince him to follow him to London, the night of Pétain's infamous armistice speech, 'It is with a heavy heart . . . ' Mandel told him that it was impossible. As a Jew, he'd be called a coward and a deserter, which they ultimately called him anyway. Mandel was with Léon Blum in Buchenwald, locked in a separate compound overlooking the camp; while hardly comfortable, their situation wasn't comparable to other detainees', but they were held in solitary confinement, cut off from the world and without news of the war. He was eventually transferred to a prison in Paris where the Milice caught him and brought him here, to Fontainebleau. He was shot just a few weeks before the liberation."

"I thought it was Jean Zay who was assassinated by the Milice?"

"Him too. In *l'Allier.* Vichy's paramilitary squad impersonated resistance fighters to convince him to join them, saying they would help him get to the Maquis. After they shot him they stripped him of his clothes and his wedding ring so he couldn't be identified. His body was found by accident two years later in a ravine and buried in the local cemetery, from which it was later exhumed. I had just turned in my dissertation when he was interred in the Pantheon, right outside my window. Sixty years later. It felt like a sign. Of what I have no idea! Or maybe, yes, that my work was not entirely in vain, that I was doing my part to rescue these figures from oblivion, from the national amnesia."

The first time I got a sense of what being Jewish might mean to you, Papa, we were at the movies on the Champs-Élysées, a beautiful cinema that no longer exists, around the corner from the office that is no longer yours. Louis Malle's *Au revoir les enfants*, *Goodbye, Children*, had just come out. I was the age my George is now. The story takes place at a French boarding school where Jewish boys are hiding during the war. You were sitting next to me in the *strapontin*—the little fold-out seat along the aisle, which you favored, however small and uncomfortable it was, so you could be closer to the exit, so you could stretch your legs and get up without bothering anyone. There was a scene toward the end of the film when the protagonist, a Catholic boy, is asked to pull down his pants in front of a German officer searching the school. I heard you stifle a sob. And then you were weeping uncontrollably, your entire body convulsed. I watched you, aghast, incredulous, and, without understanding why, I also broke down in tears. You took my hand and held it very tightly for the rest of the film. Like the boy on the screen, you later told me, you started wetting your bed in those years. And even in the theater, you felt humiliated at the memory of waking in the middle of the night, the sheets soaked with piss.

You have always claimed to be an atheist, but you have never traveled anywhere without what you call your bible, *Le guide du croyant israelite*, a collection of prayers written by your great-grandfather Lazare Wogue, known as Grand Rabbi Éléazar. You have asked us not to forget to place it on your chest when you die, that you must have it in your coffin.

Whenever I say my family name in France—to a telephone operator, at a ticket counter, at a doctor's office, to a government official, no matter the context or the situation—and I spell it out for further clarity, my interlocutor invariably responds: Huis*mann*. What I said was Huis*man*, as in *maman*, a softer *n*. I repeat it once, twice, ten times during the course of the conversation, with the increasingly ominous feeling that I am not making sense, I am not being heard, or maybe I am the one who is mistaken—perhaps my entire life I've pronounced my own name wrong? "Do you suggest I don't know my own name?" I hear you shout. For this skirmish over pronunciation is, in your mind, a little repetition of our family's banishment and flight. It's never struck me as so malevolent: I agree that our name doesn't sound very French. And indeed, it's not. It's Flemish. Georges' father, Hartog, was from Belgium, where the last syllable of his last name certainly did not rhyme with *maman*. Georges, on the other hand, was born in France; like you, he grew up in the sixteenth arrondissement of Paris. "I don't exactly know what it means to be Jewish, what being Jewish means to me," wrote another Georges—the writer Georges Perec, whose name also sounded typically French: It just missed an accent to pass as authentically Breton.

"Being Jewish is a fact, but not a very relevant fact. It is more of a lapse, a question, a questioning, a hesitation, a concern: that behind this concerning fact lies another fact whose imprecise contours weigh you down: that of having been designated as Jewish . . ."

In Marseille, where you and your family landed after you returned from North Africa, the headmaster of the Lycée Thiers called you into his office. "Tell me, *Huissemanne*, you're a Jewish national, aren't you?" "No sir, no, I'm French, I'm a French citizen. Jewish is not a nationality. A religion, a denomination, a culture maybe—a race, some might say—but not a nationality." "Okay, *Huissemanne*, don't try to fool me with word games. Are you or are you not a Jew?" "If you say so, sir. If you say so."

Béatrice Duval's dissertation focuses on Georges' work at the helm of the Beaux-Arts administration, but she also carefully describes his larger trajectory: from the vice presidency under Paul Doumer, to the Senate and on to Rue de Valois, then his family's destitute wanderings during the war, and finally, after the war's conclusion, his job on the Conseil d'État. For Georges was not restored to his former office, which he experienced as a tragic rejection. It weighed so heavily on his heart, said Papa, that he languished for ten years before surrendering to death. In *Beautiful Illusion: Culture and Politics Under the Sign of the Popular Front*, Pascal Ory, a distinguished historian and member of the Académie française, presents Georges as a key figure of the prewar government. My father's edition, its cover torn in half, distended from my compulsive note-taking, bears the following inscription: "In homage to the son of one of the most important protagonists of this book." Despite its prestige, the position Georges held within the Conseil d'État after the war wasn't, Ory writes, suited to his ambitions. There was no great mission, no overriding aim for him to fulfill there; it was ultimately a very bureaucratic position: "So little for such a man!" The quote became a catchphrase in our family. We trotted it out at every opportunity, laughing at its bombast. "Well, now, so little for such a man!"

France's highest administrative court and governmental body, the Conseil d'État advises the government on ordinances and decrees, serving as its final arbiter. Under Vichy, it distinguished itself by approving an impressive number of anti-Semitic laws. Some historians even assert that the Council epitomized the legalization of anti-Semitism under the occupation, that it became the go-to authority on the "Jewish Problem." After the war, Georges supported a bill allowing naturalized immigrants to Gallicize their names. This elective amendment was limited to spelling changes that would make a name easier to pronounce, leading the way for future laws that would broaden options for modification, such that foreigners could decide to make their name as French as they wished. Freeing oneself from the trace of otherness embedded in one's name was seen as an opportunity; assimilation was considered a basis for equality.

Primo Levi's *Survival in Auschwitz* was required reading by the time I was in elementary school. That Papa insisted so vociferously on being called *Huisman-as-in-maman*, that he preferred to sidestep his Jewish ancestry to lay claim to Frenchness, struck me, as a child, as denying himself an honor: the honor of having survived. For I grew up at a moment when the Vichy regime's culpability in the deportation and extermination of French Jews was lamented, but in a way that made anti-Semitism seem safely ensconced in the past. I was old enough to follow the trial of Klaus Barbie on television. At ten, my father had heard anti-Jewish laws pronounced on a radio broadcast in a transit shelter in North Africa; when I was ten, I watched the Berlin Wall come down in an elegant Parisian apartment while my mother was in a mental hospital. The tragedy of my father's childhood was his *déclassement* as a Jew. The tragedy of my childhood was my mother's *déclassement*, her social ostracizing not because of her background—working class, uneducated—but because of her mental illness. Contrary to Papa, Maman considered her claim to Jewishness, through her father, to be a mark of prestige. It was her way of belonging to our erudite family, of trying to weave herself into the tapestry of the Huismans, one *n*.

Béatrice advised me to dig into the Valmondois archives. "It's an enormous task," she cautioned. "I tried to organize what I could, but there was stack upon stack of boxes. I only took care of a tiny portion, selecting what seemed most relevant to my work. There are heaps of papers left to inventory and sort through. I can't promise you'll find Choute's letters." "Bonne-Maman would surely have burned them," I said. She laughed. "Well, a lot has indeed been burned. Possibly even love letters. That's not my area of expertise, though I have nothing against romance! Oh wait, now that I think about it—no, sorry, nothing to do with Choute, I didn't mean to give you false hope—but I did come across a bundle of correspondence between Georges and his mother, Louise, between Marseille and Paris."

You described your father as an incorrigible Don Juan who picked up every ballerina of the Paris Opera, seduced every actress in the Comédie-Française. Imagine, le directeur des Beaux-Arts!

He could just snap his finger and get any girl he wanted! Dancers had good technique, but he preferred actresses, who were more emotional. I ask Béatrice what she thinks about this portrayal. "Your father was the ladies' man!" she exclaims. "I don't know, I wasn't there, but it strikes me as very unlikely that Georges would have been so fickle. He was a man of deep integrity, never overbearing, never haughty." But what about Choute? "I suppose you can fall in love without being a skirt-chaser! Choute existed, that much is certain. Her name—Choute, always plain Choute—appears again and again in his diaries for 1939 and 1940 at Chaillot. 'Lunch with Choute,' or just 'Choute,' with no specific time slot. But not every meeting with a woman is an assignation. And Georges was very involved in women's causes when it was hardly the norm except, precisely, in the Front Populaire, which was really ahead of its time in that regard. Georges hired many women for his cabinet—Laure Albin Guillot, of course, but lots of others. He assigned many commissions to women artists, he wrote a radio play about Marceline Desbordes-Valmore, whose work, he believed, had been unfairly neglected. And remember that he coauthored two books with his wife, your grandmother, the little collections of tales from the Middle Ages and the French Revolution. Have you read them? Of course, they're not great works of literature, but even supposing that she was the one who wrote them, which I think is likely, how many men in 1930 would have insisted on their wives getting their due credit? He hardly ever wore his top hat. There are countless pictures from official functions where you can see him with his hat under his arm. I also noticed your grandmother mourned this habit of his in her memoirs; too often, he demonstrated a lack of protocol; he was doing himself no favors, she seemed to think. And he didn't have your father's panache from what I could gather; he always appears to be leaning back in pictures, his head tilted as if he were trying to recede into the background."

Georges Huisman authored a disparate array of works, which Béatrice Duval lists in her bibliography. Of note are a monograph of the Flemish painter Memling; a treatise on aviation in the First World War, based on his observations; a biography of Manon Roland, a proto-feminist figure from the French Revolution; and an illustrated essay on the monuments of Paris. I immersed myself in Georges' prose in search of a voice—verbal tics, metaphors, punctuation—that would rise above Papa's assertions, a grandfather's voice I could separate from my father's. Bonne-Maman had also put together a collection of speeches delivered at his funeral. *Georges Huisman par quelques-uns de ses amis* can be found on the shelves of every member of my extended family. Multiple boxes of the book can also be found in a corner of the Valmondois attic. The little bound volume features emotional tributes by some of Georges' most distinguished friends: writers, artists, musicians, officials. René Cassin, Nobel peace laureate and drafter of the Universal Declaration of Human Rights after the war; Roland Dorgelès; Georges Duhamel; Darius Milhaud. All without exception agree that of Georges Huisman's collected works, the one to endure would be his magnificent ode to the capital, *Pour comprendre les monuments de Paris*.

You, Papa, were barely thirty when your father died. You waged your battles and pursued your projects out of his sight whenever possible so as to stay free of his judgment. You would neither seek nor spurn his advice. Free from the actual man, you could mythologize him to your heart's content. You had four children already, you had published two books, and you were about to open your school franchise. You had wasted no time. I was also thirty when my mother died, but, unlike you, I didn't have children, I had published nothing.

I saw Béatrice again at my father's funeral in the winter of 2021. The pandemic had us on a kind of lockdown again. She was one of a handful of guests outside the immediate family. My two closest childhood friends were there, too—the ones who had helped me and Elsa scatter our mother's ashes in Dakar, as per her wishes—though they hadn't been invited, and, in fact, I had told them not to come. Iris and Ada said their presence wasn't optional. If they had traveled to Dakar on a day's notice, they would certainly make it to the Valmondois cemetery. Elsa and I were like sisters to them. Whether our blood relatives acknowledged it or not was irrelevant. Papa's wishes called for pomp, for crowds. Ideally, we would have had the Republican Guard follow us all the way from Paris to Valmondois: the infantry, motorcycle brigade, calvary, and mounted band, all thousands of them in helmets adorned with cockades and feathers. But that spring, even the Queen of England had to bury her king in strictest privacy. Serving as Papa's guards of honor were two lieutenants in military attire, whom a friend of Elsa's had bribed to attend. They accomplished their duty—standing beside the coffin like legitimate ceremonial guards—with a degree of seriousness that verged on slapstick. My girls were there; Tom was there. George burst into tears at the very first words of my eulogy. It did not lack pathos. I was the last to speak—as I was the last to be born. Save for the dogs, of course.

Overlooking the L'Isle-Adam forest, on a hilltop rising above the valley like an amphitheater, Papa would rest under a gray slab of granite engraved with our family name. Together with his grandparents, his mother, his father, his sons. At the foot of the slope, a far more imposing funereal monument paid tribute to a far more renowned Frenchman: Louis-Nicolas Bescherelle, the custodian of conjugation for every student of the French language. The plot that held my family's remains was also the final resting place of the guardian of grammatical time.

"How is your work on Georges progressing?" Béatrice asked after holding out both of her hands and offering me her condolences. "I can't say. I'm stuck, or I don't know—lost." "Oh, I'm sorry. It must be so hard. Trying to write the book of your father's father—and then your father passes. Give me a call. Let's make a date. We could go to Chaumont together?" I said I would love that. Again I saw the lines around her green eyes; the black of her mask felt fitting for the day.

For some reason, I was the only one to have really dressed up for the occasion, excepting the military men. (Perhaps everyone had been accustomed to lockdown attire.) I had on a long-sleeved black midi dress in silk georgette; I believed my father would have found it to be an exemplary mourning costume. I had polished my leather boots. A passage from Proust came to mind, the misogyny of which felt worthy of Papa's worst tirades: "In the lives of most women, everything, even the greatest sorrow, ends up being a fashion question." Never mind. I was prepared to forgive anything on that day. I was even prepared to be cast as frivolous. I was grateful for the chance to doll myself up for Papa one last time.

It was bitterly cold, as it had been at Georges' funeral, according to witness reports. In my mind, the two funerals were suddenly overlayed. We, my father and I, were standing before the same grave. The same vault. Armed with the same white roses. Papa, too, was dressed in an elegant suit. Except he was also down there, his book of prayers on his chest.

After the funeral we would all gather at the house, Bruno's house. We had laid out a spread of Carette tea sandwiches. I thought perhaps I would be able to sneak away and explore the attic, half imagining I might find a madwoman there.

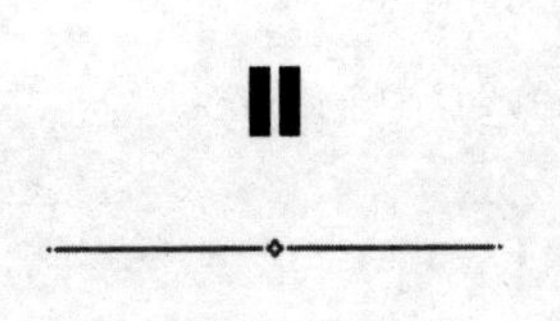

Thursday, 16 May 1940. At 14.00. The powers that be advise us to burn our papers as if the Germans will march into Paris any minute now. We're still in Chaillot, cars gassed up, all packed, but no order comes."

In her far-from-exhaustive catalog of the Valmondois archives, Béatrice Duval registered the journal that Georges kept from May 2 to June 17, 1940, under the heading "1940 Diary." She quotes this excerpt in her thesis. I know the journal is in one of the labeled boxes, but I can't find it, and I stop looking lest I disrupt her filing system. Instead, I sort through one of the uncataloged piles—as promised, there are innumerable piles. I have no idea what I'm after, so I dig around at random. A card from Léon Blum, effusively thanking Georges for his condolences on the death of his wife. A letter from Fernand Léger, written in colored pencil, peppered with puns and adorned with a turquoise border. A receipt for a lunch for two at Le Barbu, table 11, where the couple washed down a half bottle of Pouilly, a bottle of Vichy, a *café-calva*. A menu for a Christmas Eve supper—the "last Christmas before victory," it says on the little sheet of graph paper, folded in half and written out by hand: *choucroute alsacienne*, champagne, coffee ("the real thing!" underlined twice), Valmondois apples, bread (war bread or actual bread?). A calling card from the foreign minister, Pierre Laval, conveying his best wishes. Georges' business card as honorary secretary-general of the presidency of the Republic and chief of staff to the president of the Senate, at the Palais du Luxembourg. Stationery bearing the Council of State letterhead. A black-and-white photo of Georges mounted on a mat of yellowing cardboard. He's seated behind a massive desk, sporting a mustache, a bow tie (this mustache, this bow tie, appear in every single portrait), and a striped three-piece suit. His hair slicked back; broad forehead; a large, straight nose (mine?); full lips; high cheekbones. The piercing brightness of his eyes. A fountain pen in his right hand, a cigarette in his left, and his forearms are resting on an enormous stack of papers. He's not wearing a ring although he must have already been married at that time. In the background, reflected in a mirror hung above the fireplace, a woman's silhouette casts a shadow over the back of the room. The photo has been pinned to the wall more than once, as evidenced by the holes at each corner of the mat, which my father has signed in pencil with his first name. I imagine it was he, too, who drew a rosette on Georges' jacket lapel in red marker.

Following the funeral, after our modest buffet—so modest, I shivered at the thought of Papa's judgment—everyone left in quick succession, including Tom and the girls, who I encouraged to go without me. I tried to help Bruno and his wife clean up the leftovers, but they wouldn't hear of it. "Leave it, please, and go on up to the attic," said Bruno. I had not been to Valmondois since their elder daughter's wedding, twenty years before. The house had not changed, but it had shrunk, like all the places from the past. My childhood echoed in the sound of my footsteps clattering on the tiles in the entry hall. The grand piano in the drawing room, the great walnut table in the dining room, and the French doors leading to the concrete terrasse overlooking the garden were exactly as I remembered. There is but a single, solitary cherry tree at the very end of the property, but our house in Valmondois always merges in my mind with Chekhov's *The Cherry Orchard*. In the small room on the ground floor that Bonne-Maman had claimed for herself after her husband's death, the furniture and linens continued to carry the smell of her face powder and lavender water. Every object had remained in its place, almost too perfectly, too exactly, as in a museum display: the twin bed and antique wardrobe, her trinkets and toiletries laid out on top of the dresser, her soft pink quilted cotton bathrobe hanging from its peg.

Georges' first major project as the newly appointed directeur des Beaux-Arts was the reimagining of the Palais de Chaillot. In the nineteenth century, decades of urban planning had turned this hilly meadow overlooking the Seine into the Trocadéro monument and square. Inaugurated in 1878, about a decade before the Eiffel Tower (which it would end up facing), it was named after a victorious French battle against Spain. The Trocadéro Palace was a gigantic, multicolored, bizarrely byzantine, minaret-topped edifice, and unanimously abhorred. Across the nineteenth and twentieth centuries, world fairs or universal expos served as pretexts for the edification or reconstruction of monuments, some more enduring than others. Unlike the Eiffel Tower, which Parisians grew fond of over time, the "old" Palais de Chaillot never ceased to be decried as an eyesore. Taking advantage of the closest thing there was to a world fair under his mandate—the 1937 International Exhibition of Art and Technology in Modern Life—Georges promptly ordered the palace razed.

He was criticized for selecting Jacques Carlu as the architect for the undertaking. Carlu was his dear friend, a former war comrade, his former boss at the American School of Fine Arts in Fontainebleau; some kind of inside favor was suspected. "I don't think that's true," Béatrice told me when I asked her about this on our walk in Fontainebleau. "What's important here is that 1937 is a turning point. Paul Rivet's Musée de l'Homme—the Museum of Mankind, conceived as a think tank to study what defined humanity—opened in one of the wings of Chaillot that year. At the same time, Georges inaugurated the Palais de la Découverte, the Palais de Tokyo . . . This was France entering a world competition for cultural capital. The policies of the Front Populaire were decisive with regard to museums. There was the major van Gogh retrospective that inaugurated the Palais de Tokyo, Paris' new museum of modern art. Pascal Ory actually sees it as the first major modern art show, the prototype of all the blockbuster exhibitions to come."

The plan for the new Palais de Chaillot was to streamline the existing edifice rather than destroy it completely. Carlu and a team of architects, selected by a panel of experts—this wasn't a matter of Georges hiring a friend—proposed to keep the shell and decapitate the columns, plane down the bloated facades, minimize the moldings, cut the building open, and redistribute it around an esplanade. It would remain as gigantic, but it would look entirely different. It would look, that is, of its time. And indeed, few Parisian monuments showcase so prominently the most outdated aspects of the interwar style: its calcified classicism, elevated by pompously poetic aphorisms by Paul Valéry emblazoned in gold letters on the pediment.

The 1937 World Expo, which was so central to Georges' career, fanned out from Chaillot to the Champ de Mars across the Seine, along Avenue d'Iéna, and diagonally toward the Arc de Triomphe and the Champs-Élysées. The Third Reich pavilion, topped off by the Nazi eagle, and that of the USSR, featuring the colossal sculpture *Worker and Kolkhoz Woman*, flanked the Eiffel Tower. Among the fifty nations represented, the Spanish Pavilion unveiled Pablo Picasso's *Guernica*, completed in Paris just days before the exhibition opened.

At the height of his career, my father arranged for a group of his students to stand in rows on the Trocadéro esplanade to spell out the acronym of his school—EFAP—and had them photographed from a helicopter. When I picture the Palais de Chaillot—its vast marble terrasse facing the Eiffel Tower, its water fountains down below, its 1930s statues—the image I invariably conjure is Papa's promotional stunt. Papa and his extravagance, his fierce capitalism, his folly. Papa's bold revenge against the war years. Papa's personal ownership of every monument of Paris, including those in part erected by his papa.

It was as though Georges were scattered among the stones of Paris and I was on an archaeological mission. I had to excavate him from layer upon layer of memory and narrative. At Chaillot, which would become the set for the signing of the declaration of human rights in the aftermath of the Second World War, time folded in on itself like uncut pages in a book.

"While its aesthetic value is nil, its technical virtuosity is indisputable," Georges wrote of the Eiffel Tower in *Pour comprendre les monuments de Paris*. For those of his generation, the quintessential Parisian edifice remained an odious column of bolted iron that had somehow become a permanent fixture in spite of its hideousness.

Georges was born within days of its inauguration, in May 1889. His father, Hartog, a Jew of Flemish descent, was raised in Belgium; his mother, Louise, an Alsatian, was born into a family of patriots who, following France's fall to Prussia, gave up their haberdashery in Mulhouse rather than lose their French citizenship.

Hartog was mostly illiterate. A traveling salesman, he specialized in no particular goods and, depending on the season, dealt in wine, fertilizer, hempseed, or cotton. Louise, the eldest of three girls, had sacrificed her studies to help her father raise her sisters after their mother died young. Louise had been a brilliant and passionate student, and having had her schooling interrupted made her all the more ambitious for her future son: Georges would have to become an intellectual. Academic achievement was, in her mind, the most enviable form of success. Louise vowed to have an only child—they would never have the means to raise more than one—and that he would pass the *agrégation*, the pinnacle of the French education system. He would, of course, have to grow up in Paris.

Louise found a position as a nanny and tutor for a rich banker's children in the upscale neighborhood of Passy, in the sixteenth arrondissement (a few blocks from Chaillot). Mr. Hirsch and family lived in a magnificent mansion on Avenue Mozart, and the Huismans moved next door, into a simple one-bedroom apartment at 54 bis, fifth floor. I imagine they spoke Yiddish at home. According to my father's retelling, Hartog spoke a heavily accented French, either as a trace of his exile or his Jewishness, it was never fully explained. It was said that he had so little education that he had to ask his customers to write down their own purchase orders so Louise could decipher them later; he had to sign his own son's birth certificate with a cross. Louise taught the Hirsch children through elementary school and was allowed to include her own boy in these lessons. Described to me as the archetype of the Jewish mother, she was remembered as heroic, intractable, madly affectionate, convinced of the preeminence of her child, and prepared to do whatever it took to force the world to recognize the genius of her darling son.

About anti-Semitism in early twentieth-century France, Léon Blum wrote: "It had arisen in the restricted circles of Parisian society, among elitist and professional circles; its immediate cause was the intrusion and encroachment of wealthy Jews or studious Jews, which had been experienced as too precipitous." The Jew was considered a "foreign body," a "body impossible to assimilate." By virtue of an irrefutable tautology, the Jew was considered unassimilable because the Jew, by definition, could not be truly French. And the Jew who dared to think of himself as French was, of course, the most suspect of this suspicious race.

My family's Jewishness was so nebulous in my upbringing—every question I asked about it only confused me more—that I was shocked to discover, reading Bonne-Maman's memoirs as I was conducting my research, that she and Georges had been married in a synagogue. I was dumbfounded to find out that this bible my father cherished had in fact been written by my great-great-grandfather Lazare Wogue, chief rabbi of Paris, a renowned professor of theology and Hebrew in the French Israelite seminary. The Huismans I knew were secular Jews; we were barely Jews. The notion of Shabbat was mentioned to me for the first time at seventeen by a classmate explaining why they couldn't go out on Fridays. Being Jewish was such a distant, imprecise reality in my life that Iris and Ada, attending my father's funeral, were stunned to see, propped up among the photos that Bruno had placed on the mantelpiece, the fake identity cards that my father and his mother had used during the war. "Look at this," Bruno said, pointing to our grandmother's signature. Marcelle Georges Huisman, renamed Alice Cécile Henriquet, had mistakenly signed her real name, "M. G. Henriquet." The photo showed her in profile. Details of her identification included the shape of her nose, the dimensions of its bridge and base. Hers was straight, of average length. Partially buried among the jumble of pictures and keepsakes was also Georges' ID, under his real name; as well as his card as mayor of Valmondois; a photo of him in the village square, by the municipal building, looking jubilant among a group of uniformed soldiers; and an undated, partially filled-out and unsigned form with a picture on the top right corner in which he appeared emaciated. "Hook nose," the form said.

"Is that your father?" Iris asked about the identity card in the name of Denis Antoine Henriquet, tilting to one side to adjust her angle and read through the glare on the glass. "Well, yes." "Henriquet?" Iris asked again, as if I might be mistaken. "Yes, his assumed name during the war." "That's so crazy!" Ada said. "Haven't you ever heard my father tell the story of the *Massilia*?" Sure, they had heard the story of the *Massilia* countless times over extravagant meals where Papa was ecstatic to watch them lick the plate of profiteroles. It never made much sense to them that my father was Jewish, or it was irrelevant. Besides, no one ever pretended to understand the story of the *Massilia*. It wasn't taught in school; it wasn't a famous episode of the war, a war that to them, to us, belonged to our grandparents' generation. It was impossible to imagine my father in hiding—"*Your father!*" they exclaimed; their emphasis was resonant. More than anything, my father was to my friends a paragon of Frenchness, the very essence of Parisian chic, if also a caricature of its excesses. The underlying and almost subliminal message that Jewishness and Frenchness were incompatible endured, even in Iris and Ada, who had known me almost since birth. "You did know my father's family fled during the war," I replied. Still, they couldn't imagine it. And I, too, felt unimaginably distant from his persecution. Even now I feel reluctant to lay claim to this history of discrimination, even if my family's experience is intimately entangled in it.

Georges had no burning political ambition. He passed his *agrégation*, as his mother wished; his top choice over all other elite schools was the École des Chartes, an institution whose founding mission was to revive the study of archives. (What would he have made of his granddaughter searching among these piles?) He won a prize for his thesis titled "The Jurisdiction of the Municipality of Paris from Saint Louis to Charles VII." And thus he became an *archiviste-paleographe*. ("What a bore!" I could hear my father exclaiming.) Georges envisioned an academic career for himself and hoped to publish a few books down the line, maybe write a review here and there to keep current with the work of his contemporaries. And that is, in fact, exactly how he started out.

Drafted into military service as a penniless student—weighing barely one hundred pounds, never eating a square meal—he was soon sent home for health reasons. This provisional discharge was a cruel debasement. A man of that generation, even an intellectual, needed to be seen as virile, stalwart. He recuperated at his mother's and returned to serve under the flag. "I can still see him," said his army buddy Pierre Nathan, son of the publisher Fernand Nathan, with whom Georges would sign his first book contract, "holding his rifle in a droll sort of way, standing as straight as he could, head tilted back, chin out, managing to look both martial and debonair at the same time." (I am quoting from *Georges Huisman par quelques-uns de ses amis*, the compendium of speeches given at his funeral.) Georges worked hard at being a soldier, but by all accounts his military service was not his moment of crowning glory. It did, however, give him an opportunity to make friendships that would last him a lifetime: among them, Fernand Nathan and the architect Jacques Carlu.

When Germany declared war on France in August 1914, Georges dutifully answered the call for general mobilization. He enlisted in the aeronautical service. This new branch of the military had a particular cachet; the whole world was fascinated by it, as the notion of flying still possessed a magical quality. Yet his aerial debut ended in a failure even more humiliating than his early days in training. His very first foray into the air concluded with a crash that destroyed his biplane and almost killed him and his copilot. He was awarded the Croix de Guerre for bravery but was sent back to base and reduced to office work, where his talent for compiling reports proved far more convincing than his ambitions as a soldier or pilot. In the enlisted man's vernacular, he was a "goldbrick," a dainty man held in contempt by the valiant, by the real men. He was chickenshit.

Infantryman or chickenshit, however, the war forged unbreakable bonds among these men. There, too, Georges made a friend who would stand by him for the rest of his life: Roland Dorgelès, author of the novel *Wooden Crosses*. (To this day, it is taught in schools all over France as an exemplary account of WWI.) Dorgelès would rescue Georges from the Évêché prison in Marseille in 1942, a few weeks after the first roundups, convincing the head of the prison to release this particular Jew. At the funeral of his dear old friend in the Valmondois cemetery, Dorgelès later recalled—in a novelistic turn of phrase that finely glossed the real—that Georges had saved him first:

> Forty years ago, a young second lieutenant from aeronautical general headquarters, who had recently returned from squadron duty, where he had enlisted as a volunteer and been awarded the croix de guerre, drew up a list of combatants from all branches to be called up as student pilots in the aviation service. He noted the name of an infantry corporal whose stories he had read in literary journals, and spontaneously added him to the list. The young lieutenant was Georges Huisman; the foot soldier he raised up from the muddy trenches was me.

Meanwhile many women of the time experienced a kind of wartime emancipation. They found jobs and wore their hair short, their skirts calf-length, their husbands' clothes when necessary, and, for those who had taken jobs in a factory—the *munitionettes*—overalls. They served as nurses, laborers. They could not afford to wait at home, as their husbands, fiancés, and suitors would have preferred them to do. A staggering number of veterans later accused these women of having partied while they were getting butchered. Men were duped, gamed, diminished by these whores who had used their absence to cast them aside and enjoy their independence. The suffering men endured was deep and penetrating, but it carried within it terrible violence, as if they were replicating the savagery to which they'd been exposed, inflicting it on "their" women. (Dorgelès's writings offer a strong example of such misogynistic displacements.) There are, of course, exceptions to the brutality in the wartime literature. Apollinaire: "Four days my love no letter from you / The day has expired the sun is drowned / The barracks have become a house of horrors / And I am as sad as a convoyed horse." I trust Georges was more poet than fighter; I like to imagine him siding with Apollinaire.

In the little notebook with the word *Souvenirs* scrawled on the cover—notes for the memoir Georges never got around to writing—he recalled: "The casemates, the beauty of the land / The blue line of the Vosges." My grandfather, I believe, possessed the authentic passion for the arts my father merely performed.

Georges' experience at the front gave him the topic of his first book: on the function (and dysfunction) of his aeronautics base from 1914 to 1917, *Behind the Scenes in Aviation (Why Haven't We Maintained Consistent Air Superiority?)*. An in-depth examination of the new technology of air combat published in 1921, it evidences an interest in structures of command and administration, with precise ideas on execution; it does not reveal the soul of a poet but of an administrator. Upon his return from the front, Georges was awarded the Legion of Honor for his bravery in combat, but he felt that he didn't deserve it. ("What a fool!" my father exclaims in my head.) He married Marcelle Wogue in 1920, a year before his book came out. Her family was far more sophisticated, wealthy, and assimilated than his. She was a real catch for someone who, at that time, was merely a high school teacher.

Of her first meeting with Georges, eleven years her senior, Bonne-Maman wrote in her memoirs: "A voice like a cello, dazzling wit, no arrogance—in short, the timid young woman that I am is in awe. Will Georges Huisman compromise his precious freedom, take the plunge and get married? His mother strongly advises him to do so. The daughter of an associate professor, a graduate from an elite university—what more could she want for her son? Then one fine day he makes up his mind and tells me point blank that we are to be married. He's so sure of himself that he doesn't even ask for my opinion." A few pages on, Marcelle describes their wedding, a religious ceremony required by both families, a condition to which Georges submitted grudgingly, with a sneer for the inept speech delivered by the rabbi cousin. "The poor bride has a nasty head cold. The festivities are a success but she can't enjoy them, busy as she is drenching one handkerchief after another," recalled Bonne-Maman in the third person. "A lot of relatives attend, as do many girlfriends, who Georges Huisman finds very much to his taste."

My father often complained that his mother paid very little attention to her looks, that she hardly ever wore makeup, that she had no idea how to dress. No matter what Béatrice Duval may say, it seems likely that Georges didn't sleep in the bathtub when he found a pretty girl in his bed—to quote one of my father's favorite expressions. He referred to Georges' womanizing ad nauseam (and with admiration, and in front of his daughter). Georges' own wife seemed to admit it openly in her memoirs: "From late 1917 to the armistice in November 1918, Georges Huisman devotes himself passionately to his military duties, but he is in Paris. The handsome blue-eyed lieutenant has a lot of women chasing him and—why conceal the fact?—he no doubt takes advantage of it." The newlyweds spent their wedding night at the Hôtel Lutetia, a quarter of a century before the return of the deportees, of those lucky enough to return. The hotel is situated near a little square with a pretty carousel, a square where one is surprised to find odd palm and pine trees in the heart of Paris, and where one encounters a rarity among Parisian monuments: a statue of a woman—the founder of the Bon Marché department store. In the years after Maman returned from the mental hospital until I left home and left France, Maman, Elsa, and I lived in an apartment down the street from the Lutetia. I smoked my first cigarette in that little square, then my first joint, and had my first kiss. Paris and its surge of signs.

Between Béatrice's thesis, my grandmother's memoirs, and Papa's memories, I began to piece together an account of the series of events and favorable encounters that led Georges to his position at the Élysée. His wife, Marcelle, appears to have been heavily involved, partly through her family's influence, partly thanks to her own ambition for her husband. She would certainly not allow him to languish in some provincial high school—he began his career in Douai, in Northern France, where he was born—nor would she settle for the distinctly more reputable Lycée Janson de Sailly, in the sixteenth arrondissement, nor even for the prestigious École alsacienne overlooking the Jardin du Luxembourg. No, like his mother, his wife had visions of Georges becoming a great man, far more than some teacher. Perhaps without their ambition on his behalf, Georges would have settled for a modest life, far from seats of power. But he did have passionate political ideals; a sweeping vision for the France to which he so desired to belong; and a love of action, of travel, and, it seems, of women.

I hear the old wooden staircase creak. Soon Bruno's head pokes through the hatch in the attic: "Are you okay? You're not dying of cold? It's almost eight o'clock." It's February, and the attic isn't heated. Night must have fallen some time ago, fallen on my father's grave—I came up here in the early afternoon and hadn't noticed the sky growing dark. (Time slows in the attic; whereas for my father, it has stopped.) "Can we drop you off in Paris? We're about to head back. No rush, just in a little bit. You know you're welcome here whenever you like, none of this is going anywhere. Nobody has looked through these boxes since Béatrice was last here. But you should get back to your husband, your girls? Hm? What's that?" I notice that Bruno has inherited Papa's verbal tic of pretending not to have quite heard a response that was never uttered. "Come again?" Papa would ask whenever I failed to offer my immediate assent. "Yes, of course, you're right," I tell my elder brother. "I found an extraordinary letter by Fernand Léger. I'll bring it down. Perhaps we should have it framed?" "There must be treasures in there," Bruno replies. "We really ought to sort through it all." I suppose that by *we* he means me. But I can already tell I won't have the courage to come back; there are too many ghosts in the attic, too many mythological fathers, and I fear becoming their secretary, their archivist-paleographer. "Do I have another few minutes?" A few minutes before I have to reenter the world of minutes, clocks, tenses. "I'd like to take some pictures." "Sure, no rush. We'll close the shutters. I left the light on in the stairwell. Don't forget to turn it off behind you. The only working switch is on the landing."

I use my phone to photograph documents more or less at random: Léger's letter, the pages of a travel diary on a transatlantic cruise to New York—Georges' only trip to the United States, where he was greeted by the literary agent I would meet so many decades later. I don't try to decipher the barely legible handwriting. I make sure the photos are sharp, then I close the notebook and return it to the box. Just as I'm about to stack another box on top of it, I hesitate.

What if this is the one? The box with Choute's letters? (Now that I'm about to leave the attic, all the disorganizing emotion of the funeral returns; it's as though I'm fleeing the arrival of an occupying army—"The powers that be advise us to burn our papers"—and I can't choose what to carry with me, what memories to preserve.)

My hope, even if I half hid it from myself, was to find some trace of Choute among the clusters of boxes, to infer her presence. Quietly, but obsessively, my mind kept circling back to her role in Georges' life, no doubt because I associated Choute with my mother. To be sure, Maman had no aristocratic name, no education, no social standing, but I imagined that she and Choute shared the same insolence, the same disruptive beauty. These women seemed like the key—the discarded key—to the official history from which they'd been excluded by the celebrated men of my family, a family wherein my own legitimacy had often felt in question. Choute, my mother, and I, did we form, for all our differences, a kind of shadow lineage? The secret lover, the cast-out wife, the exile. Of course I was projecting, exaggerating, metaphorizing, mourning, or refusing to properly mourn—but yes, if I were being honest with myself, it was the fantasy of summoning Choute that led me from my father's graveside to his father's papers in the attic of a house where my mother was never welcome. Our family had omitted my mother from its archive. It was through the fictional retelling of her life that I had forced her back into a recorded narrative. If Georges' prominence within French cultural history had been erased, it still existed in official, authoritative sources: It could be resurfaced. In fact, Béatrice had successfully reinscribed it within a documented historical legacy, within an academic framework. Choute was irrecoverable except through the prism of fiction, through creative invention, through love.

Béatrice had disabused me of the idea that I would find a trove of letters at the bottom of a box. Choute was only discreetly and cryptically mentioned in the pages of Georges' diary in Chaillot—nothing more. And this diary was also irrecoverable it seemed to me as I looked at pile upon pile of boxes. When I pictured Choute, I saw Bathsheba in a Flemish painting at the Louvre: blond tresses, tiny breasts, wide hips, dainty ankles, eglantine skin. And layered on top of it, as if superimposed, I saw my mother in a photograph taken by my father when they were married. After my mother died, over a restaurant lunch, Papa had brought me an enormous leather-bound picture album of their best years. In it was as chaotic and incoherent a medley as could be found in the attic: Polaroid prints and glossy rectangular photographs, the kind one had printed from rolls of film in my youth; pictures of Elsa and me as babies in our mother's arms, of us as toddlers, of us four as a family, and then images of adult costume parties, of women I didn't know, with no semblance of chronology, no order at all. Some photos were stapled on the large horizontal black cardboard pages, and many more were loose, erratically placed there. A shocking number of them featured Maman naked: One page pictured us on vacation, our mother lying on her stomach in the grass with Elsa and me in arm floaties sitting on her sun-soaked bare ass, and immediately next to it was a black-and-white artsy shot, which had her posing nude in an armchair, light gently shining on her elaborately made-up hair. And so when I pictured Choute, I saw a fantastical mash-up of eras, an alarming jumble of family roles. I saw my mother through my father's eyes, through his suffocating, eroticizing gaze, and yet still my mother. My beloved, adored mother and her frightening beauty, her devastating beauty, with all the damage it caused her.

Inside the second box was no more Choute than in the first, just the same unfathomable mess: flyers to art openings, an application for a card identifying the holder as a member of the Resistance, a rent receipt from the mansion at the Manufacture des Gobelins, where the family moved in 1938. As I keep digging, I happen upon an envelope—small, thick, and roughly the dimensions of a postcard. "Papa" is scrawled across it. My breath catches. I recognize my father's handwriting, which I experience, impossibly, as fresh, the ink barely dry. A few hours ago I kissed his cold forehead; now I have found him again, or at least the trace of his living hand. (This envelope will contain the secret—of Choute, of my family. Whatever it is I'm searching for, surely it is here.) But wait, no—this isn't my father's handwriting, it's Georges'.

Marcel Proust made of his hero, Swann, a student of the École du Louvre and a biographer of Vermeer," Georges mentions in passing in his introduction to *L'Histoire générale de l'art*, a four-volume encyclopedia published under his editorial guidance in 1939. Georges, a student of the École des Chartes and a biographer of Memling. I couldn't have made him up.

Choute first appeared in Georges' life at one of his on-site seminars for the Université des Annales, shortly before his tenure at the Élysée. He had been conducting a series of classes organized around visits to artists' studios, galleries, museums, and notable architectural landmarks. He often taught with his friend, the architect and designer Robert Mallet-Stevens (best known for his black lacquered metal dining chair). They called these courses "Instantanés modernes." On Saturday, January 25, 1930, Georges lectured twice in the same afternoon at Maison La Roche, designed and built by Le Corbusier and Pierre Jeanneret in the neighborhood of Auteuil, in the sixteenth arrondissement. (We are still within the same one-mile radius of Chaillot.) He praised his dear friend Corbu in no uncertain terms; Georges was a great admirer of his work and wished he could have supported his design proposal for the Musée d'Art Moderne. It was incontestably the most original, and posterity would no doubt have preferred it to that of Dondel and Aubert, but Le Corbusier was Swiss. The same problem had arisen with Picasso as a Spaniard. No official national commission of such scale could be offered to a foreigner.

"Notice how we find the five points of a new architecture," Georges told his students (on this day all girls from a local school). He was as precise and erudite in his analysis of the work of his contemporaries as of the Renaissance. "Note the open facade, the open floor plan, the horizontal windows, the roof-garden and stilts." In accordance with the wishes of the villa owner, a banker and collector, a section of the house was dedicated to an impressive art collection including Braques, Légers, and Lipchitzes. "You'll see throughout the house many works of art that may challenge your preconceptions," Georges warned the fifty-two girls at the two p.m. session and the forty-seven girls at four p.m., "but remember that from its onset, art has always been revolutionary." His speech was both pompous and casual, pronounced with ease and detachment, a mixture of aloofness and grandeur that earned him enamored glances of admiration. But Choute's gaze cut through the forest of chignons and ringlets. She was nineteen years old, with a Louise Brooks bob shaping her thick, strawberry-blond hair, and willowlike eyelashes hanging over bright green eyes. Or not exactly green—a disconcerting color, bronze or gold—a hue whose name eluded him, despite his familiarity with color charts. Standing before a Juan Gris washstand, Georges declared: "One must feel a sympathetic admiration for those who ascribe themselves to such a practice. For ultimately, such paintings speak to our intelligence as much as our senses." Who was she? Her name appeared twice on the register. After the first session, she had stood aside as her friends swarmed the lecturer. She had watched them leave and had then signed up for the second session: Choute de Troguindy.

He was forty-one and deeply uncomfortable at the idea of being smitten with such a young woman, the chaste neckline of the sailor collar above her perfectly round, perfectly high, perfectly firm bosom; her charming little cherub fingers; her plump hands that evoked the child she still was. He would not have allowed himself to fall for her—of that he was quite certain, similar situations had presented themselves countless times—if she had not sought him out with that shameless gaze (whether it was the shamelessness of innocence or of experience, he couldn't quite tell). Of course, he noticed how she stayed for the second session. He tried not to repeat himself or fall back on hackneyed catchphrases, but she looked so distant, so pensive, he doubted she was listening. Had he been less disorganized by her presence, he would have done what he usually did with brazen girls: put her on the spot by asking her to elaborate on his remarks, or by soliciting her opinion of an especially challenging painting. Instead, he ignored her—that is, he pretended to ignore her, he tried hard to make her understand that she was being ignored. Another mob of girls surrounded him at the end of his second lecture—giggles stifled behind handkerchiefs, the rustle of dresses, the clicking of heels—but she had vanished like a sylph among the chestnut trees lining the avenue. He could have run after her through the Bois de Boulogne, chased her all night long, but instead he returned on foot, sheepish, to his home on Rue La Fontaine, stopping at his parents' on the way. His mother, of course, sensed his distraction. He fell into her arms. Louise still babied him, despite his graying mustache.

Once married, Georges and Marcelle had moved into a modest apartment at 8 Rue La Fontaine, the first address my father mentioned in the conversations I recorded. The last of the three boys, the baby of the family, my father was born at home, with the help of a midwife who filled water basins from the apartment's sole tap, at the kitchen sink. In her memoir, Marcelle bemoaned the lack of amenities; not only was there only one source of running water and no bathroom, but there was no electricity either. Gas lamps provided the only lighting, which threw the young mother into a panic lest the child's cradle catch fire. As for Georges, he was delighted to be just a few blocks from Louise and Hartog. My father recalled having composed a little song for his mother—since she composed no song for him—a lullaby he would make her sing as often as possible. Perhaps inspired by photos of himself as a baby in frilly frocks, his face framed by thick brown ringlets, he claimed to have been forced, like the young Rilke, to dress up as a girl to please his mother, who didn't want yet another boy. Georges, too, would have preferred a girl, a little princess with round pink cheeks to peck.

Marcelle was a mixture of anxious vigilance and distance. She had been raised in a bourgeois household where pampering was frowned upon and children were handed over to nannies who were expressly advised to fondle them as little as possible, to watch out for germs, and above all to avoid growing attached. Eight decades later, Papa still remembered the name of his caretaker: Cécile Ratteau, like *râteau*, meaning rake. Bonne-Maman instructed her to be as firm and cold as possible. And Madame Ratteau was icy indeed. As their standing (and housing) improved, my father recalled his mother being wholly taken up by the worldly duties imposed by her husband's professional positions; he recalled endless nights when he lay in bed waiting for her in vain, and the nanny, Madame Ratteau, being "as sweet as battery acid!" At least his mother would sing the little lullaby he wrote before she left the house. It was his way of making her pledge her undying and unconditional love for him, of making her swear that, no matter how lavish and exciting the parties she was required to attend, she would only be thinking of her darling little boy. "Poor Cécile Ratteau, she was found hung from the rafters in her mansard room." My father reminded me of this tragic event over the phone on the day of my mother's death. What I was supposed to make of this information, I still don't know.

Georges took refuge in his work. Paul Doumer was running for president, he would join him at the Élysée if they won the election, and an unimaginable opportunity was opening up before him. But since that "Instantané moderne," he spent hours every day staring at the walls, where he projected the silhouette of a young girl in a navy blue dress. He worked nevertheless indefatigably; he'd become oddly irritable, finding himself suddenly overcome by sadness or wild joy. No matter how much he beat himself up for the absurdity of his infatuation, it only intensified. He wandered the endless corridors of the Élysée Palace, where he never felt at ease nor at home, ignoring his wife's admonishments about his wardrobe, his thoughts occupied with a mysterious blonde whose eyes mirrored the depths of an alpine lake. Had he been Cocteau, he would have turned it into a movie or a play. But his work was in archival documents, not sentimental nonsense.

The extraordinary splendor of the Élysée—especially in contrast to 8 Rue La Fontaine—was always prominent in my father's reminiscence. Papa was two years old when they relocated: his brothers, seven and ten. The staff residence at the Élysée had seventeen rooms, a liveried attendant in almost every one, French gardens (of course) as far as the eye could see, and a swan pond. My father felt like a little prince in that Parisian palace with impenetrable gates. The place would become his paradise lost, from which he was exiled by the sudden and senseless death of President Paul Doumer. Georges should have been with the president that day in the spring of 1932 but was asked to represent him elsewhere. Doumer was irritated by the squad of bodyguards who followed him everywhere. It was a waste of the state's precious resources, the president believed, and he dismissed the unwanted escort. As a result, Papa insisted in his retelling, Doumer was assassinated in broad daylight by a madman armed with a pistol! Georges had hastened to his bedside. Too late. Almost a century later, I was able to hear my grandfather delivering a radio eulogy to Paul Doumer on my laptop, via the French National Archives' streaming service. Despite the crackly recording, Georges' voice is so similar to Papa's that I experienced a moment of vertigo before I could tell them apart. With antiquated grandiloquence, Georges described attending to the president on his deathbed. "Following a night haunted by excruciating death rattles, dawn broke over Paris in mourning, giving way to a day of heartbreaking splendor, a dazzling morning of May, with deserted avenues lined with chestnut blooms and filled with the scent of lilacs."

It was three and a half years before Georges would again encounter Choute, this time on the coast of Brittany; to say he remembered her instantly would be to understate the shock his body registered at her presence. Only her name had changed. Introduced to him in the drawing room of their mutual friends, the Seignobos, she had become Choute de Montmoreau, earning the title of duchess, the highest rank in nobility, by marrying the man who now held her arm. Born a marquise, one rank below, her father was an aristocrat who had expanded his family fortune thanks to wise investments and inordinate luck at the racetrack. Her parents had been dangerously permissive, some said, and encouraged her to pursue her studies as long as she wished, to be her own person, to build a career if she so desired; being a talented musician, a talented sketcher, they had imagined she might become an artist. As a little girl, she had a constant look of mischief about her, which she had never fully lost, her father said. Her mother had cautioned her not to marry too young, to take her time. As an only child, she had everything she could ever have hoped for, including doting parents, a respected name, and a lofty inheritance awaiting her in the future. Nobility had become entirely obsolete, they added. Money was far more useful, but they themselves were not venal, and she would have more than enough to support herself. And yet she married the first provincial duke she came across. (While her father claimed to care nothing for titles, he was vexed that his daughter had chosen a nobleman one rank above his own.) She imagined that she might be freer attached to a man for whom she cared little, as opposed to a father whom she loved madly. And so she appeared—in this rustic drawing room of ancient Breton stone, behind its burgundy shutters overlooking the beach at Launay, with a fire blazing in its immense hearth, as if to symbolize its hospitality—with golden hair cascading to her shoulders and her sea-green eyes just as Georges remembered them. (Her eyes are changeable in my imagination; I'm no archivist.) On the drawing room wall, there hung a canvas by Maurice Denis, *Saint Georges et le dragon*, featuring the pink boulders of Bréhat island against the ultramarine ocean. Amid flat planes of color, a tiny knight on a bright white horse charged at what looked like a kind of prehistoric bird. To the right, a princess in profile, hands joined in prayer, resembled a stained glass icon. Georges would later persuade Charles Seignobos to bequeath this painting to the French state, intending it for display at the Musée du Luxembourg. Georges bowed to Choute with detached gallantry, but his heart beat so strongly in his chest that he could almost hear the white horse at full gallop, feel his fist gripping the spear, with victory or death in sight.

Charles Seignobos, a distinguished scholar well into his eighties, was known as "Captain" along these shores as he loved nothing better than to take his many guests sailing. From the prison of Riom, Jean Zay would recall the long and merry evenings in the house of crimson shutters dancing "the polka or the waltz, roaring with laughter, while the Captain played the piano." Seignobos was an early supporter of Dreyfus and, like Georges, of the ideals of the Front Populaire. The Captain had been the first to attract their little clique of intellectuals and scientists—Paul Langevin, the Curies, the Perrins—to the peninsula. They were constantly in and out of one another's homes. No hedges or fences separated the gardens of those who owned property; those who didn't have a house in the region were invited to stay indefinitely. Most days were spent cruising aboard the Captain's sailboat, the *Églantine*, named after the flower that was then the symbol of workers' rights and socialism. All were members of the League of Human Rights. Their children, dressed in sailor suits, chased one another on the beach at low tide, while the youngest despaired of keeping their muddy sandcastles intact, screaming as their elders or giant crabs ran past. One had to watch that babies didn't swallow pebbles. Women tended to the children, with the help of local hired girls. Women, of course, were in charge of meals and all domestic tasks. With the exception of a prominent writer—pompously and sardonically referred to as Madame the writer! And with the exception of Choute, who had no obvious reason to excuse herself and never provided one. Growing up several decades later with a sister who didn't concern herself with household chores provided me with a powerful—if eminently frustrating—example of how femininity can absorb social norms without questioning them. I felt guilty if I didn't help clean up, while my sister couldn't have cared less. She followed my father's example—and of most boys of our generation. There was no question that housekeeping was a girl's duty, unless a girl simply didn't identify with the role and just didn't do it. It might have long been condemned, scorned, reprimanded, and chastised, but in the context of my childhood as in Choute's, one didn't get hung for defying sexist norms. One had to have the gumption to stand apart.

In 1933, Georges was hard at work on his *Histoire générale de l'art*, a massive encyclopedic project for Aristide Quillet covering art throughout the world, a sort of prewar prototype for André Malraux's collection *L'Univers des formes*. The unemployment rate in France peaked at 15 percent (in the United States, it reached 37.6 percent as the dollar collapsed). Fernand Léger delivered his famous lecture on "The Wall, the Architect, the Painter," on murals, a topic dear to Georges' heart. In January of that year, Hitler was appointed chancellor of Germany; in March, Violette Nozière attempted to murder her parents in the first installment of a major national drama, featuring incest and parricide, that would captivate and divide the country; and in July, Georges, on vacation at the Seignoboses' in L'Arcouest, chanced upon Choute for the second time.

I could always say that I was pressed for time, that in my haste I had pocketed it by mistake. And anyway, it was unlikely that anyone would notice the disappearance of a brown envelope untouched for seventy years. I filched a few photos of which there were multiple copies. I stole a handful of letters from my father to his mother, paying no attention to their dates. I was collecting a random sample of the boxes' contents. I had no idea what I would do with them yet.

In addition to the huge, full-length portrait of Georges, Papa had given me another painting that had once hung above his desk, in which Georges is depicted enthroned behind his own desk in the Rue de Valois. My father and the portrait of his father therefore formed a *mise en abyme*.

Papa also gave me a photo by Laure Albin Guillot in what looked like its original frame—a wide tortoiseshell ornamental molding chipped at the corners. The picture mounted on a linen board was neither sepia nor black and white, but of an indeterminate color that I imagined might have changed with age. My father inscribed the photo to me with a sweet little note, which I found both touching and odd—odd that he would deface a historical photograph, a valuable artwork. It was a sign of affection and of recklessness, I thought. I thanked him effusively as he handed it to me. It was a wonderful gift, a very beautiful and significant gift. The picture was not so large, about letter-sized, and Papa encouraged me to pack it away among my clothes as a carry-on. "It feels a little like I'm smuggling it," I said, only half joking, but I did as he suggested. It wasn't until I was back in New York that I realized the note on the picture was not addressed to me. It was from Georges. I believed my father was unique in addressing me as his "beloved little darling" and signing off "Your loving father." Apparently, he had learned it from his father; their handwriting was nearly identical. The photo was dated May 1935. My father would have just celebrated his sixth birthday.

From 1934 to 1940, Laure Albin Guillot photographed Louise and Hartog multiple times at her Paris studio on Boulevard de Beauséjour, in the sixteenth arrondissement, a five-minute walk from the apartment where they still lived, on Avenue Mozart (and, yes, still within walking distance of Chaillot). Albin Guillot ran the photographic archive service of the Beaux-Arts administration and also took the official portrait of the new director—different from the one my father had given me, which is distinctly more romantic. Mine is a three-quarter close-up, Georges' blue eyes staring off into space, an enigmatic smile on his lips; he's wearing his signature polka-dot bow tie, an unfiltered cigarette, as ever, between his fingertips. Laure Albin Guillot photographed the entire family—Papa, his brothers, their mother, the grandparents—which was highly unusual, Béatrice Duval notes. These portraits are reproduced in the family tree in the appendix of her thesis. The originals must be in one of the Valmondois boxes. I'm familiar with the image of my father: For as long as I can remember, it had been hanging on the wall of his living room on Rue Erlanger. He is the six-year-old little boy who has just received his father's portrait as a gift, his face still framed by heavy brown curls, in his hand a large glass ball, which I associate with Chardin's *Soap Bubbles* and which I can picture clearly at the Louvre, even though it's actually at the Met.

In 1937, the year Chaillot was inaugurated for the World Expo, Laure Albin Guillot coauthored a book with Henri Verne, director of national museums—*Le Louvre la nuit*—on the electrification of the museum, which, in an amazing innovation, was then open to the public at night. The volume shows theatrically lit black-and-white images of the antiquities galleries and the *Winged Victory of Samothrace*, among other masterpieces. In a fabulously oneiric setting, the reader feels invited to travel through the ages of creation, as if art history were being narrated by a statue coming to life. This was the first "nocturne" in the history of Paris museums.

To understand Georges' vision, his grand plan, for the Beaux-Arts, you must read the lecture he gave at Salle Pleyel on April 19, 1937, said Béatrice Duval. "The New Relationship between Art and the State," reproduced in its entirety in her thesis, was the cornerstone of his cathedral.

A few days earlier, on April 13, his youngest son had turned eight. The boy had not seen much of his father lately. On the night of his birthday, he had begged his papa to read him the speech he'd been working on for weeks. The child insisted with such adamant emotion that the directeur des Beaux-Arts agreed to skip (yet another) art opening and grant the boy's wish. Plus, it was good practice. Upon leaving the Élysée Palace, following the death of Paul Doumer, they had moved to a very comfortable—if hardly as extravagant—apartment on the third floor at 102 Rue d'Assas—an address to which the boy would return, twenty years later, four stories higher, with his own four children, after trying his luck going door to door and asking the old concierge, who vividly remembered his brown curls; his big, dark eyes; and his excellent, if flamboyant, manners, if there were any vacancies. Reading the speech to his son, Georges paused to correct a few typos, the fault of his secretary. True, she wasn't terribly experienced; she'd only recently been hired. She had an odd first name and a duchess's title and unusual green eyes, which could turn into the color of solid gold. She was recently widowed, had no children, and wanted none.

When he looked up from his lectern in the Salle Pleyel, he met the blinding ray of Choute's stare. How could a man withstand the lightning strike of her gaze? The woman was unbearably beautiful. Never mind the actresses and their tragic swoons and the corps de ballet dancers and their firm thighs and their inimitable way of shaking their hair as they undid their chignon . . . The story of Georges and Choute, as I narrated it to myself, oscillated between romantic fairy tale and steamy erotica. As if the novel of my father's father—set in a time before my time, a time abstracted from lived timelines—could somehow adjoin both childhood and adult fantasies of what love might represent.

Georges' lecture is more than inspired—his fervor startles and then convinces his audience. To say that he was invested in his mission hardly expresses the extent of his commitment. His belief in the importance of the arts to the Republic, the unity of aesthetic and national experiment, was religious; he was in his pulpit, but preaching the gospel of art. He began by chastising his predecessors, who knew not what they did. To think that the State refused to purchase some of Cézanne's best work! He quotes a letter from Gauguin to the direction des Beaux-Arts describing the bewilderment with which his work was received: It was rejected, of course. As was Monet's, Manet's, Pissaro's, Sisley's, Degas's, Van Gogh's, Toulouse-Lautrec's, Renoir's . . .

> In past times, the king of France upheld the bold and the revolutionary over the retrograde, and it is to that aesthetic policy that we owe the chateaus of the Loire, the Louvre, Versailles, Poussin and Le Brun. [I realize that men of that generation were not afraid of bombast, but even so, the floridness and fanaticism strike me as a little excessive, a little reminiscent of his youngest son.]
>
> It is thus indispensable for the state to purchase or commission with fervor and passion.

There you have it: fervor and passion.

His program promised to reestablish the role of the artist in society and the place accorded to art in public spaces—streets, monuments, and national collections—and ultimately to promote the teaching of art and aesthetic taste to the public. What is the point of supporting culture if the people don't understand it, are not interested in it, and, above all, don't have the leisure to participate in it? Georges' speech, delivered just as Léon Blum and the Front Populaire were embarking on a vast reform program, was part of a drive to ensure equality in knowledge and free time—time freed from the slavery of work—and national harmony based on pride in a shared national legacy and the collective joy that the French, workers and bourgeois alike, would take in celebrating it: "What is the point of leisure and shorter work hours if the State fails to condition future generations to enjoy France's culture which its artistic richness and the talents of its creators can deliver so magnificently?"

Georges—veteran, (agnostic) Jew, worshipper of beauty (old and new and Choute)—believed in his homeland as an aesthetic ideal, for its cultural heritage and treasures of refinement, no matter that those were so often built on its glaring social inequalities. To understand the citizen of the Third Republic, one had to picture a country that had not yet been divided by collaboration and Vichy; a country where universal education was still a new concept; where the dissemination of the French language through colonial conquest was a point of uncontroversial pride. One had to picture a citizen who believed unequivocally in the verticality of power and of education. A citizen, the unadulterated product of French meritocracy, who believed in progress as the outcome of knowledge acquired in books and study. Neoclassical architecture could coexist with advanced painting so long as it was in the service of France—of its bright future and imagined past. The arts were the meeting place of spirit and politics, the crucible of the nation.

Georges' lecture, delivered a month before the opening of the Universal Exposition, expressed the cultural ambitions of his political party, the French Popular Front, or Front Populaire, a coalition of left-wing parties, including the Communist Party, whose rise to power in May 1936 had been greeted with a massive strike wave. In a jubilant celebration of working-class strength, identity, and visibility, major social reforms were proclaimed almost immediately, including the introduction of a forty-hour working week, paid holidays, and collective bargaining. Léon Blum, as the party leader, conducted these negotiations that to this day continue to define the French republic. Blum was also a notable poet, the first socialist to ever become prime minister, and the very first Jewish prime minister. The Front Populaire included among its party members Jean Zay, minister of national education, a brilliant scholar in his early thirties, and Jean Perrin, a Nobel laureate in charge of state scientific research. Also both Jews.

When he took on the direction des Beaux-Arts, Georges scandalized the old guard by visiting art schools and attending shows by emerging, unknown artists, encouraging them personally. He also organized unprecedented contemporary music concerts in the offices of his cabinet in the Rue de Valois. Large state commissions became a hallmark of his policy as a way of creating jobs for artists and craftsmen, supporting creation in practical terms. Léon Blum called for art to be "freed from mercantilism." As nationalist fanaticism swept across Europe and a new world conflict was brewing, the patriots of the Front Populaire championed the need for artistic creation, for celebrating beauty and the beauty of getting together. Art and joy to avert war.

Contrary to Papa's claims about his father's inflexibility, it seems that Georges made a great many concessions. I am thinking, for instance, of the enormous decorative motif he commissioned from Évariste Jonchère, an homage to Apollo and the theatrical arts, for the Palais de Chaillot—a work I struggle to believe Georges chose sincerely, out of pure admiration. Before coming to the Élysée, before the Senate, before the direction des Beaux-Arts, he had been interested in artists far more innovative than those whose work he commissioned or bought on behalf of national museums. More than ten years before the inauguration of the Musée de l'Homme,

Georges had written an article on the history of African art, in which he declared it essential to study that continent's artifacts as seriously and thoughtfully as if they "belonged to early Roman art." In 1930, he organized an exhibition of the work of the Sudanese artist Kalifala Sidibé, unknown to European audiences at the time.

Among the state acquisitions that Georges could confidently assume would not be controversial was the Château de Chaumont, the luxurious residence of the Princesse de Broglie, expropriated for public purposes. On August 1, 1938, the octogenarian princess officially handed over the keys to her castle to Georges—and to Choute, who knew a thing or two about castles, having grown up in one of her own in La Roche-Jagu, Brittany, on the estuary of the Trieux, between Pontrieux and the Bréhat archipelago. That is where she was staying on the evening she spent with the Seignobos—slumming it with the commoners, as Georges would tease her after their love was consummated, after he had recovered his sense of humor. They often spoke of that meeting in L'Arcouest, how she had arrived on her husband's arm; they enjoyed revisiting the awkwardness of those conversations, when desire made small talk, or talk of any sort, difficult. Choute seemed more at ease than this celebrated, grown man; how could he act so childish, so bashful?

The Captain had taken them sailing on that visit. A sudden squall overtook them, and the boat heeled over violently, throwing her against Georges, the skirt of her dress lifted in such a way that she had found herself half naked in his arms. Neither the wind nor the water splashed in his face could mute the scent of her hair. She wore Mitsouko by Guerlain—a secret accord of peach and rose, a legend of impossible love, said its advertisement. While reefing the sail, the Captain had shouted at Georges to help the poor young woman. But Georges had stood paralyzed, stricken like the dragon under the spear.

Choute had written to him after his nomination to the direction des Beaux-Arts. Since the sailing incident, six long months had passed—months during which, she would later assure him, she had been waiting for him to call. She had only just gotten married; she had scruples, however mild, about cheating on her husband, and wasn't a woman supposed to wait to be seduced? Georges had replied to her note by suggesting that she join him on one of his visits to the studios of young artists. In the Seignobos' dining room, she had stood transfixed before the Maurice Denis painting, Georges' hand not quite brushing hers, as he lectured her on the evolution of pictorial representation since impressionism. In her opinion, the Nabis had challenged form even more than the Cubists. Despite being figurative, the painting relies entirely on the power of its colors, the true subject of Denis's work, Georges interjected: Here we have a painting whose focus is really abstraction wrestling with representation. Jacob wrestling with the angel, Choute suggested. The comparison moved the art historian. Georges evoked Delacroix, Baudelaire's writings on art, Fra Angelico, the Sainte-Chapelle. The most modern works of all had been prefigured by stained glass pierced by sunlight, transcendence reliant not on the human figure or landscapes but pure light. He glanced at her furtively, his cheeks burning. Since that encounter, his dreams had been haunted with fragments of their conversation, details of paintings—the hem of a dress, an ankle, a wrist, Choute's eyes staring him down, fixing the ground, putting an end to their interview, corridors of the Louvre, corridors of the underworld, Dido and Aeneas.

His response to her compliments was sober. He was thinking of commissioning murals for his old school, the Lycée Janson de Sailly, from two young recipients of the Prix Blumenthal, and he would value her insight. He liked what she had said about emerging artists. Perhaps they could go see the latest works of Odette des Garets? Did she remember that the Seignobos owned a still life of hers, very reminiscent of Cézanne? The salon for women artists was scheduled to open the following month. It was to include some truly outstanding work, painters of great vitality. Suzanne Valadon—what a wonderful discovery! The young generation had moved to studios behind Montsouris Park, south of Montparnasse. Artists were constantly relocating, establishing new outposts farther out of the way. The state should freeze their rents and offer them affordable live-in studios. Otherwise, they would all flee the capital. And where would they go after Rue d'Alésia? Montrouge? Malakoff? One creates differently in the aura of exquisite monuments. Art conceived in the shadows of a seventeenth-century chapel—how could the artists be impervious to such influence? He had called her from the black Bakelite telephone resting on his Empire desk—walnut with gilt bronze and mounted green leather top. His voice was composed, poised, but his speech was a little hurried. If they had time, they could stop by Georges Braque's studio, an architectural gem, a personal Auguste Perret commission, did she know it? A wonderful example of the use of concrete and bricks, the epitome of elegance, but with marvelous skylights . . .

Choute and her husband were renowned patrons of the arts,

Georges would say to himself, justifying their meeting on professional grounds; it was his duty to cultivate such relationships! But he surely did not have the time to spend a whole afternoon visiting studios or idling around Paris like a flaneur. They could walk from Rue de Valois, if she wanted to meet him there. From the gardens of the Palais Royal, it would take an hour to walk to Boulevard Arago. It was February. Leafless chestnut trees lined either side of boulevards, reminding him of the marble columns of the Mosque-Cathedral of Córdoba, he said aloud while silently recalling his visit to Andalucía—his honeymoon. Walking through the Cour Carrée, the Louvre esplanade, he suggested they take a slight detour to the Sainte-Chapelle before crossing the Seine. The Sainte-Chapelle, which appeared to be standing only by some miracle, its ogive-vaulted bays supported only by buttresses of incredible delicacy and banks of multicolored glass of exquisite craftsmanship. All here is grace, light, and air! Inside, he took her to the Judith window, bay eight. The story unfolds from bottom to top. Here is Judith, in her medieval coif, decapitating Holofernes—right there in the middle of the eighth row, the most beautiful medallion, isn't it? The pink of Holofernes' blanket, incarnadine like a spring garden rose. It's obviously a contemporary interpretation: biblical characters dressed in the clothes of Saint Louis's era; we are watching a play, aren't we, it's all a stage. And see how the pink is picked up again in the roof of the funereal monument where our heroine is laid out, high up on the left? The people cry over the death of Judith, proclaims the banner in white letters against a royal blue background. In French, not Latin! The use of the vernacular; the use of narrative ellipsis; the use of the *mise en abyme*; the use of synecdoche—Georges' commentary surpasses any guide's to any monument in Paris. Look down:

The floor would have been as white as alabaster when it was first built. In the shimmer cast by the light shining through the windows, the faithful would have found heavenly Jerusalem at their feet, the holy city descended from the sky.

In *contre-jour*, all you see is the tin surrounding each piece of glass. In full sun, all you see is light. You need softer light for each image to appear distinctly. Every passing cloud taints the story with catastrophe. As if each interruption of light prefigured the apocalypse.

The weather had clouded over during his discourse. He suddenly worried that he had bored Choute. She had silently drifted over to the opposite bay, the Book of Job. Under the Judith window, Georges positioned himself between the Jewess and the Assyrian general. The decapitated Holofernes loomed like a cautionary tale. He watched Choute facing away, her blond hair mottled by the blues and greens of the stained glass, her dress like purple jasper, speckled, marbled. With his hat in his left hand, he kneaded his neck with his right, pulled at his collar, and loosened the bow tie pressed against his throat. Choute abruptly turned around as the sun reemerged. He felt himself falter. The violence of his desire was a blade at his throat. The golden sword of Choute's eyes. He looked back at the bay. One medallion depicted Judith in her bath. His Bathsheba.

Once again pontificating so as to regain his composure, Georges fell into step with Choute in front of the Conciergerie: "Paris did not become a capital until Clovis, in 508." He had written a popular guide to these streets that appealed to novices and scholars alike and had been reprinted multiple times. Under the Carolingian emperors, three centuries later, Paris grew from a little Gallo-Roman citadel into a large, heavily populated city, humming with commerce and resplendent with glory and opulence. The Musée de Cluny holds the most relics from that time, as so little of it remains visible in the city. Erudition had restored his confidence, and now he was getting carried away. So little history has been preserved, he repeated. And then he quoted his own *Pour comprendre les monuments de Paris*: "At the hands of vandals, ancient and modern, almost all Parisian monuments built before the twelfth century have been entirely erased."

At the hands of vandals. Throughout Georges' archives, there were pockets of fervor at odds with the bureaucratic impersonality required of a government position. I recognized his passion for his role, how seriously he took it. How driven he was, surely. Yet his sentences—in speeches, in publications—seemed punctuated by oddly strident notes, something slightly unhinged.

Georges was elected mayor of the little village of Valmondois in 1932, the year of Paul Doumer's assassination, the end of his tenure at the Élysée. Early in their marriage, he and Marcelle had acquired a fine bourgeois home in the center of this tiny village. Half a home, really; they co-owned it with another family, who they bought out ten years later. Marcelle's dowry, their only fortune, offered them a chance to get Louise her dream garden. She had always wanted to grow her own vegetables, raise roses, and gather flowers that she herself had sown. Georges took great pride in his position as mayor, in addition to his duties at the Beaux-Arts. A chauffeur from his cabinet drove him to the village twice a week, unless he took the train. (Did Georges already buy Carette tea sandwiches then?) Through the windows of the quaint little commuter train that left Paris from the Gare du Nord, one could see in those years a new experiment in urban development spreading beyond the walls of the capital, neither quite the city nor yet the real countryside: the suburbs. Those suburbs housed workers who voted en masse for the Front Populaire.

Choute lived in a mansion on Rue Jacob, a fifteen-minute walk from Rue d'Assas and the same distance to Rue de Valois in the opposite direction. She and Georges would always part outside the *porte cochere* to her building before he returned to his family. Choute could barely be bothered to respond to her husband's recriminations about these suspicious outings; after all, he spent the greater part of his time on his estate in Charente. He was only reproaching her for the sake of appearances, she claimed, when Georges insisted that she at least keep up appearances, that she play by the rules of the game. What a hypocrite. You have some nerve, pretending to be a paragon of virtue.

Then the duke was thrown from his horse to his death. This was a little less than two years into their marriage. Choute was hardly devastated. She spent only one month in mourning; her outraged parents were no more able than Georges to make her see reason, to observe convention: A widow must wear crepe for a year. (Bonne-Maman often scolded Elsa and me for wearing black, which was shockingly inappropriate for girls who had not lost their parents.)

In 1937, Choute was a twenty-six-year-old widow, fabulously wealthy, officially untethered, but hopelessly attached to an aging, married father of three, a bureaucrat whose work took precedence over everything. Why? How? And he still had the impudence to harass her with his morbid jealousy. Rue Jacob had become a second home for Georges. A third, or a fourth, after Rue de Valois, Rue d'Assas, and Valmondois. He showed up at all hours to make sure she was waiting for him, to monitor her visitors. A Gitane forever between his lips or fingertips, he burned with suspicion, fear, desire, panic, and devotion. "Whatever you want, my little angel," he whispered, breathing in her hair, or burying his head in her blouse, or counting out a rosary of kisses along her leg, the arch of her foot in the palm of his hand. He would have welcomed her most despotic command to prove how much he loved obeying her. Had he not plucked the moon from the sky for her? For her, had he not illuminated the *Venus de Milo* at night in the Louvre? "Look, my beloved, see how beautiful she is? How she looks just like you?" It was unclear who was the prisoner of whom.

In her memoirs, my grandmother described a stray cat that had been found wandering into the garden of Valmondois. Georges had adopted her and named her Vergère because she liked to hide in the branches of the apple trees in the orchard at the far end of the property, beside the little shed that, half a century later, I spent hours decorating with scraps of fabric and cushions pilfered from the drawing room so I could stage plays for my dolls. That cat became Georges' pet. Not the family's pet; Georges and Choute's pet. Their cat-child.

From a box reserved for state officials, Georges and Choute applauded Darius Milhaud's *Médée* and Yvette Chauviré's breathtaking performance in Serge Lifar's *Giselle* before returning to Vergère, on Rue Jacob, before returning to his wife and children. The box assigned to Monsieur le Directeur des Beaux-Arts at the Palais

Garnier, at the opera, was a not an unwelcome perk. As was the table awaiting Georges across the street at the Café de la Paix. Quintessential examples of the Second French Empire, these monuments invariably set off Georges' wrath. I can hear him muttering under his moustache about those vandals who disfigured Paris! Napoleon III and Haussmann being the worst. What they called the embellishment of Paris was merely a comprehensive plan to control crowds. The Attila of the straight line!

Paris's wide avenues were indeed a useful setting for demonstrations of political or military power. When Georges was put in charge of welcoming King George VI on his first journey abroad in 1938, my grandfather took full advantage of the layout of a city intended for parades and lavish spectacles. He had barely two months to prepare the festivities around a visit that was to seal the entente between the two nations on either side of the Channel. Two short months to organize galas, museum visits, concerts, and pageants; plan the sovereigns' itinerary through the capital; and select the artists to be featured and the flowers to be presented to the queen. More than one hundred staff members participated in choreographing the pageantry, but it was to Georges that the minister expressed his "personal gratitude" in a letter dated July 29, 1938. The sovereigns themselves asked that those responsible for their wondrous reception be warmly thanked. "The decorations throughout Paris, the various spectacles, and in particular the Opera gala, the luncheon in the Hall of Mirrors and the wonderful afternoon in Versailles were all your work," said the minister's note. This directeur des Beaux-Arts was more than a little proud to have so valiantly served the Franco-British friendship. And he was proud to have had at his side a woman on whom all eyes converged at the Bagatelle garden party, a woman who outshone the twenty most beautiful dancers in the *corps de ballet* as they performed on the stage built over the little pond—a woman who outshone even the queen.

The program devised by Georges (and preserved on yellowing sheets typed out by what I surmise to be Choute's energetic fingers) laid out the sovereigns' itinerary from Porte Dauphine to the Palais d'Orsay in four movements, as four acts of a ballet, each intended to showcase the might and poetry of France. Upon their arrival at the Bois de Boulogne, the sovereigns would be welcomed with a dove release and a children's choir that would follow their motorcade all the way to the Place de l'Étoile. From there, they would drive down the Champs-Élysées, which would be decked out in the colors of the two countries and lined with attractive, carefully curated crowds. At the bottom of the avenue, by the Petit Palais, pretty girls in party dresses would embody Parisian elegance in the midst of water fountains, topiaries, lilies, and gladioli. Place de la Concorde was reserved for the army; on the Tuileries terrace was a staged display of French cities and their specific attributes. Crossing the Pont de la Concorde, the royal procession would finally reach the Quai d'Orsay, their ultimate destination, which they were to call home for the duration of their stay. The minister approved the program in a handwritten note scribbled on its first page, albeit with a sarcastic comment on the floridness of its prose.

Only a few months after Hitler had annexed Austria, France spared no expense in receiving George VI. A special budget had been allocated in two separate votes by both houses of legislature. Some 90 percent of a total of 24 million (old) francs was spent to "beautify the streets of Paris." The other 10 percent was to go to parties, entertainment, publications (programs, menus, invitations), and propaganda films—although nobody would use the word *propaganda*. As indicated in the minister's note thanking his director, officials were all deeply satisfied with the event. "Did the expense seem justified as a peacemaking effort? Did it seem appropriate in response to the Nazi war drive? The magnitude of the outlay is perplexing, but no contemporary response could be found in the documents consulted." (I am quoting from Béatrice's thesis.)

At a secondhand bookstore during the erratic course of my research, I came across a pamphlet titled "The British Sovereigns' Visit to France." On the cover, a zeppelin floated above the Place de la Concorde. The Roman columns of the Hôtel de Crillon and its counterpart La Madeleine—both masterpieces of Ange-Jacques Gabriel, Louis XV's architect—framed the background. In the foreground stood the obelisk of the Temple of Amon from Luxor, presented to the king of France by Egypt a century earlier and officially consecrated as a historical monument in 1937, making it the oldest monument in Paris. Off frame, to the left of columns of soldiers on the ersatz-Roman bridge, is the Élysée Palace; to the right, the Tuileries; and beyond the lindens and chestnuts, the Louvre. Just around the corner of La Madeleine was the restaurant Lucas Carton, whose wood-paneled, wainscoted room made it an official monument, too. Leafing through the booklet, I stumbled upon Georges in a photo of the queen visiting a special exhibit of English paintings at the Louvre: Georges and his mustache and his bow tie and his slicked-back hair; Georges in profile, in patent leather shoes, standing apart from the other dignitaries milling around Her Majesty, who wore a big white capeline. Georges, deep in contemplation of a painting. The photo, reproduced from *The New York Times*, has him standing in the background. I'm not sure I would have recognized him had it not been for his mustache, his bow tie, and his posture: His bearing is exactly the same in the portrait that hangs in my living room.

In a diary entry from May 1940, Georges wrote: "Two hours at the Louvre. Essential to take advantage of the war to change the layout of the galleries. Have the Waterfront Gallery become an overview of masterpieces in chronological order, not organized by country. Other galleries would be dedicated to national paintings. Very important." One month before German troops invaded Paris, this was his most pressing preoccupation.

When Georges purchased the Château de Chaumont on behalf of the French state, it was not simply, or not only, to impress his mistress. The official reason was a plan for the safekeeping of national treasures. If art couldn't prevent war, let it at least be protected from human folly. The chateaux of the Loire Valley were designated as warehouses and triage centers. If Paris was under siege, it was to these chateaux, including Chaumont, that artworks would be sent. To these country houses the administration would retreat.

Every morning for many months, Georges would gather his colleagues on Rue de Valois to draw up meticulous plans for safeguarding invaluable works of art. Georges would tell the story in 1949, in an article written for a journal edited by a Belgian curator, how he had worked in 1940 to hide the van Eyck brothers' *Adoration of the Mystic Lamb* altarpiece, better known as the Ghent Altarpiece. Nevertheless, the fifteenth-century polyptych—one of the most important artworks, Georges believed, in all of human history—was later stolen by Hitler with the collusion of Pierre Laval and concealed in a Bavarian castle. Toward the end of the war, in the midst of air raids, it was abandoned in the Altaussee salt mines, in Austria, where it suffered abominable damage; only later was it recovered by a group known as the Monuments Men.

"It was critical to record not only the duration of each journey by car, but also the time needed to take down, crate and load each artwork," wrote Georges. "The curators from the Louvre and their scientific colleagues calmly undertook a task that they might have to re-enact the next day in an air raid, in a Paris seized by panic and terror. While government agencies are often criticized for allowing themselves to be taken by surprise, we anticipated developments and stayed one step ahead of them."

Or almost. Géricault's *The Raft of the Medusa* was stood upright in a trailer, held in place by straps, and enclosed in scaffolding so precarious that it swayed in the wind. Despite the meticulous preparations, it had occurred to no one that the height of the cargo as it jounced along the country roads might expose it to power lines. Near Versailles, on the way to Chambord, the frame cut through the dangling cables of the Seine-et-Oise tram, setting off a fountain of sparks. The nightly expedition caused a blackout across several surrounding towns. The electrical company had to be sworn to secrecy as it restored the lines, the mysterious shipment and its conveyors standing by for untold hours.

Men and women raced against the clock to crate the *Winged Victory of Samothrace* in the corridors of the Louvre; they removed the windows of the Sainte-Chapelle and the cathedrals of Chartres and Reims one by one—a total of fifty thousand square meters of stained glass, dismantled according to a numbered grid to keep them in the right order—barricaded each window frame with planks of wood, and swaddled each opening, each ornamentation, in padded blankets. Ultimately, these largely nameless men and women shipped 5,201 crates over 238 journeys by truck or freight car to eleven different chateaux in the Loire Valley.

At the same time, preparations were afoot in Cannes to host the largest film festival ever. The success of the British royal visit, judging by the joy it brought the French people and the alliance it sealed with the British empire, had convinced the government to go all out.

As Georges left no written account of the creation of the festival, its origin story belongs to Philippe Erlanger. "We literally challenged fate," Erlanger wrote in *La France sans étoile* (*France without a Star*). "In August, ignoring the looming threat of war, Cannes launched the grand parade." Hollywood's leading stars crossed the Atlantic on an ocean liner chartered by Metro-Goldwyn-Mayer. Their French hosts spared no expense to welcome them and acceded to their every wish, except when it came to erecting a life-size reproduction of Notre-Dame Cathedral on the beach in honor of the movie based on the novel by Victor Hugo. Tyrone Power, Gary Cooper, Norma Shearer, and George Raft were among the distinguished guests. On the program were *The Wizard of Oz*, original works by Walt Disney, and Frank Capra's *Mr. Smith Goes to Washington*.

Before there was a Palais des Festivals, the Cannes Casino served as the main venue for the festivities. A temporary thousand-seat theater equipped with all the latest technology was built facing the sea. The International Film Festival was declared open in neon letters on the pediment of the municipal casino, at the foot of the pier for the Lérins Islands ferry. The illuminated letters, reflected in the water, blurred as pleasure crafts glided over them, like fireflies fluttering over the waves, disappearing beneath the foam.

Louis Lumière, the godfather of cinema, had accepted the honorary presidency of the first festival. There is a photograph of his arrival at the Cannes terminal, which seems to allude to his own recording of a train arriving at La Ciotat, a couple of stations away—a short film often credited with inaugurating the new medium. "It is a great honor and, more, a great joy for me to be associated with this apotheosis of cinema on the Côte d'Azur, where my earliest work was made," Lumière told the journalists in his radio address from the platform. "May this coincidence be an auspicious sign!"

The Cannes Film Festival, it has been said—my father said so, and so did Erlanger—was established in response to the cultural influence of Nazism throughout Europe, as manifested at the 1938 Venice Film Festival. Since Béatrice Duval had defended her dissertation, her research had paved the way for other historians, including one who devoted an entire book to the aborted first edition of the festival. It provided the exact date of Louis Lumière's arrival. It also described with great earnestness the placing of the plaque in honor of Georges Huisman at the Palais Croisette, along with Jean Zay's. It gave a thoroughly researched critical analysis of Philippe Erlanger's memoirs. The festival had been a collaborative effort in which a good many people had participated, including René Jeanne, a film journalist and French jury member at the 1938 Venice festival; Harold Smith, an American festival juror; and Henry Gendre, owner of the Grand Hôtel in Cannes and member of the Resistance, who was arrested by the Gestapo in 1943. This was not a festival for which any one man could reasonably take credit (especially given that it was organized within a few months).

Cannes was indeed a response from liberal democracies to autocratic dictatorships. The festival was meant to strengthen the Franco-American entente, thanks to what France was known and loved for: elegance, luxury, and landscape. Galas and other unforgettable soirees on a sublime waterfront, with no shortage of palaces to welcome its guests—these were its main assets. The tourist season on the French Riviera typically ended in late summer; a film festival swarming with the rich and powerful, a vast beach party attended by celebrities of all sorts, would be a useful way to prolong it. Various cities were considered as potential hosts for the future international film festival, but the top priority was that Americans love it. The hoteliers of Cannes, Henry Gendre in particular, proved themselves to be powerful lobbyists. In a note to Jean Zay, who in May 1939 was in the United States for the New York World Fair, Georges reported: "Cannes' hotel capacities are more or less unique; it offers the great advantage of being a transatlantic stopover, so any festival held there would be guaranteed an elite audience from the outset." The reputation of the French Riviera was already well established. It was renowned enough to compete with Venice.

"We here thank cinema for having become the number-one entertainment available to the anxious and beleaguered citizens of our age," wrote Jean Zay in the weekly *Marianne*, announcing the festival launch. "We know that it is a way for each country to make itself better known, to assert through spectacle its ideas, its labors." As opposed to propaganda, a concept he reviled, Zay praised film for its educational value and took advantage of the festival to unveil an extensive series of short documentary films promoting France's tremendous scientific discoveries, the richness of its cultural history, and the strength of its army. France was best prepared to stand up to the German and Italian offenders, the festival would assert on its screens. But the lights went out before a single film could be shown. On August 29, 1939, the festival was called off. For the next five years, France failed to distinguish itself for any of the values it had so adamantly defended.

If I still had doubts about Georges' role in the creation of the event, they were laid to rest when I came upon the official paperwork describing the rules governing that first aborted festival. Its introductory paragraph mentions three names: Louis Lumière, honorary president; Jean Zay, executive president; and Georges Huisman, chairman of the production committee. Not a single mention of Erlanger! I was inordinately pleased yet oddly surprised. Papa must have been right, even if he told it all in a jumbled, incomprehensible way, mixing up dates and names, and emphasizing all the wrong things. No, Papa hadn't made it up. Papa remembered everything.

Georges spent the weeks leading up to that first festival, in the summer of 1939, at his home in Brittany with family and friends. He had his picture taken for *Paris Match*, which ran a piece on their cohort in the village of L'Arcouest, renamed Fort-la-Science or Sorbonne-Plage. Georges must have had little time to spare for his sons, despite the relaxed pose he assumed on a chaise longue, his trousers rolled, his bare feet propped up before him. The dozens of letters he wrote on a daily basis bear witness to the furious sprint toward the festival's finish line. The family had moved into the lavish house connected to the Manufacture des Gobelins in Paris—official housing provided by the ministry—but in Brittany, they made do with a humble dwelling built three years earlier by an amateur landscape architect, with an espalier garden rare for the region, where pines, hydrangeas, rosebushes, and white laurel overlapped against the backdrop of the ocean. They were landowners in a remote little corner of the country that was neither touristy, nor chic, nor luxurious, but simply magnificent. By the time I knew the house some four decades later, the bathroom still featured its vintage claw-foot tub and the great concrete trough that served as the kitchen sink. Water had to be pumped by hand. The wiring was even more obsolete than in Valmondois. Papa eventually bought himself a house on the other side of the bay—"across from my dear old mother's place," he continued to say long after her death when describing its geographic location—after his wife had spent many years complaining that this house was uninhabitable. She could live with the nonstop rain, but it was too much to ask her to spend all summer bathing in a bidet. Whereas my father was happy to get by on a little trickle of water and a big splash of eau de cologne. (I now wonder whether Papa was uniquely bizarre in his horror of showers or whether there were other Jews who shared this phobia after the Holocaust.) My father could imagine vacationing nowhere else but on this coast. Brittany was the only place he was able to rest—the only place where he seemed truly at home, peacefully at home. More so even than in Paris, because it represented his childhood before the catastrophe. It recalled that summer of 1939, far from the capital, when everything, including the Festival de Cannes, still seemed possible.

The family was still in L'Arcouest when Georges left for Cannes in early August, and later that month he convinced his wife to move with the children to Rennes, where a friend had lent them an opulent home. The boys would be able to pursue their education there. Each was at the top of his class, it went without saying. They all studied Latin and Greek. One played the trumpet, another the violin, and the third the cello, as seen in the spread of *Match* photos. Apparently, they dutifully practiced their instruments on summer vacation. All were able to recite the longest monologues from *Le Cid* and long poems by du Bellay. Georges adored his children. He called them "his greatest pride."

Georges took the little Micheline railcar from Paimpol to Guingamp, where Choute picked him up in a car from the ministry's fleet. Choute drove. They turned this most serious of journeys into a romantic jaunt, stopping off at a small hotel near Le Mans to see the cathedral again before boarding the Train Bleu bound for Cannes. Choute followed Georges to the room he was assigned at the Grand Hôtel, the Croisette's premier luxury hotel, notable for its eclectic, rococo style. Through an elaborate gate, past a mini-savanna of palm trees, past a grandiose pink marble entrance hall, up two flights of stairs in an elevator upholstered in dark green velvet, down a blue-and-gold-carpeted hall, Choute walked across their room to step out onto a balcony overlooking the beach. She would have liked to look more in vogue than her slender shape and opaline face allowed; without makeup, her face looked four centuries behind the times. The fashion was for shape-fitting draped fabric; she wore the famous "La Sirène" dress designed by the great New York fashion designer Charles James, in regal, deep purple silk. Choute undulated above the Mediterranean. Georges had turned fifty in May. His mistress had plied him with perfectly extravagant gifts, including a Boucheron cigarette case in eighteen-karat gold, engraved with his monogram. "My adorable beloved cherished darling, you have definitely lost your mind!" he had cried, admiring the yellow-and-pink checkerboard on one side, the cabochon ruby inset in its push button. He had kissed her feverishly to conceal his confusion, attributing his blushing cheeks to the desire she provoked in him. Georges had little taste for pomp and displays of wealth. As a newlywed, he had refused to let a friend of his wife's family invite them to dinner at La Tour d'Argent. But everyday life is nothing but habit. Even luxury can be taught. Since taking up his post on Rue de Valois, he had made himself at home in the silk-hung salons of Le Grand Véfour, to which he preferred the gastronomy of Lucas Carton, the Art Deco monument opposite La Madeleine. He had chosen Monsieur Carton for the banquet for the English sovereigns.

(Lucas Carton was also my father's favorite restaurant, so I could simultaneously conjure the building, the ironwork of the storefront, the taste of the lobster salad and of the rack of lamb, and the look of dismay on my father's face the night I joined him, at seventeen, on the arm of an actor ten years my senior with whom I was madly in love, and who, to honor these official introductions, had donned a Hawaiian shirt.)

On August 22, 1939, at the Palm Beach on Pointe Croisette, the tables were set for a thousand people at a thousand francs a head. The event—the Bal des Petits Lits Blancs, a charity gala in aid of young tuberculosis patients—was intended as a kind of dress rehearsal for the official inauguration of the festival the following week. Men wore white suits, black bow ties, and patent leather loafers. Choute was resplendent in her salmon strapless dress, topped with an emerald green cape made of a wrinkled silk taffeta, an exclusive Schiaparelli creation. The garment proved its worth when, following Fernandel's song recital, the lobster flambéed in Mexican tequila, and the Prunier caviar—"Prunier, inventor of the Paris oyster bar!" Papa cried in my head—a spectacular thunderstorm, a veritable deluge, let loose over the party. Choute held her cape out at arm's length as a canopy to shelter Georges, while poor old Charles Boyer and a princess no one could identify were left terrified and shivering. Then all the notable guests made a break for it, fleeing the storm as if scattered by an air raid. It took the entire hotel staff six full days to repair the damage. Even attendees less superstitious than Georges took it as a bad omen. The German-Soviet pact was signed the next morning. Posters announcing the festival, featuring a drawing of Choute seen from the back in her orange-pink dress, holding the arm of an elegant man to whom a pair of binoculars added a touch of seriousness—every one of them disappeared in a single day under the general mobilization order plastered across the city walls.

The next day, September 2, 1939, all eligible Frenchmen were summoned to report to duty, failure to do so being "punishable to the full extent of the law." Under a decree with immediate effect, the president of the Republic ordered the mobilization of the armed forces—land, sea, and air—and requisitioned all animals, carts, harnessing gear, aircraft, motor vehicles, ships, and watercraft, as well as anything else that could supplement the standard armaments and provisions.

Did Jean Zay come to see the resources devoted to the festival—which he called a "gathering for peace" and a "peaceful September oasis"—as excessive? He resigned as minister to join the army; although not compelled to do so by law, he chose to "share the fate of the young Frenchmen on whose behalf I worked to the best of my abilities in the government." He was commissioned as a second lieutenant and adjutant to the colonel in charge of logistics for the Fourth Army. On June 19, 1940, with his commanding officer's approval, he left his unit for Bordeaux, where members of Parliament had assembled, before embarking on the *Massilia*.

During the eight months of the Phony War (known in France as the *Drôle de guerre*, a term coined by Georges' friend Roland Dorgelès), the Beaux-Arts leadership worked out of the bomb shelters in the Palais de Chaillot, where Georges oversaw the transport of artworks while hundreds of his colleagues set up temporary offices in the Château de Chaumont. Under a new supervising minister, he sought to maintain the collective endeavor of the Front Populaire that he had made his personal duty to fulfill: supporting artists and championing creation on social and moral grounds as a way to uplift humanity.

France had never seen a colder winter than that of 1939–40. In January, the heating system at the Palais Garnier, which had been perpetually under repair—to the point that the boiler repairs had become a joke worthy of the satirist Courteline, whom Georges admired greatly—broke for good, shutting the opera down for months. Georges resumed his round trips to Valmondois, with Choute as chauffeur, and visited his family in Rennes twice, which was already a lot, he said when Marcelle complained. Parisians huddled at La Michodière for vaudeville and at the movies for dramatic love stories and news reports; Erlanger could be found dining at Prunier or Le Grand Véfour most nights. Lucas Carton was always packed. Parisians carried on with their lives. What else was there to do? Georges and Choute set up a home in the bowels of Chaillot. Georges had finally gotten over his morbid jealousy, an anguish almost as oppressive as the vise closing in on the borders of France. They were finally living together. He no longer worried about where she spent her nights. Choute had been working for him for the past two years. He wanted her right there, by his side, her hand in his at all times. "Look at me, my darling, let me see your eyes. Open them, open them wide." He decided they were the color of tree lichen, or the color of moss that grows on stone monuments.

On May 10, 1940, the armed forces of the Third Reich entered Sedan. Luxembourg, the Netherlands, Belgium, and France were all invaded at once.

Erlanger again provided the best account of the flight to Chaumont: "On 8 June, a wave of panic overtook Chaillot." At that time, the military governor of Paris ordered for the bridges to be blown up, but his order was never carried out for lack of ammunition. Georges was disappointed. How he would have loved to see the Pont Alexandre III bridge destroyed at last! In his lengthy and highly detailed account of the day, Erlanger writes that they all met up at Prunier, where Georges informed the last remaining colleagues that the situation had suddenly improved, and the government was no longer considering abandoning the capital. The news was celebrated with champagne. But plans were made and changed from one minute to the next. "Unfortunately, a few hours later, I received a call from Huisman urging me to get to Chaillot as soon as possible. We leave for Chaumont at lunchtime."

The exact date of Georges' arrival in Chaumont varies depending on the account, but it must have been a day in early June, when the banks of the Seine were covered in poppies and wild irises. On that last stretch of gravel to the castle, the history teacher treated Choute to a lecture on the rivers of France. The young woman squeezed his hand and shut her eyes—her way of lovingly asking him to shut his mouth. She had cut her hair short, as she'd worn it when they'd first met at Maison La Roche. The slate steeple of the Blois Cathedral gleamed against the crisp blue sky. From a distance, the cathedral looked more like a factory than a place of worship. Georges remembered the strikes orchestrated by the Front Populaire. "We did well," Georges said out loud. "Yes, we did our duty."

In the castle's magnificent park, endless banks of peonies scented the late spring air. Hands on her hips, Choute watched the chauffeur unload her trunk from the luggage compartment at the front of the car. It would take two men to carry it to the far end of the castle, through a maze of corridors and a succession of rooms occupied by ministry staff. Chaumont had been the first castle in the Loire Valley to be fitted with modern amenities, including running water and electricity. With a flick of a switch, Georges would be able to read and write at any hour of the night. The director and the duchess claimed the most beautiful bedroom for themselves, that of the lady of the house, the late Princesse de Broglie, in the west wing, with windows in every wall overlooking the Loire River between two corbelled towers. The princess, before leaving her property, had held an auction at the foot of the drawbridge and sold off most of her furniture. The state had bought some lots, pieces of historical interest and paintings, including one of Saint Jerome, the translator, one hand resting on his book, the other raised in warning, that hung opposite the bed. Choute drew herself a bath in the adjoining bathroom. Modern amenities—but perhaps of modernities past. Choute had not seen carved wooden toilets since her childhood in her own castle, La Roche-Jagu.

The bustle of busy civil servants echoed within the stone walls. Panes of pale yellow and blue glass in the windows along the corridors of the princess's wing mirrored the alternating colors of the wild irises that lined the road. The day of their journey had been one of radiant sunshine. The weather had deteriorated since, but the blue-tinted windows robbed the sky of its clouds.

Erlanger visited the princess's chamber at the hour when the setting sun cast two long rectangles of light on the floor, the shadow of the elongated window frame spanning the room. Georges, sitting at his desk facing the eastern flank of the castle, squinting behind whorls of cigarette smoke, gray stubble on his chin, shouted at his cat, Vergère, to get down from his desk, while with a flick of her paw she made an even greater mess of his papers. Unkempt, he furiously scrawled out illegible memos. Shadows cast by the windows' latticework, now aglow with the red of early dusk, crisscrossed his back. Coming upon Georges as he was turned to the side, Erlanger shuddered—there appeared to be a gallows hovering over Georges' head. One could already hear the creak of tank tracks on the levees of the Loire. "We need to get the fuck out of here, old boy. Take what you can carry, the RAF will provide transportation . . . Yes, the RAF! Everything must to be shipped to North Africa. Do you hear? The RAF, the RAF!" And as I read this testimony, I wonder again: Why not go to London if he already knew that the Royal Air Force was the only way out?

Marcelle drove the three children in the family car, a Citroën Traction Avant, from Rennes to Chaumont. On June 14, 1940, days after Georges' departure from Paris to Chaumont, the French capital was under the control of the Nazi army. It was urgent to regroup with the rest of the government in Bordeaux, halfway across the country, as far as possible from the marching troops. General panic had set in. Where was everyone to go? What was everyone to do? The RAF was nowhere in sight, and there were no more orders for Georges' hundreds of colleagues in Chaumont. There was no safeguarding plan for the people who saved the art.

In front of the castle, there is but one car to pile into: It belongs to the Huisman family. Erlanger cannot believe his director's blank stare, as he begs to be taken along. "What do you want me to tell you? Go on foot!" Aghast, Erlanger watches his once-effusive director hustle his children, his wife. As he prepares to flee, he is abandoning several hundred staff members, many of whom start surrounding the car, hurling insults, pleading, begging.

In their Traction Avant are two front seats, a wide banquette in the back, and a very small trunk. The entire vehicle is filled to the brim with belongings Marcelle packed for their unpredictable journey, as it is impossible to tell how long they will be gone for or what they might need. She remains in the car, behind the wheel, waiting for Georges to take his place next to her. Their three sons are huddled between pieces of luggage in the back. Papa, eleven, is carrying his suitcase of zinc car models and tin soldiers on his lap. At the start of the war, he had stashed it under his bed, in case they had to flee in haste, to be sure not to lose it, and now he is holding on to it, his hands firmly gripping its sides, when Georges orders him to make room for Choute and Vergère. "What's all this clutter! Get rid of this junk immediately!" cries Georges, clearing space for Choute's enormous trunk. Papa gets out of the car with his suitcase in his arms. He does as the director commands: He drops it to the ground, next to the car, and returns to his seat, Choute pressed against him. She kisses him on both of his cheeks, ablaze with shameful, babyish tears. The ravishing Choute. How is she to take precedent over his most valued treasure? he fails to ask out loud. And how is she coming along, with Vergère, a stray cat everyone had forgotten about for years? The explanation doesn't come as the eleven-year-old boy watches in disbelief as the brown leather of his toy trunk vanishes in the dust. In their wake, rebellion erupts in full.

"Against whom? Against the government, against the traitors of the fifth column, against the cowards, and above all against the Jews. Huisman is a Jew. Once again, the Jews had fled before the evil they themselves had precipitated. These were the same Jews who had held every important post, especially in the Beaux-Arts administration," wrote Erlanger in *La France sans étoile*.

In the aftermath of Kristallnacht (the "night of broken glass," known as the first mass killing and deportation of Jews across Germany and Austria) just two years earlier, in 1938, the French government found itself having to entertain Hitler's emissary, Joachim von Ribbentrop, who was in Paris to sign an accord that would turn out to be as empty as all the others. It had determined that the galleries of the Louvre, recently electrified, would be a perfect place to receive him. Ribbentrop, who had just ordered the murder of twenty thousand Jews, was greeted at a museum without a single Aryan at its helm. The minister of education, Jean Zay, was Jewish. His chief of staff, Marcel Abraham, was Jewish. The director-general of the Beaux-Arts, Georges Huisman, was Jewish. The honorary director-general, Paul Léon, was Jewish. The president of the National Council of Museums was, too . . . Conversely, at Chaumont in June

1940, out of more than four hundred civil servants, only two Jews remained: Georges Huisman and Philippe Erlanger.

The exodus from Chaumont was not a turning point; it was a definitive break with the world that preceded it. Papa, squeezed between his two brothers and a duchess in the back of the family Traction Avant, knew this intuitively. It was here that his destiny was fractured, amid the scent of his father's cigarettes and the Guerlain perfume of his father's mistress, as he ran his fingers through Vergère's fur.

On the road, disbanded soldiers and military trucks stumbled among hordes of civilians on foot. Marcelle drove all the way to Bordeaux. Papa didn't remember whether they had stopped in Poitiers or Angoulême. They must have stopped at least once overnight. Walking would take three and a half days without pause, and cars were often slower moving than pedestrians on this terrible exodus. As the family finally arrived in Bordeaux, Choute and Vergère in tow, an elegant mansion awaited them belonging to an old Chartes schoolfellow of Georges'. Only then did Marcelle allow herself to lose her composure. "Make her leave immediately!" she screamed. "Right now! I don't care where she goes, I will not tolerate her a second longer."

For the first time in six years—six years of intimacy, crises, reconciliations, secrets, routine, boredom, doubts, and passion—Choute felt the precarity of her situation. She held no status in Georges' life; there was no way to explain her position to his family. What had he been thinking, bringing her to Bordeaux? That his wife would welcome his concubine? That his children would tolerate a polygamous father? That Choute would agree to live as Marcelle's guest? He had probably not thought it through at all. He needed Choute by his side. He needed to save his family. He was anxious enough about his parents, whom he had left to fend for themselves in Paris. Choute had promised that her butler would look in on them and supply them with anything they needed. From Chaillot he could get to them on foot, walking down Avenue Paul Doumer, the former Avenue de la Muette, renamed on the first anniversary of the president's assassination.

On June 16, the French prime minister resigned; two million men, women, and children left Paris within a matter of days, joining six million more fleeing south or west, away from the German troops approaching from the north. The mass movement was so great and unprecedented, it quickly became known as the Exodus. Public services—firefighters, police, schools, hospitals—ceased to exist; supplies of weapons, food, medicine, gas, firewood, and paper were depleted or nonexistent. In Bordeaux, tens of thousands of desperate refugees roamed the city in search of shelter.

Marcelle demanded that Choute leave that very night—it must have been the 16th or 17th of June—in the middle of chaos. No one had ever seen anything like it. Even those who, like them, had survived the Great War, and who had heard countless stories from their parents about the Prussian invasion, knew that they were living through something without precedent. Especially for Jews. The city's hotels were filled beyond capacity. It was impossible to find a room, impossible to call anyone. Georges was compelled to obey his wife. He took Choute by the arm, and she took the cat in hers. Wracking his mind for somewhere safe he might send her, he suddenly remembered the housing development that Le Corbusier and

Jeanneret had built on the outskirts of the city—the urban utopia of Fugès.

Thirteen years earlier, the year the complex had been inaugurated, Georges had written an article for *La Lumière* praising the aesthetic qualities and democratic potential of the Quartiers Modernes Frugès. Designed as functional housing for workers, not for fleeing duchesses, the buildings had been conceived as works of art in their own right, in a variety of colors and layouts in six different models based on a standard module. One of the residences had suffered water damage several years before, and Georges had raised the money for its renovation. The Quinconce housing module had been left empty to serve as a model home for special visits and educational purposes. The furnishings, designed by the architects themselves to match the angles of the walls and the colors of the surfaces, gave the impression of a three-dimensional painting whose vanishing perspective had materialized into real space.

And so Choute, sprawled in a canvas-covered armchair inspired by Eileen Gray, looked as if she had stepped from the frame of her portrait in the Louvre. Georges leaned against the wall to keep himself from falling over—his chest was heaving with pain. They had walked almost two hours on foot through the staggering throng. "Choute, my love, I beg you!" Georges suddenly burst into sobs, collapsed to the floor, his knees pressed against his chest, and curled into a ball. She had seen him weep at the opera, during *La traviata*, or at a concert of Beethoven's Seventh, the most sublime of human creations, he claimed, but never like this, bitterly, like a child, his face buried in his crossed arms. "My love, I beg you, I beg you." She stroked his hair. "I implore you, Choute. Don't leave me."

At two p.m. on June 18, the president of the National Assembly summoned two deputies to announce that the government was preparing to evacuate to North Africa. The president of the Republic, the presidents of both chambers of Parliament, and all those deputized with executive power were duty-bound to evade the enemy. "All are in agreement. The Head of Government unreservedly concurs." Only Pétain and three ministers would await the Germans in Bordeaux. However, that very night Bordeaux was bombed, and the urgency of establishing a government in North Africa became even clearer, lest the Germans take the French president prisoner or the conditions of the armistice, which had not yet been signed, deteriorate still further. On June 20, Admiral Darlan wrote the following memo: "The government, with the assent of the presidents of the Chambers, decided yesterday, the 19th of June, that the members of Parliament would board the *Massilia* today, the 20th. The river having been mined at Pauillac, the *Massilia* has been unable to reach Bordeaux and has remained at Verdon. Public officials must therefore travel to Verdon in cars to be provided by the government." Verdon-sur-Mer was a hundred kilometers from Bordeaux, and a bus and two cars were made available to those departing. The chaos in Bordeaux was so widespread that few parliamentarians could be informed of the plan. Out of 846 members of Parliament in France, only 27 met the bus at five p.m. on June 20. Georges and his family were among them. Georges, poor slayed dragon.

Choute, in her modernist residence with her cat and her trunk, looked like the heroine of an unfilmed Eisenstein movie. Choute in exile from her Rue Jacob, from her bunker in Chaillot, from the bedroom of the Princesse de Broglie at the Château de Chaumont. Choute backlit against a horizontal window, her blond hair gleaming under the artificial light. Georges had told her he would come back for her, or that she would join him in Algiers, that they would work it out. "Who, exactly, is abandoning whom?" she had asked him when his tears had dried. "Georges, you're being dishonest, you are only lying to yourself. You need to divorce her. We could get married, you could take my name. I would hide you. I could adopt your children if anti-Semitic laws were enacted in France." Georges didn't have the courage to ask her what would become of Marcelle.

The majority of parliamentarians who embarked on the *Massilia* were on the left and virulently opposed to an armistice that would repudiate the alliance with England. Strategically, the rationale for moving the government to North Africa was that the German army had no experience conducting naval invasions. In all likelihood, it could not prevail even against feeble opposition. France would also enjoy the support of the Allied navies, and of course of its colonial troops. Among those who stayed behind, the most vehement advocate of an accord with the Germans at any price was Pierre Laval.

The armistice signed on the 22nd of June in Rethondes ratified the occupation of three fifths of France by the German armed forces, across a territory divided into zones, including one designated "free"—that is, not occupied by German troops, with its capital at Vichy, under the authority of Maréchal Pétain. Laval was named vice president of the Council of Ministers on June 23. On July 10, 1940, Laval called a vote in Parliament to delegate full powers to Maréchal Pétain to draft a new constitution. The result was 596 votes in favor to 80 against. Léon Blum was among the minority dissenters. "This Constitution must guarantee the rights to Work, Family and Fatherland." A *coup d'état*.

With the distance of history, the episode of the *Massilia* fails to convince as the single most climactic event of the war. And yet, for Papa, it remained the epitome of betrayal.

The *Massilia* carried 506 passengers, including some 200 Jewish families fleeing Nazis. There was tension between the civilians and the parliamentarians, who were seen as having precipitated the disaster. That hostility was the least of their worries. With its three tall smokestacks, the majestic vessel—176 meters long, the width of the Seine under the Pont Neuf—represented, in June 1940, the last hope of those opposed to the armistice.

As the passengers began to board, a hysterical woman, disheveled and wailing, grabbed Marcelle by the sleeve in front of her terrified children. "Don't get on! This ship is a trap. Don't get on, Madame! Turn around while there's still time!" Bonne-Maman describes the episode in her memoirs (which my father pretended to publish). Mendès-France recalled having seen and heard this oracle as well. At that very moment, they ran into the Perrins in the crowd.

They had not known that the Perrins had also fled to Bordeaux. They, too, were leaving for Algiers.

Georges had many acquaintances on board the *Massilia*, all of them traveling with their families: the composer Jacques Ibert, director of the Villa Medici in Rome; Jean Perrin, a friend from L'Arcouest and colleague in the Blum government; Julien Cain, general administrator of the Bibliothèque nationale; the well-known actor Béatrice Bretty, member of the Comédie-Française and partner of Georges Mandel. A sculptor, a painter. A fashion designer, a travel agent, a veterinarian, a lieutenant in the Spahi, several lawyers, an aviator, a postal worker, a window-dresser, a cleaning lady, and a nineteen-year-old student social worker who, thirty years later, would become Pierre Mendès-France's second wife. The archived list of passengers includes Georges Huisman, directeur des Beaux-Arts; Marcelle Huisman, a writer (the children's books she coauthored with her husband give her a claim to the title); and the Huisman children, including one young schoolboy.

The *Massilia* weighed anchor at 1:30 p.m. on June 21, 1940. The first leg of the crossing was risky; once beyond the Gironde estuary, they had to hug the coast to avoid mines. A few mines exploded in the open water nearby, and the *Massilia* sailed past a burned-out freighter. Fortunately, the weather held. Those who kept journals aboard noted that there was a certain elegance to mealtimes and that the food was excellent. The women took pains with their appearance and spent their afternoons lounging in rocking chairs on the promenade deck and indulging in worldly small talk. The parliamentarians gathered in groups to engage in animated discussions as if they were in the halls of the Palais Bourbon.

Yes, following its chaotic departure, the *Massilia* settled into something that might have been mistaken for a pleasure cruise. The most eminent passengers, Georges Mandel and our Georges, were authorized by the captain to access the bridge. The children had a fun time playing together. Caught in the social whirl, their mothers watched them distractedly. The smoking lounge was the arena of choice for political discussion, and it was there, on the night of the 22nd–23rd, that they heard the first news of the armistice broadcast on the radio. It was their call to action. Pierre Laval's joining the government convinced the parliamentarians that they had been set up. The liner changed course and made a beeline for Casablanca, the nearest port in North Africa.

Mandel sent a telegram to the commander in chief of the North African forces to alert him to the imminent arrival of twenty-seven parliamentarians, who had "set sail by order of the government," and asked him to make "immediate provision for transport to Rabat 120 persons with luggage." From Rabat, the administrative capital, there was still a chance to rectify the situation. At 7:45 a.m. on June 24, as a foggy, ochre dawn rose over a glassy sea, the *Massilia* docked at the Casablanca trading pier.

At 11:15 a.m., the acting minister and secretary-general of the General Residence of Morocco came aboard to explain the conditions of the armistice to the parliamentarians, who had remained on the ship. Their despondency was overwhelming, although it did not keep them from their lunch. They were the only passengers left on board. A few headed into town to do some shopping—Mandel, who was notorious for his vanity, supposedly bought himself a closetful of shirts at a shop called Le Carnaval de Venise before returning to his cabin. On the 25th, he paid a call on the British consul in Casablanca.

Churchill sent two emissaries to take him to England. That very night, Mandel was arrested onboard. The British mission had failed. On the 27th, the rest of the parliamentarians finally disembarked.

A fractious crowd, alerted to the presence of the ship by the press, which had accused the passengers of desertion, cornered and threatened the parliamentarians. The threat of violence was very real. No sooner had they reached the dock than the resident-general whisked them away, for their own safety, to an upscale hotel in Casablanca. Counterorders followed from Bordeaux and Vichy. From that moment on, the parliamentarians' journey diverged from Georges'. Those who were considered to be mobilized officers, including Pierre Mendès-France and Jean Zay, were arrested on August 31, 1940, in Casablanca, repatriated to the home country, brought before a military tribunal in Clermont-Ferrand, charged with "desertion before the enemy," and sentenced two months later to prison terms and a ten-year deprivation of civil rights. Georges Mandel, who had been at sea the day the armistice was signed by order of the government, was nevertheless accused of responsibility for the country's defeat and tried in Riom in 1942, alongside Léon Blum. That iniquitous verdict was overturned in 1946, but by then Mandel had already been assassinated by French paramilitaries.

The families on the *Massilia* couldn't let go of the idea that there had been some sort of misunderstanding. If only they could hurry home and seek clarification, justice would be done. Georges insisted on calling for orders from the government he worked for. The resident-general was very uneasy about their situation and sought to find ways to distract them and at least make their stay as pleasant as possible. No one was quite capable of being distracted. No one, that is, but the children, who invented new games inspired by the exotic setting, which they'd previously only known from the storybooks about the Orient. They discovered guavas and kumquats. Papa remembered vividly his short-lived idyll with the little Mandel girl: At night, they slipped love notes under each other's doors across the corridor. The family had more luggage than sense, stuffed with items that were perfectly useless in these circumstances. What they needed was cash, which they lacked, but they felt (delusionally) confident that their bank accounts were still good in North Africa. Georges wrote to Pétain. He wrote to Laval. No response.

From Casablanca, Georges and his family headed for Algiers, despite the sobs of their little boy, who was head over heels in love with his new companion. Their farewells in the hotel lobby, under the eyes of parents more concerned with affairs of state, would have been heartrending in less dire circumstances. The lovely eleven-year-old girl, in her floral dress with balloon sleeves and ribbon cuffs, could not have imagined what fate had in store for her sweet papa. Georges and Marcelle temporarily put the Bordeaux incident behind them. Their situation was critical, and this was no time for squabbling. Georges wrote to Choute, care of Édouard Barthe, that he would be returning to France as soon as possible and that above all she should stay put in Bordeaux. He was on his way. That is, he was on his way from Casablanca to Algiers to Marseille, the only remaining open route to France: twelve hundred kilometers of the North African colonial empire by train, stopping at every station, before crossing back over the Mediterranean.

In the Hollywood version of our story, Choute would have surely met Georges in Casablanca.

In Algiers, the only hotel available to the family was cramped and shabby, but never mind; the important thing was having somewhere to lay your head. Georges knew everybody—people he had met or helped while in office. He ran into them on every corner. One, a film producer and friend of Harold Smith, offered him a little radio set to listen to the BBC; another, a painter married to an Algerian woman, found them a fine apartment belonging to some absent English friends in the hills above the Telemly neighborhood, at the far end of Rue Saint-Saëns. The Perrins, the most well-to-do among their comrades in misfortune, were staying at the Hôtel Aletti, a jewel of Art Deco architecture with its own cinema and casino. A feeling of unreality pervaded their sojourn. In his inventory of all the places where he had lived, my father would recall with dreamlike vividness the opulent Algiers apartment with a breathtaking view of the white city and the cobalt blue sea that separated them from Europe.

Georges had no need to wait for racial laws to be adopted to grasp the violence of his reversal of fortune. As the daily headlines accused the parliamentarians of desertion, on July 12, 1940, the *Journal Officiel*—the government gazette—published the new law concerning the staffing of ministerial cabinets: "Only those born of French parents may hold a post in a ministerial cabinet." Georges did not meet that criterion. Hartog had been naturalized and barely spoke French. On July 17, a new law limited access to public positions "exclusively to born Frenchmen." On July 22, a commission was established to review naturalization policy. This was just the first phase of the Vichy policy to rid France of the plague of "foreigners of Jewish origin."

The next day, the *Journal Officiel* announced that "any French citizen who left metropolitan France between May 10 and June 30,

1940, will forfeit his nationality . . . This measure will take effect on a date set by decree and may be extended to the wife and children who accompanied the person concerned." The property of the parties concerned would be sequestered and liquidated. Georges had protected his personal art collection by storing it with the treasures from the national collections. He did the same with the contents of the studios of Fernand Léger and Georges Braque, whom he had personally visited in order to persuade them to safeguard their work.

The law's primary targets were rich Jews, such as the Rothschilds, who had immigrated to the United States. Georges could not understand what this had to do with him. He had left the country on the authority of an official travel order; his actions had been unimpeachably legal. But the Vichy government denied ever having issued such an order. Pétain washed his hands of the matter; Laval welcomed it. Georges was a deserter. His—my—family was no longer French.

Thus, three weeks after having embarked on the *Massilia* at the port of Verdon, Georges found himself fired as director-general of the Beaux-Arts administration by one law, banned from holding any public position by another, and stripped of his French nationality by a third.

He was dismissed without pension. There was no question of remitting any back pay he was due. He was banished without further legal recourse. It all felt like one big heresy. A charade. An incomprehensible misunderstanding. A nightmare from which he would surely wake. Despite all the racist abuse he had suffered throughout his life, he could never have foreseen the extent to which he would be affected and ruined by anti-Semitic hatred.

The Huisman family returned to mainland France, where the first thing Georges did was to hasten to Vichy to clear up this whole mess. Obviously, the family could have remained in Algiers and lived more or less peaceably and comfortably. They had friends there; Georges would have found work of some sort; Choute could even have joined him as they waited for the allied landing. They could have gone to Portugal and on to Brazil; to the United States with the Perrins and Fernand Léger; to England. They still had options. Things might have gone otherwise. But then, they could have all ended up in Auschwitz.

What part did politics play in the decision? What part emotion? Georges' parents were old; they had rested all their hopes on their only son, who had made them proud and prosperous. Could he, in good conscience, have chosen to abandon them for the duration of the war or taken the risk of their dying in his absence? And what about Choute?

In October 1940, the *Journal Officiel* published the law on the status of Jews, prohibiting them from working in education and the press, among other professions. The police initiated a census of Jews, French and foreign alike. That was followed in short order by a law authorizing and organizing the immediate internment of foreigners of Jewish origin; the requirement that Jews have their identity cards stamped with the word *Jew*; the establishment of the Commissariat général aux questions juives (CGQJ, or Commissariat-General for Jewish Affairs), charged with implementing applicable discriminatory measures; a ban on Jewish property ownership; the mandatory registration of all relevant charitable associations (children's centers, nursing homes, etc.) with the Union générale des israélites de France (UGIF, or General Union of French Israelites), overseen by the CGQJ; the banning of Jews from public places; the mandatory wearing of the yellow star; a curfew for Jews in the occupied zone;

limited access for Jews—one hour a day—to food shops; the proscription of Jews from the artistic professions; and the prohibition of the use of telephones by Jews.

Any failure to obey these laws was punishable by incarceration, the legal route to Auschwitz. Although French Jews, veterans in particular and so-called assimilated Jews—the very description of Georges—were not yet the targets of raids, no Jew in France could consider himself or herself safe. None could feel in any way "protected." Nevertheless, the response of most to the new circumstances was one of incredulity. This simply could not be happening.

One month before the status of Jews was announced, Pétain had another law promulgated in France, which gave him permission to jail and try those he deemed "dangerous to the national defense and public security." The law authorized him to put away his high-profile political opponents—the perilously decadent Leftists of the Front Populaire—including several passengers of the *Massilia* and obviously Léon Blum. The accused were tried in Riom, near Vichy, before a jury of staggering bad faith, where Léon Blum and Georges Mandel in particular were found guilty of having precipitated France's defeat in June 1940. The Front Populaire's focus on leisure! The extravagant social concessions that hindered the war effort! The moral decadence of all this merriment, these festivities, concerts, museum outings, festivals, and holidays! Having won all these cultural battles (or were they only social events?), they had lost the war.

Several months before his election six years earlier, Léon Blum had been beaten in the street by a mob of far-right extremists. The notorious anti-Semite Charles Maurras, a founder of Action

Française, had labeled this "naturalized German Jew, or son of naturalized Jews" a "monster" and "human garbage," concluding that he was "a man to be shot in the back." Maurras was sentenced to eight months in prison for "incitement to murder." When he was released from prison, it was outside the Vélodrome d'Hiver that his defenders organized a celebration for his release.

As I write this, eighty years after the Vél d'Hiv roundup, the largest French deportation of Jews during the Holocaust, when thirteen thousand men, women, and children were sent to concentration camps, historians continue to find victims' letters and physical evidence of the atrocities inflicted on tens of thousands of persons who the literature describes, again and again, as "innocent"—as though they might have committed some sin that would have otherwise justified mass murder and so this qualification is necessary. It was only on the fifty-third anniversary of the Vél d'Hiv roundup, on July 16, 1995, that then–French President Jacques Chirac acknowledged the role that France and its police had played in the persecution of Jews and other victims of Nazi occupation. "France," Chirac said, "land of the Enlightenment and of Human Rights, land of hospitality and asylum, France, on that day, committed an irreparable act. It failed to keep its word and delivered those under its protection to their executioners." For more than half a century, my grandmother—who died, at ninety-seven years old, a couple of months before Chirac's speech—had endured the fiction that France had been forced by the Nazi occupant to deport its Jews.

The Vél d'Hiv stadium, built to host major sporting events, stood on Rue Nélaton (named for a pioneer of plastic surgery) in the fifteenth arrondissement of Paris, between Pont de Bir-Hakeim and the Île aux Cygnes, just south of the Eiffel Tower. Nicknamed the "temple of sports on Boulevard de Grenelle," it was the venue of cycling competitions between the First and Second World Wars and later, under the auspices of an American promoter, of basketball games, boxing and tennis matches, and international figure skating competitions. It was there, on the sidewalk opposite the memorial garden dedicated to the children of the Vél d'Hiv, that during the year when we were separated from Maman, when she was committed to a psychiatric asylum, José, on Papa's orders, used to stop to buy us a snack at the bakery, which has since become a Japanese restaurant, on our way home from school. I never wanted that snack. I was a spoiled child heartbroken by her mother's absence. I had no idea at the time that thousands of children had been forever separated from their own mothers on that very site.

The stadium, illuminated by a gigantic skylight, included five toilets, roughly one for every twenty-five hundred "human scum." Those who were able to recount their experience of the velodrome in July 1942—social workers and handfuls of survivors—remember above all the suffocating stink. The facility was restored to its original purpose immediately after the war, until it was torn down in 1959. Perhaps the smell was not entirely gone. And stones, however silent, bear a kind of witness.

Léon Blum's defense in his trial in Riom was astoundingly eloquent and heartfelt. He vehemently refuted the accusations against him. Nothing could justify the spite and vitriol he faced: "As I see it, I prepared French minds for the idea of a kind of French unity that could have and should have been as beautiful as it was in the early months of the war of 1914." The spirit of prewar socialism radiates from the oratory of the leader of the Front Populaire before his judges. Georges shared in that same legacy. After the war, that French unity, an ideal cherished by veterans of the Third Republic, had become a cruel anachronism.

In Marseille, Georges and his family, suddenly destitute, were hosted by Dorgelès, himself married to a Jew, as later recalled by Bonne-Maman. There, Georges ran into his old friend Gaston Castel at the Old Port. Castel was the chief architect for the Bouches-du-Rhône department; Georges had helped him finance numerous projects and done him many a good turn. Castel was one of the very few who was honest and brave enough to acknowledge his debt to the fallen man. He found them an apartment, modest but habitable, at 5 impasse Croix de Régnier, across the street from his own home at number 2. Marcelle furnished their two-bedroom apartment with whatever she could find at the Red Cross. (For the rest of her long life, my grandmother was a fervent supporter of the Red Cross and the Secours populaire français, among other nonprofits to which she donated a significant portion of her money.) The boys shared a room. Those Castels did us *many a good turn*, Papa recalled on his sickbed, using an expression that I had never heard him use before. I was later surprised to read the same phrase in Bonne-Maman's memoirs. The precision of memory. Perhaps they were both quoting Georges? In a few weeks, Fernand Léger would set sail for America, followed by the Perrins. Varian Fry, a journalist from New York and a scholar of classics, arrived in Marseille at the same time as Georges, in the summer of 1940. He had been sent by the Emergency Rescue Committee, established, with the support of First Lady of the United

States Eleanor Roosevelt, to help prominent intellectuals and artists who were stranded in France and threatened with arrest and deportation. With no experience in such work, much less in clandestine operations, Fry opened a rescue center to assist not only the most famous refugees but also the greatest possible number of people in crossing the Atlantic. Lacking any documentation to verify who was actually in danger, Fry admitted that they could only guess and that, given the gravity of the situation, each refugee should be given the full benefit of the doubt. "Otherwise we might refuse help to someone who was really in danger and learn later that he had been sent to Dachau or Buchenwald," he wrote in *Surrender on Demand*. By his own estimate, his underground operation took up some fifteen thousand cases between his arrival in August 1940 and his return home in May 1941. Marc Chagall, Hannah Arendt, and Victor Serge were among the four thousand people who were able to covertly flee France thanks to Fry's work, by means as complex as they were varied. But Georges and his family remained. They had to clear their name. They still believed in a misunderstanding. They still believed in justice.

As to Erlanger, he had finally managed to leave Chaumont: "I had thought myself abandoned when a big black Citroën that did not belong to the administration suddenly pulled up." The car belonged to Laure Albin Guillot, Georges' official photographer and archivist, impeccably coiffed and dressed, who was traveling in grand style, accompanied by her chauffeur and her housekeeper. "What are you doing here? Get in! You only have one bag? Perfect!"

The Huisman family scraped by in Marseille, in the so-called "free zone," until July 1942. Thanks to a buddy from the previous war, the recent director of the Beaux-Arts found work processing sausage casings. Papa was in seventh grade at the Lycée Thiers. "What will we do when we run out of money?" he recalled asking his father. He would have to get through the winter with nothing but his boy scout cape to keep him warm. As Bonne-Maman recalled in her memoir, and my father confirmed—unusually enough, they concurred on that particular anecdote—Georges had calmly responded: "We'll all throw ourselves in the harbor." Papa demonstrated a precocious entrepreneurial spirit, his mother recorded, by offering a friend, the son of a grocer, to share his Latin homework in exchange for a few cans of food.

Months went by with very little news of Georges' parents. The news was bad in any case. That first winter in Marseille, the schoolboy in his scout uniform was caught unprepared by the ferocity of the seasonal mistral. In a photo dated December 1940, the Transporter Bridge is seen looming over the harbor under a deep layer of snow.

For weeks following my father's funeral, my thoughts returned again and again to the manila envelope from the Valmondois attic. My short visit with the family archives had convinced me that I must get down to work, but what that work might entail was still as vague as ever as I alternated between Béatrice's thesis, the stack of books I had selected from her bibliography, Bonne-Maman's memoir, and Papa's rambling stories. Every day I put off opening the old envelope, which I had tucked away in a clothes drawer, conscientiously wrapped in a shirt as if it were highly breakable or a sacred relic. I feared it contained a secret or revelation that would somehow invalidate my project, somehow undo me. The envelope, larger than I had remembered it, was folded in half. I finally set it on my desk, reached my hand inside, and slipped out a pile of note-cards. They were the size of postcards but had no images on them, just blank space, prepaid with a postal stamp of Pétain's face. It took me a minute to understand that the cards had been meticulously arranged in chronological order according to the postmarks. In other words, among that enormous mess in the Valmondois attic, in a box no less disorganized than all the others, the contents of this particular envelope had been arranged with specificity and care. "My Papa / in the Occupation," Georges had written on the other side of the fold.

Papa had told me that, because Hartog was barely able to read and write, his grandmother, Louise, had been in charge of all the household's administrative tasks and maintaining the couple's correspondence. As I glanced quickly through the stack, I noticed that all of the cards had been sent from the same address, on Avenue Mozart in Paris. I was not surprised to find that the first card had been written by Louise, or Amère as her grandchildren called her. She only ever wrote in purple ink, Papa had told me once, associating the color with his set of Larousse Classics. The card was partly prefilled, with sentence starters and phrases to choose from, like some kind of perverse Mad Lib. They were "reserved strictly for family correspondence," the header advised in an intimidating tone. "WARNING—Any card whose contents is not exclusively related to family matters will not be delivered and is likely to be destroyed." The other instructions said to "cross out what does not apply. Do not write outside the dotted lines."

Paris, 30 April 1941

I am not in good health. . . . . *very*. . . . .
tired. . . . . slightly, ~~seriously~~ ill,
~~wounded~~. . . . . ~~killed~~. . . . .
~~prisoner~~. . . . . ~~deceased~~. *I have had* ~~no~~ some
news. . . . . of. . . . . *you*. ~~The family~~. . . . .
~~is well~~. . . . . . We have. . . . . *no*. . . . . need of
provisions. . . . . *or*. . . . . of money.

News, luggage. . . . . will be back on. . . . .

. . . . ~~working at~~. . . . . ~~will start school at~~. . . . . ~~has been accepted~~

We are doing all we can to come to you. . . . . on. . . . . as soon as possible

but it will be long, I will leave everything behind once we are able to go because I still have no strength. Will be happy to see you again.

Warm thoughts.
Signature
Amère

The fact that Amère did not add her personal fond farewells to the government-approved "Warm thoughts" makes me wonder about how "slightly ill" she was. Amère was eighty years old in May 1942. In Laure Albin Guillot's photos, reproduced in the annex of Béatrice's thesis, Amère is a very old woman with a mysterious, intelligent smile, her face haloed by a frizz of hair as white as foam, her eyes bleary with age and circled with dark rings that in no way dim their vivacity. Her youngest grandson would remember her wonderful, enveloping embraces until his dying breath. And her son was devoted to her beyond words, beyond reason, beyond danger.

Georges did not wait for a second postcard. He left Marseille for Vichy in order to request a *laissez-passer* from former colleagues who, until recently, had claimed to be in his debt. Surely they wouldn't dare refuse him his *Ausweis*? His identity card had not yet been stamped with the word *Jew*. He reached Paris just in time to witness the first roundup, on May 14, 1941. The so-called "green ticket" roundup, named for the summons sent to men—Polish immigrants for the most part—to present themselves for a "verification of status." The capital was awash in red flags bearing swastikas. At the Palais Berlitz, preparations were underway for an exhibition called "The Jew and France," presented as an educational initiative to help the French identify Jews by their physical characteristics—hook nose, greasy hair, clawed fingers, thick lips—and their moral traits of cupidity and duplicitousness, and to highlight their widespread, corrupting influence on the nation. The Jew Georges Huisman was prominently featured in the exhibition.

In vain, Georges searched Paris high and low for Choute. She was not on Rue Jacob. She had left no forwarding address anywhere. She had responded to none of his telegrams, none of his letters, none of his calls. Where was the woman who had promised to hide him, who had begged him to marry her? Even Choute had turned her back on him. Yes, even Choute.

Louise was dying. Georges was aware of it, but he was aware that overstaying the expiration date on his *laissez-passer* could mean death for him, too. If the *Massilia*, the racial laws, and the reversal of fate he had experienced in just a few months had not yet convinced him of the peril of his position, seeing the French police deport refugees the country had sworn to protect made it real. He felt he had no choice but to abandon his mother to her agony. His ancient father, bewildered, utterly confused, and accompanied only by one lone distant cousin, buried her in the Valmondois cemetery, as his son instructed.

Papa often repeated that his grandfather Hartog could barely read or write. Even so, his stories had not prepared me for the scribbles on the postcards that followed Amère's in the manila envelope.

The cards were no longer pre–filled out. On one side was the name and address of the sender and the receiver, seemingly transcribed by a post office employee. On the other side, a rectangle of blank space was covered in what I came to identify as Amère's purple ink, appearing as tangles and blobs, largely indecipherable. Only the first card offered a legible note: The cousin, taking over from Apère, who was in no condition to write, in his overwhelming distress, described the utter sadness of the funeral. As I shuffled through the stack, I managed to make out only a few words, drawing on my experience of my girls' whimsical spelling. Mostly mentions of the weather. During the week of July 10, 1942, Hartog sent four cards. Meaning he walked to the post office four times as ten thousand foreign Jews like him were being rounded up a few blocks from his apartment. At the bottom of the cards, he signed: Apert or Aper or Apèr. And on every one of them: *Je vou embrase de tou mon coeur.* I kiss you with all my heart.

I read these postcards again and again, turning them over in my hands. It was as though the blotches of purple ink were transferred to my mind, becoming Rorschachs in which I saw images, characters, scenes.

In the fall of 1942, three consecutive postcards did not reach their destination. They were returned to the post office. There was no Georges Huisman at the address provided, impasse Croix de Régnier. Had the apartment been raided then? Marcelle, in her memoirs, described telling the Gestapo that she had no idea where her husband was. She described her youngest son, Papa, terrified, awkwardly trying to hide his drawing of the inglorious end of the *Admiral Graf Spee*, a German ship scuttled off the coast of South America. Georges, carrying a little bag of figs for his wife and children, had been arrested outside the Marseille train terminal and sent to the Évêché prison. On what charge? Were his papers not in order? In their search of the home, the police had found compromising names, such as those of Jean Zay and Georges Mandel, in his address book. The trial in Riom had just concluded. Thankfully, Roland Dorgelès, who knew the chief of police in Marseille, managed to get Georges out within a couple of days. (Perhaps this is why Papa became so intent on being inducted into the Legion of Honor, so that he could never be arrested in the middle of the street.)

In endlessly rereading the notes, I have shuffled them like playing cards. They are no longer in chronological order. As I try to get them back in sequence, I see that the Marseille address on several cards has been crossed out in sky-blue pencil and replaced with "Hôtel Le Lion d'Or de La Clusaz." But this is earlier. April 1942—several months before the Évêché prison episode. Papa would have just turned thirteen. An archival website tells me that this hotel was one of the fanciest ski resorts in the Alps. Georges didn't ski; it was springtime. Who could it be if not Choute? I am convinced that this deck of postcards, of tarot cards, has led me to her—she who, in my imagination, in my heart, is the secret architect of Georges' story.

In 1942, after two years of silence, Georges had received a telegram through Gaston Castel. Choute had run into Jacques Carlu on his return from the United States; he had filled her in on Georges' misfortunes and given her his address in Marseille. She was sorry about Louise: "Heartbroken for you," she wrote. Her father, too, had fallen gravely ill. He had succumbed to cancer in a matter of months, although she did not tell Georges in that note; her message was laconic to say the least. She soberly asked him to meet her at the Lion d'Or. The hotel was in the free zone; he should be able to get there. She said nothing further. There was no need for words.

After the dreadful saga of the *Massilia*, after months of filling Choute's deafening silence with desperate explanations, Georges had come to wonder if it had all been mere fantasy. If he had dreamed up that lavish life of theirs, rich with luxury and honors, those idyllic afternoons with the most beautiful woman in the world—a duchess!—those strolls through the Palais Royal gardens, those rendezvous under the stained glass of the Sainte-Chapelle. If he—the son of an illiterate tradesman, a little Jew sprung from nothing—had simply enjoyed a long hallucination before the world crumbled around him.

Her legs crossed at the edge of an armchair upholstered in beige velvet in the lounge of the Lion d'Or, Choute—who had scarcely worn mourning for her husband—looked like a blackbird perched on a winter branch in her black crêpe dress. A tulle veil covered her face and chin, revealing, on either side of her oval face, two little diamond pendants in her ears, gifts from Georges in the early days of their love. She was sitting in silence, staring into the void, both hands on a knee. Her story would take several days to unfold, but he could almost read it on her face, her tight lips, her eyes lost in the distance. Georges remembered all those nights when he visited her in dreams, his suitcase in hand as he ran for a train, his lost suitcase, their misplaced luggage, roaming homeless in the labyrinthine streets of a strange city, storms on the open sea, huge waves smashing their raft, she in a white dress, her perfume mixed with sweat, her makeup running down her cheeks, her purple lips, the raft on which they clung to one another, transporting the Géricault along country roads, the fireworks at the Eiffel Tower to celebrate the British royal visit, the stars over the garden in Brittany, stars vanishing in the smoke from his Gitanes, stars tumbling down in a cascade of ashes. Had he gone mad? He had left his home, his family, in mad haste, like a thief.

Choute told him that day—a day of hope hemmed in by disaster—that she had lost their child. They'd had a daughter. A girl, at last. She had been born two months before Amère's death, in Choute's own castle in Brittany. The family doctor had tended to Choute, whom he himself had delivered. She had named the child

Manon, like Madame Roland, the iconic figure of the French Revolution of whom Georges had spoken so much and to whom, he had often said, he wanted to devote a book. She had thought her choice of name would please him. Manon de Troguindy. In the absence of a father to recognize her, she would bear her mother's name, and title. She was about to tell him when she'd learned of Louise's death, and the first roundups. She had seen that awful exhibition at the Palais Berlitz. She was scared for her daughter; her only concern became to keep her safe. The child was delicate. "How I prayed! I prayed for her, for you!" cried Choute. "To think that the last time I'd been to church was to admire the stained glass of the Sainte-Chapelle. With you. I kept thinking back to those verses you taught me. I'll know them by heart to the end of my days. Some listen to God; I listened to love, / And your lightning-bright eyes all but blinded me, / And so when your soul had seized my entire being, / You were my devotion! My heaven! My poetry!"

Manon had been born with a heart defect. And she was so tiny. Choute had hired a wet nurse to supplement her own milk; it had dried up after her father's death. The sorrow had been overwhelming; it was just too much grief. And then Manon had contracted typhoid fever. Choute had told the household to filter the water, which was known to be teeming with bacteria. She kept a close watch, looking after everything, never letting the baby girl out of her sight. "The child was never out of my arms for more than an hour; even at night, I held her hand through the bars of her crib, I watched over her constantly, I thought my gaze could protect her, I was confident I would keep her safe, I was totally convinced of it. But then she lost so much weight in just a few days. And she was so little to begin with. All I could see was the precipice, the abyss. I watched her go under, her hands limp at her sides, her damp curls, I could tell she was dying before my eyes. I screamed. I screamed for hours, day after day. My mother was there. They wanted to stop me, stop me from breaking the windows, from throwing myself out. I wouldn't stop. I screamed and howled through Manon's last breath but she died in silence, without a sound. She wasn't even a year old. Do you hear me, Georges? Your daughter! Our child. She died in my arms, her tiny, blue body in my arms. I beg you, don't leave me. I wouldn't survive it, don't leave me again, please!"

In two years, Georges had lost his work, his identity, his friends, his nation, his mother, his great love, and now his daughter.

Georges and Choute spent two weeks at the Lion d'Or, according to the dates on Hartog's postcards. Motherhood and sorrow had changed Choute's body, made it more angular, revealed the outline of her ribs. His clothes were all too big for him. His trousers belonged to a man who had been well-to-do, an important gentleman with a rich man's belly. An arrogant man. He had come to think of himself as a permanent fixture, a monument. He had come to believe that his social status belonged to him, that he'd been born to it, that he was at home on Rue de Valois, at the Gobelins mansion, in the Princesse de Broglie's bedroom. Now, of course, there was no money for new clothes. He would have to make do with the hand-me-downs from his former self, his former bourgeois life. Every fortnight he had to punch a new hole in his belt. He had found his wife, Marcelle, to be a true companion in these long months of exile in Marseille. He had almost forgotten her completely. She laughed at his mildly smutty jokes, loved to hear him whistle, thrilled at his (now vanishingly rare) good moods. He had not yet taken the cigarette case that Choute had given him to the pawn shop, even though he could get enough for it to feed them all for weeks. He carried it with him everywhere like a talisman, like a pledge that he would someday return to his former life. The children learned to share their day-to-day existence with a father they had previously barely known. Their father who was no longer the elegant and exalted man he once was but now an exile in his own country. But he was also the father who cajoled and entertained, who could make history come alive and feel present like no one else, whose wit and erudition might still light up a room.

"He entered the room briskly and the whole class fell silent." (I am quoting from one of Georges' former pupils from the Lycée Janson de Sailly, in an homage preserved in *Georges Huisman par quelques-uns de ses amis*.) "He never forced his students to cram; instead, he enticed and dazzled them. During his lessons, those fifteen-year-old boys, who were on the cusp of young manhood and liked to act tough, suddenly felt like kids listening to a master storyteller."

For the first time in two years, Georges ate his fill in the dining room of the Lion d'Or, where there seemed to be no restrictions of any kind. How could two totally disconnected worlds and realities coexist so closely? Choute regained her appetite, too. The two castaways devoured each other. For those brief moments, all their hardships seemed to be behind them, the anguish of their journey all in the past.

Choute had money. Lots of money. Her fortune had thrived in the war; already a prosperous widow, her father's death had made her a fabulously wealthy heiress. Georges could marry her, she suggested. She would give him her name. He would be safe. They could go to England, or to the United States! Papa would go with them, while his two older brothers stayed behind to look after their mother. Carlu would find work for him. And anyway, the Allies would get to France at some point. It was only a matter of days, maybe weeks.

Choute was prepared to sacrifice almost everything for her great love. Everything she owned—her safety, her well-being, her future, her ambition—but not her pride. She would not wait in vain. She had Vergère to remind her of their romance, and their cat alone confirmed that she hadn't dreamed it all. Papa said no. (Right, Papa? At the center of this family chronicle, this composite of fact and fiction, is that "No" you never tired of recounting.) Never, not in a million years. His older brothers called their father a traitor, a scumbag. The delusional, treacherous plan wasn't spoken of again. The family fell silent. Choute didn't try to find Georges, didn't wait for his answer. She knew the moment they parted that he wouldn't come back. And Choute vanished completely. For all eternity, Choute disappeared from public records, from written accounts, from photo albums, from archival footage, save for that image of her back and her updo on the poster of the Cannes festival that didn't take place. I wish I could hold on to the seams of her dress, keep her from fleeing. Grab her ankles with both hands, wrap my arms around her knees, and beg her to stay. But Choute is a comet that can only be held in the fleeting glimmer of the imagination, that can only exist in fiction. *Fugitive parce que reine*—fugitive precisely because she was queen, to quote Proust, as I did for the title of my first novel, a book about my mother.

Following Georges' arrest and his mercifully brief detention at the Évéché prison in the fall of 1942, after the Allied landing in North Africa and the end of the free zone, the family settled in Vaison-la-Romaine under assumed names. Marseille had become too dangerous, roundups had intensified. Georges had to go into hiding. In Vaison, he joined a network of Resistance fighters in the medieval village of Rasteau, which brought him into contact with a farmwoman named Madame Duc—not exactly a duchess but worth a thousand of them—who allowed him to stay in her cellar until the Liberation. The correspondence she and Georges kept after the war revealed her incredible kindness and selflessness, despite the risks she ran. In response to a letter in which Georges bitterly recounted his fruitless efforts to be reinstated to his old Beaux-Arts job, she wrote compassionately: "Remember, dear Monsieur Huisman, on January 27 it will be exactly one year since we met in such trying circumstances. You came to my door one night, dripping with sweat. I have not forgotten. The worst days of your life were upon you. That nightmare is now over."

The Liberation took place in August 1944. Georges made his way back to Paris. As instructed by the local authorities, he went to the Claridge Hôtel on the Champs-Élysées. He is unlikely to have made use of the swimming pool in the basement, where a vaulted ceiling tiled in blue mosaic reflected the water. Was there something morbid about suddenly finding himself in such sumptuous surroundings? At least he wasn't at the Lutetia. Marcelle had returned to Paris a year earlier, as Georges was in hiding in Madame Duc's cellar, and had moved back to Rue d'Assas, this time to an apartment owned by the Catholic Church, where a charitable priest had discreetly offered assistance to the wife of the former directeur des Beaux-Arts and brilliant Chartist alum. Papa was enrolled at the

Lycée Henri-IV under his assumed name: Denis Antoine Henriquet. The school accepted students through an entrance exam, so he did not have to provide school transcripts, which did not exist under that name. That year, my father recalled paying frequent visits to his old, uneducated grandfather Hartog. One afternoon, he noticed that Apère, alone and confused, kept both his identity cards, the real and the false, in his jacket pocket, along with his yellow star, rolled up in a ball. Dumbfounded, he screamed at his grandfather, who had no idea why his teenage grandson was so angry. Papa grabbed the hateful items from Apère's pocket and ran to the nearest public toilet, where he burned the real identity card and threw the scrap of yellow fabric into a urinal.

Hartog died three years after the end of the war and was buried in the Valmondois cemetery alongside his beloved wife. Georges would not be reelected mayor. The Beaux-Arts administration was broken up into four separate departments, including a film division, which Georges coveted. Instead, the new government appointed him to the Conseil d'État, the highest rank in the civil service, the state body that also epitomized the legalization of anti-Semitism under the occupation. "So little for such a man!" One friend and colleague reported (in his eulogy, reproduced in *Georges Huisman par quelques-uns de ses amis*) that Georges was visibly overwhelmed with boredom in this position, exasperated by what he called its "administrative viscosity." He did make friends, though, as he seemed so prone to do. Through his camaraderie with René Cassin, he started to engage with the international Jewish community. He who had felt Jewish only by virtue of an insult now joined multiple associations and became a fervent Zionist. He supported the creation of memorials to the Holocaust. He participated in many radio programs, which I was able to listen to on the French archival streaming service. His voice carried the same fervor and exaltation I read in his speeches. And he lectured around the world, including in New York.

The Compagnie Générale Transatlantique had suffered heavy losses in the war. Two thirds of its fleet had been destroyed, including its crown jewel, the *Normandie*. And so Georges made the crossing not on the *Normandie* but on the *Île de France*, a floating emissary for the Art Deco style, designed by Jacques Carlu. The streamliner's grand foyer, with its perfectly symmetrical polygonal apertures and arched staircase, recalled the bridges of Paris. Gustave Louis Jaulmes's interiors for the dining room and the first-class salon were so similar to the furnishings and frescoes of the Palais de Chaillot that one could be forgiven for confusing them. One wall was adorned with a mural of a hunting scene at Fontainebleau. Georges kept a travelogue in a graph-paper notebook, which I had hurriedly photographed before leaving the attic in Valmondois. "I'm not sure I like to travel anymore. There comes a time in a man's life when he takes more pleasure in working his thoughts out on paper than in the vain distractions of external stimuli. But can one live and understand the times we live in without getting to America? Well then."

First day at sea. At eight a.m. precisely, he went to the dining room in his dressing gown. The crew had to explain that he was required to dress appropriately for meals. Never mind, he would eat in his cabin. The cuisine was of the highest quality. The liner was rightly known as a temple of French gastronomy. Compared to this floating palace, the *Massilia* was a torpedo boat, he wrote. Papa, conversely, remembered the *Massilia* as being as big as the *Titanic*.

"I feel like a fossil on this ship, where every passenger is a businessman. I, a mere civil servant who never knew how to 'make a buck.'" The grand political project of his generation, the vast moral enterprise of Léon Blum's socialism, was already obsolete by the mid-twentieth century. In the evenings, after dinner, he put on his best face and dove into board games, dancing, and attending film screenings. "My god these young people are so poorly dressed!" The only person he enjoyed talking to was a young Haitian returning to her island to open a beauty salon. Bedtime at 11:30 p.m. Seven days after they set sail, at dawn, the skyscrapers of Manhattan finally appeared on the horizon.

Georges summarized his observations on the fly in a series of eloquent adjectives: "Monstrous, gigantic, mind-bending, sprawling . . . uncanny impression of immensity beyond all human reckoning." And then the Statue of Liberty emerged through the fog atop her enormous pedestal, symbolically connecting New York to the City of Lights. At a dinner held at the famous restaurant La Grenouille, in midtown Manhattan, he met once again with the artists he had selected for the French Pavilion at the World's Fair of 1939. Harold Smith organized a banquet in his honor. "Remember that crazy storm at the Palm Beach in Cannes?"

In the years following the war, Georges also joined the world committee for the Memorial to the Unknown Jewish Martyr. And a little over a decade after its inauguration for the Universal Expo, on December 10, 1948, beneath the stage pediment designed by Évariste Jonchère, the Palais de Chaillot theater became the stage for the signing of the Universal Declaration of Human Rights, solemnly adopted by the United Nations in a plenary session. The United Nations' permanent headquarters in New York were yet to be completed, and Paris benefitted from a temporary waiver to host one of the key moments in the history of the modern world. The text represented a global extrapolation of the humanist principles of the French Revolution. It would become the model reference document for democracies worldwide, supporting the fiction that France had been one of them all along.

The Cannes Film Festival opened barely a year after the Allied victory. The alliance envisioned by Jean Zay, Georges, and others had come together at last. In an archival photo, Georges can be seen on the arm of the divine Michèle Morgan, back in Cannes with the film *La symphonie pastorale*, adapted from the novel by André Gide, in a role that earned her the Best Actress Award. The flags of nineteen nations fluttered over the Croisette. The beachfront outside the Grand Hôtel and the Carlton was studded with stars, while reporters and photographers captured their unprecedented glamour. Bathing suits in the day and ball gowns in the evening clearly demonstrated that peace had at long last been won. And with the glitz of one of the most spectacular events of the postwar years, France pulled off the tour de force of whitewashing its years of collaboration with the Nazi invader. Even as rationing persisted, the cinema and its dazzling power of propaganda and fantasy shone brightly above the ruins of a country divided and depleted, covering its trauma under a blanket of stardust. France had immediately regained its status as a global model in defense of the arts and human rights.

Georges, too, was depleted. Since the Liberation, life had lost its flavor. He found himself in a world that was no longer his. He wrote the following words a few days after his sixty-fifth birthday, sitting at his sun-drenched desk in Valmondois. The lilacs smelled lovely, and Louise's rosebushes had born new buds. "Last night, while taking a walk, I remembered a night in May 1944, when I was hiding at Madame Duc's outside Vaison-la-Romaine. I would go out at dark in her moonlit garden, filled with the scent of lilacs and peonies. I was filled with hope that night, that I would survive, that I would escape the Krauts, my heart buoyed by a boundless hope that I would work to build the new France." Instead, France had been butchered or straightjacketed by imbeciles and traitors, Georges added. He wallowed in his bitterness three more years. If there was no mention of Choute in his notebook, I suppose it was because—no, I have no idea why. I can hear her steps shuffling between the lines. In Madame Duc's garden, I can see Georges caressing the oxidized gold of his cigarette case at the bottom of his pocket, catching the scent of his sweet beloved in the night air, confident that they would be reunited one day.

Georges died just after Christmas 1957 of occluding gangrene; one leg had been amputated at mid-thigh, then the other had also been removed. In May of that year, still standing, but on failing legs and grimacing with pain, he had gone to the Cannes Festival one last time as a member of the tenth-anniversary jury composed of the first ten presidents, including Jean Cocteau. The festival had become a showcase of French culture. Georges' suffering was excruciating, but Cannes offered some glimmer of redemption, salvation, as if association with the festival might keep him from oblivion.

Papa often spoke of his father's agony in his final hours, his body mutilated and shriveled in his hospital bed, a trapeze bar hanging from a bracket overhead. His efforts to pull himself up were futile. "It was terrible to see him like that!" Papa burst into tears as he remembered—heavy tears running down his withered, grizzled cheeks. My darling papa. I took his hand, a hand as gnarled as the roots of a tree under bare earth, and showered it with kisses, like an April rain that coaxes dandelions and daffodils from the ground at winter's end, a child's fantasy. At the very end, he was just one long, tortured death rattle, interrupted by a few incomprehensible words. He never spoke of Choute. Had not said one word about her since the spring of 1942. There was no way of knowing if he still thought of their love. Nothing remained to bear witness to it. No one knew what had become of her. Her castle in Trieux, the Château de la Roche-Jagu, was bequeathed to the department of Côtes-du-Nord one year after Georges' death, in 1958. One can visit it. One can take little girls on a tour of the property and tell them that a princess named Choute once lived there. Her mansion on Rue Jacob was sold and converted into luxury apartments. I believe Choute must have fled to Buenos Aires or to Dallas, somewhere grandiose and absurd, or somewhere worthy of televised dramatization. Or no, she must have settled somewhere with a sea view—in Rio, in Goa, or in Dakar, by my mother's ashes.

It could only have been Choute who had discreetly buried Vergère while the war was still raging, while Georges was hiding in Madame Duc's cellar. She buried the cat beneath an apple tree at the foot of the garden of Valmondois. One day a child would come upon the small skeleton while digging a secret tunnel to the house.

Christmas 1957 came and went without presents, without a tree, without a party, not even for the little little ones, who had been more or less left to their own devices. They called Georges "Apère," like Hartog. Scenes from the First World War haunted the dying man. His phantom limbs itched dreadfully, but there was nothing there to scratch but absence, lost time. He thought he was in a biplane, doing aerial acrobatics over Japan.

There was no national funeral. Georges Huisman is not buried in the Panthéon. A narrow alley in Valmondois is named after him. It leads to his house, or that of his grandson, the mayor. I gently placed Papa's "bible" on his chest. The book was in tatters, coverless, held together by loose threads. It looked as if it would fall apart at the lightest touch. I had found two bookmarks inside: an old, dirty Band-Aid, and a photo of Georges at around fifty, a broad smile on his lips, his hair tousled by the wind. Behind him one could see mountains.

When I left the Valmondois attic, securing the trapdoor behind me, I was unsure what I would do with the manila envelope, the letterheads, or the pictures on my iPhone, but I felt as if this smaller, haphazard archive both connected me to the past and lightened its burden—as if history, national and personal, had become a weightless stack of papers and images. I walked over to Bruno's car, amazed to see him holding an enormous, antiquated key to lock the squeaky gate. He and his wife drove me back to Paris. I took one last photo of the plaque at the corner of the former Rue du Verger, now named after our ancestor: Georges Huisman, Mayor of Valmondois from 1932 to 1940, founder of the Cannes Film Festival, etc. To make conversation, I asked Bruno what was his favorite route when he drove back to Paris. "Well, it depends where you want me to drop you, but typically, I'd take the Porte Maillot. That would get us to Avenue de la Grande-Armée all the way to the Place de l'Étoile, then down the Champs-Élysées to cross the Seine. But from l'Étoile, if we were going to Papa's, I'd take Avenue Kléber to the Trocadéro, then Avenue Paul Doumer, then turn left. Remember Avenue Mozart is one-way . . ."

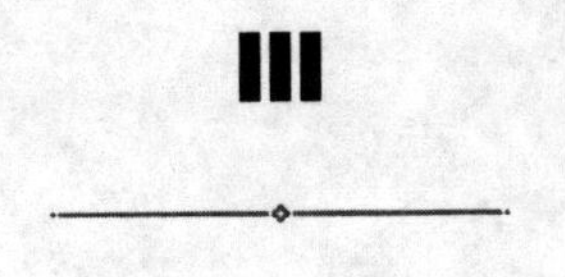

Around the time of my father's funeral, a new ad campaign took over the streets of Paris. Hundreds of posters materialized seemingly overnight—under every bus shelter, across every public billboard. The ad, from the New York tourism board, showed the Empire State Building lit up against a purple sky, with a slogan written across in bright white all caps: "NEW YORK CITY MISSES YOU TOO." COVID restrictions made it nearly impossible to travel internationally, especially to the United States. Who could this lavish marketing folly be addressed to? I felt cruelly picked on. During my entire adult life, I had never been away from the Manhattan skyline for so long. One day, waiting for the bus, I came face-to-face with this image of New York's iconic monument and realized how much I missed the city's geography, what to me amounted to a place of selfhood: I missed it viscerally, physically. I pictured myself exiting the automated doors of JFK's Terminal 1. I could smell that awful mix of asphalt and exhaust and hot dogs and garbage and ocean wind. Its stench grabbed me by the throat, with the overpowering force of a lover's arms. Arms that reeked of sweat, stale cigarettes, bad breath—no matter. They were the arms I loved.

I sat down on the bench beneath the bus shelter, despondent, tears streaming down my face. It was pouring rain, and I was grateful for it. I was living in exile in my mother country.

My father had died eight months after our move to France, in the heart of winter—"the heart of a winter," an overwrought phrase that nevertheless lodged in my chest. As the season changed, the beauty of spring in the French countryside only further articulated my sorrow. Next to the vermillion roses and carmine poppies, my puffy, dark-circled eyes and sallow skin made me look actually ill. My dear friends Iris and Ada were worried about me. Nothing seemed to cheer me up. We were on semi-lockdown once more. Meaning there were restrictions on how far one could go beyond one's home. My friends offered to get me a fake travel authorization to join them in Marseille. France required official paperwork during lockdowns for people to travel within the country. "Think of it as a doctor's note!" said Iris. "You've got to take a break, *Chouchou*. I'm not even kidding, it's like vital at this point." Three dots on my screen told me she had something to add. But she didn't. I pulled on a thread sticking out of a hole in the knee of my jeans. "OK," I replied. Heart emoji. The few clothes I had packed on our move from New York had become loose and baggy. Elsa had given me a pair of vintage jeans, and these became my uniform. Dressing up was something I had done for my father. There was no point to it any longer. I was suddenly aged; my hair had grayed all of a sudden. I had no idea how to go on.

All my life, my girlfriends had always been there to help me recover my sense of self when I got too lost. Despite having left France so many years earlier, and in spite of family life and romantic attachments, we had remained as inseparable as the teenagers we once were. Iris had become a film editor; Ada was a director. I was a writer in mourning, chasing a ghost.

Iris and Ada had recently become artistic collaborators, completing a film together before COVID arrived. Neither had asked for my opinion at the time, but had they done so, I would surely have told them it was a bad idea to work together. Each of them cared as much about their friendship as their art. Now Iris was set to edit Ada's first feature film. To make matters worse, Ada's project was an experimental film, totally unpitchable. It was a fantasy, loosely based on a book by James Baldwin and an obscure historical event: in 1944, in Thiaroye, a suburb of Dakar, a group of Senegalese Tirailleurs—the name given by the French army to the African infantrymen—were assassinated by the French colonial police after the Tirailleurs staged a protest demanding their promised wages. Ada had translated this historical event into a North African present—young men constructing a futurist tower in downtown Dakar were having their wages withheld by the project's bosses. The young men, in a hopeless, impulsive move, decided to embark on a dinghy to seek a better life in Europe. They all died at sea within days, only to return as spirits inhabiting the bodies of their former girlfriends, who rose at night, their eyes gone entirely white, to terrorize the rich developer.

After street casting all over Dakar, Ada had found her lead actress sitting on a stoop, zoning out. She was seventeen, didn't speak French, and was a genius. With her star on board, Ada managed to get her movie made, her barebones crew shooting mostly at night, as if in a long collective dream. Film distributors had had a hard time imagining how the movie would sell—or "find its audience"—until it was selected for the 2019 Cannes Film Festival. At the award ceremony, no one had skimped on glitter. Ada, Iris, the two female producers, and the complete cast glowed on the red carpet with heroic insolence. Their very presence looked like a fuck-you to all the assholes who had told them the movie would never get made. I had watched the award ceremony on my phone, from my couch in Brooklyn, on a Saturday afternoon, below the portrait of Georges. At that time, the very notion of COVID was still inconceivable. The girls were pretending to be ponies, taking turns riding on each other's backs. "Someone's going to get hurt! I don't want to hear any whining!" I shouted. Sissi cried, in jest, crushed under her big sister's weight, laughing hysterically. The evening was drawing to a close. On my tiny screen, there was only one prize left before the Palme d'or.

I had also ended up working on the film, late in the process, in its editing phase. Ada wanted a voice-over to accompany the last sequence of the movie—a dreamy love scene. She hadn't figured out what the voice-over would say; she had imagined a poem, a poem she felt she knew; she could hear it in her head but not quite make out the words, and she couldn't find it in any book. She had debated writing it herself, but the movie was almost done, the editing almost finished, and she still had nothing. "Couldn't you write it?" Iris had asked me. "That would be incredible!" Ada had added. I didn't bother telling them I wasn't a poet. The sequence would have the words unfurl on screen as they were spoken in Wolof, since the movie, wherever it was shown, would be subtitled in either French or English. Ada asked me to give it a try. As a starting point, she offered me a line from Derek Walcott: "sunlight on the seafloor." I watched the scene more than twenty times on my laptop, before, suddenly, entire paragraphs appeared before my eyes. I typed them out and sent them to Ada and Iris. Precisely, said Ada, they were precisely the lines she'd had in her head the whole time. I had dredged them up from her imagination. Yes, it was magic—it was crazy, really—but none of us was shocked. We were on our topic. We were one with our dead. If the supernatural visited only those who welcomed it, my hospitality had been confirmed many times.

Ada had been the first Black woman to ever enter the official selection of the Cannes Festival. Her films are militant, experimental, and unapologetically hybrid; her art makes no attempt to respond to the pressures of the marketplace. But explanations on the inner workings of the arthouse film industry would have to wait for another time: "What's *impossible*, Maman?" had asked the girls, befuddled. "What? Tell us! What's going on?" I had leaped off the couch and started screaming that it was *pas possible*, that it was *impossible*. "We won!" I yelled, pulling them into my arms, squeezing them hysterically. "I can't fucking believe it, they won!" Looking confused, and alarmed, the girls asked me once more: "What, Maman? And why are you crying?" The Palme d'or. How could I explain what it meant? "*Mes amours*, I'm sorry you can't understand, but it's wild, it's totally wild, it's historic, it's a game changer, it's so incredible." Ada had been the first Black woman to ever be nominated and the second woman in the history of the festival to win the Palme d'or. The prize would open all sorts of doors for her, and wherever she went from that day on, she could expect a red carpet to be rolled out beneath her feet.

There they were, onstage in Cannes, through my screen. At the festival my father always insisted that his father alone founded, Iris was wearing an off-the-shoulder vintage Saint Laurent dress that had belonged to my mother, in black crêpe printed with white butterflies. Iris responded to my dozens of messages with a call from the ceremony on her way to the after-party: She couldn't stop laughing. She was so giddy, she kept repeating on a loop that it was crazy, it was so crazy, and however gorgeous Ada was in the sequined dress Chanel had lent her, my mother's dress was even more beautiful, and they missed me, and she was so proud, so proud of all of us. "Okay, *Chouchou*, I'm going to hang up now because I have to party and I'll start crying if we keep talking." "Yes, you go now. Drink lots of champagne. I'm going to get some myself to toast you with my girls."

Ada, Iris, and I had traveled to Dakar together, a decade earlier. Senegal was Ada's father's country, and it was where my mother had settled in the last years of her life. Maman had wanted her ashes to be scattered there. Ada and Iris would come along to accompany Elsa and me in our grief, in a state of distress that rendered us incapable of exercising anything like judgment. We had improvised a ceremony, in a place whose customs we were ignorantly violating. In addition to Thiaroye, Ada's movie was shot at night in the neighborhood known as Les Almadies, on the beach where we had offered my mother's remains to the elements.

In the spring following my father's funeral, Iris and Ada didn't wait for my permission to get me a fake travel document to meet them in Marseille. They sent me a picture. "See you there," said the caption on our WhatsApp thread. The plan was to stay at an old guesthouse in Marseille called Hôtel Peron, a 1930s building that had recently been acquired by an English luxury brand that planned to turn it into a resort. They wanted to film the house before its destruction, which was of course described as its renovation, to use it as an illustration of the social fracture that defined our era. This modest yet cozy guesthouse dated from the time of the Front Populaire's labor laws—paid leave, free vacations for all. It was about to become an international hangout for the jet-set. "Nobody gives a fuck about the past," cried Ada when she described the project to me over drinks on a Parisian terrasse—she was on a Parisian terrasse, I was at home on FaceTime. "Nobody gives a fuck about the collective anymore, nobody even bothers to pretend, and the worse is that history didn't teach us shit." After what looked like her third mojito, she started mistaking me for the hostile hordes of assholes she was trying to convince. "I'm with you, *Chouchou*!" I unmuted myself to tell her. (*Chouchou*, our collective pet name, distributed across us indiscriminately.) I didn't think she could hear me, so I nodded my head in what I hoped would express solidarity. ARTE had offered some financing. I could help them think through the structure, they suggested.

My father had spent two years of the war in Marseille, and my mother had lived there for seven years, with her first husband, before meeting my father. I only knew the city from their intersecting and unreliable narratives, thirty years apart, and through the touristy images of the press. Tom had encouraged me to go join my friends. Iris was right, he said, I had to take a break from mourning. I felt guilty leaving him alone with the girls in the middle of a dump, as Papa had so often described Fontainebleau. French bureaucracy had outdone itself during COVID: one had to fill out a form to send kids to school and another to actually physically transport them there and back. There were different, specific forms for grocery shopping, and yet more to get gas. "You think you can manage?" I asked Tom. Was I insulting his French? he suggested in response.

His French was very impressive, I assured him, it was just all the byzantine administrative stuff. We'll be fine, he said. "*Ça va aller*, just fine!" he insisted. "Girls, tell Maman we'll *aller*! Tell your mother you love her."

Officially, Hôtel Peron had already been closed for many months, but the owner had given Ada and Iris a triple room, a sort of fancy dormitory with three twin beds and matching nightstands, a large wardrobe, and a tiny desk. The lime-green bathroom had a sink color-coordinated with the tiling, vintage faucets, and a claw-foot tub like Bonne-Maman's in L'Arcouest. Uniquely positioned at an angle along the corniche, the hotel had a spectacular view of the sea—the best view in Marseille, boasted the website, which looked like it hadn't been updated since the early days of the internet. Ada and Iris were housed for free, and the owner herself served them breakfast in the dining room. They had been there for a week by the time I was to join them. They had sent me dozens of pictures: from the macramé curtains and the wainscotting, I extrapolated scents of cleaning products mixed with fresh bread and dust. I would take my computer so I could work on my own memorial project while my friends were filming. My writing was stalling. I was obsessed with my grandfather's story, and its contradictions, but couldn't figure out what to do with any of it. This hotel had been built in his time. He could have stayed there. He could have met Choute there. I felt the spectral presence of this mythic family figure follow me in my dreams, on my walks. I felt constantly shrouded in it, *it* being not him exactly but the nebulous narrative that surrounded him. His life appeared as a poorly lit shadow puppet show: its contours illegible, the light too dim or the light sources too scattered to make sense of it. In contrast, my parents' ghosts were unmistakably sharp, like holograms of themselves. I could conjure them easily—but why conjure them, when they kept showing up uninvited?

Social distancing was still a thing. For the most part, Ada and Iris weren't concerned. We would share a room, three stories above the owner's apartment on the parlor floor. She was old and unvaccinated by choice: We would do our best to keep her safe. "Your obedience prolongs this nightmare," said a graffiti protesting the state-mandated lockdown along the railroad tracks from the window of my train with nonstop service to Marseille-Saint-Charles. I was halfway across France when I received a call from Iris. It could only be bad news. Talking on the phone was something our generation had outgrown and only resorted to under exceptional circumstances, for emergencies or life events. "Everything okay, *Chouchou*?" I asked. As required on French trains, I took the call from the vestibule between cars, duly masked. "Actually, we've got a bit of a situation," Iris replied.

Madame Peron was the name of the owner of the hotel, the granddaughter of the original founder. Selling this place was a tragedy she wasn't prepared for. She didn't have a choice, she had explained to Iris and Ada. The maintenance, her children who didn't want to take over the business, the financial pressure, fatigue, the extreme fatigue of these last few years, her old age. She was vehemently anti-vaccine. The pandemic had destroyed all she had ever owned, all she had ever worked for. She was convinced it was all a ploy, the virus merely an evil scheme to control people like her—modest, hard-working people—and then she got sick. "The thing is," said Iris on the phone as I held on to the steel rail on the train, thinking I should remember to sanitize my hands, "she doesn't seem to want to get tested or even see a doctor. She described her symptoms, and it's textbook COVID, and bad, really bad. Ada and I have obviously been exposed. You really shouldn't come." I reminded her that I was on the train. "Right, shit, of course. Well, I don't know what to tell you."

After the Palme d'or, Ada's film had been shortlisted for an Oscar in the best foreign film category. Hollywood producers had lined up to make her all sorts of offers. Instead, she'd decided to pursue a self-produced documentary on an old hotel in Marseille. Nevertheless, she was in high demand, and she couldn't just sit around and wait for Madame Peron to recover. Iris had postponed another job to help out Ada on this trip, but she could still get it back on track. They were both single, childless, untethered. In short, they were leaving. The triple room was mine to keep if I wanted to stay, and they hoped not to contaminate me. We barely had time to give each other air hugs in front of the hotel. "You sure you'll be okay?" they asked. Grief was infantilizing. Everyone treated me like a child. An orphaned child. "Of course I'll be fine." Iris made me promise to call her if I got too sad. "I'll text you tonight in any case," she added, handing me her key.

Don't you just want to come back?" Tom asked me. "It doesn't sound like a great place to hang out." There were places I'd been meaning to check out in Marseille, I insisted. I wanted to visit the building where my father had lived, the high school where he had been enrolled, see the Old Port, walk down the Canebière. Get a feel for the city. I was looking for a way into my story. Perhaps Marseille would give me clues, or metaphors. I had started wondering whether Papa hadn't invented Choute to allow his absent father to have preferred his little boy, his family, to a maddeningly gorgeous duchess. The choices his father had made had eluded him then. When Papa reinterpreted them, decades later, his own life experiences had gotten in the way. I was aware that it was just as impossible for me to draw a portrait of my parents distinct from my own emotions, my own trajectory, my own beliefs.

And so I found myself alone in my room in a condemned hotel with a breathtaking sunset view, next to two empty beds. I gave up on dinner. I had half a sandwich leftover from the train ride, but I wasn't hungry. I felt so weary suddenly. Tom put the girls on the phone on FaceTime. I showed them the sea, and the child-sized bathtub. They asked me who the two extra beds were for. "For you!" I replied. "And what about Papa? Where will Papa sleep?" Good question. "We'll just have to snuggle very tight." We laughed, imagining all the different ways the four of us could sleep in three twin beds. Dusk had repainted the room bright pink. Ada and Iris had obviously not trained in the military or in the hospitality industry. Their beds were a mess. I chose the one that was still neatly made, with a washed-out yellow blanket folded on top. I was going to sleep. All that was left to do was sleep. Six days in a row if necessary. I was exhausted.

"Whose beds are these?" I asked myself in the middle of the night. My first thought was that they must be my daughters', my two beautiful girls who I so loved watching sleep, their little fists pressed against their temples. Wait, no. I was also in a single bed. Didn't I have a partner? Didn't my girls have a father? Of course they did. Tom was his name. I had even married him. Jesus, married life. These beds must be my parents' then. Papa and Maman, side by side in their hospital beds, where I had looked after them so often. "Let me help you sit up," I would offer. One would kiss my arm. The other would grab me by the shoulders to embrace me. Wait, no. My parents were dead. Remember, stupid, your parents are dead. They're all dead. Parents, grandparents, uncles, brothers. God, please help me. I could see them all distinctly, all the ghosts, and then the two of them. Papa, Maman. There they both were, in their single beds, staring at me. Please, I beg you, please go away. Please leave me alone, please go for good this time. Haven't I written down your stories so you could rest? I could see my mother in her stretcher at the morgue; I could see my father in his open casket. The beds of my dead. Help, for heaven's sake. I got up abruptly. I pushed away the nightstands, I pulled the beds together, I stacked the mattresses on top of one another, and I toppled the second bed frame next to the side of the first one as if I were erecting walls, a separate room with a door I could slam shut. There were dust bunnies on the floor. There were seagulls outside. Just shut up. Please just shut up now.

I fell back asleep. I dreamed that I had started smoking again. I was trying to light a cigarette with a blowtorch. Despite the size of the flame, it wasn't lighting up. I was sucking on the cigarette compulsively, the torch inches from my face, to no avail. I suddenly realized that I was wearing a white dress, the kind I hadn't even worn at my wedding, a beautiful gown with big muslin ruffles moving in the wind. I kept trying to pull on this damn cigarette as the wind picked up, blowtorch in hand, but it still wasn't working, I couldn't get the cigarette to light, but then my dress caught on fire and I was engulfed in flames. All the accounts had described Georges as a compulsive smoker. That cigarette always dangling from his lips in photographs, in paintings. Toward the end of his life, giving up his

Gitanes had been a nightmare for him. I thought of the hero of Albert Camus's *The Stranger* in his prison cell. I thought of the hero of Thomas Mann's *The Magic Mountain* in his sanatorium. Memories from novels seemed more real than my life. I looked at the strange installation of bedframes I had made in this borrowed room in the middle of the night. It seemed a fitting representation of my current state of mind.

I stepped out onto the balcony and stood there for a while. There were ferries bound for Corsica or Algeria. I walked out of the hotel and went along the corniche. I found a sidewalk café and tobacco shop called Monument. I bought a pack of Gitanes blondes. I sipped my espresso from a paper cup and lit a cigarette on the sidewalk. There was indeed a monument across from the shop. A monumental arch rose on a promontory above the sea. In front of the arch was a statue of a woman, also monumental, draped in a sort of toga, arms held to the sky, her pose and oxidized green patina strangely reminiscent of the Statue of Liberty. The cigarette had made me nauseated and dizzy. I should eat something, I thought, then ignored the thought. I paid for my coffee and walked toward the monument. It was a monument to the dead of WWI, like so many across France. This one was dedicated to the "heroes of the Orient and distant lands." It was signed Gaston Castel, the man who had housed my father and his family in 1940. It looked as if the arch was facing west, toward the sunset I had seen from my room the night before. If the arch was meant to address the former French colonies, it was pointing in the wrong direction. In fact, it was facing New York. For me, the monument triangulated grief: New York, Dakar, Marseille.

As I wandered in this familiar unfamiliar city, I found the building where my father had lived during the war, impasse Croix de Régnier. The Lycée Thiers was a few blocks away. Gaston Castel's own home had become a museum. I could come back to visit it. For now, it was closed. At number 5, to the right of the entrance door, a little heart had been etched into the stone wall. To the left of the buzzer, there was another heart, this one red, stenciled. Underneath, in a childlike handwriting in black marker, I read "MAMAN."

"I'll come home soon," I told the girls on FaceTime after a week. I had taken up smoking again with a vengeance. "You're smoking, Maman?" asked George. "No, not really," I replied. "Isn't it bad for you?" she continued. I made a vague hand gesture, like I was brushing away her question, or my cigarette smoke. George said she didn't like that I smoked. "I understand, *mon amour*, but it's not your problem to fix." The girls had made tremendous progress in French. Their school also offered chorus and violin lessons. Georges, in his famous speech delivered at Salle Pleyel, had underlined the importance of musical education for the intellectual and artistic development of the nation's pupils. He would have been proud of his great-granddaughters. I had developed a routine in my Marseille sanatorium, my cell. Nobody seemed to care about my comings and goings. I had no idea whether the owner's case of COVID was better or if she had ended up in the hospital. I hadn't run into a single soul in this hotel since my arrival. "When are you coming back?" asked Tom. "Soon. I'm not sure yet. I still have a few things to do." "Like what," he asked, reasonably enough. I didn't have a clue.

The weather was beautiful. I could at least have gone to the beach. I had even packed a bathing suit, at Ada's and Iris's insistence. I had never spent an entire week away from my daughters; I couldn't remember the last time I had been away from family emergencies or domestic chores for so many days; when in my life I hadn't been called on to take care of someone. Even Elsa hadn't been in touch. I hadn't told her that I was in Marseille, to avoid dealing with her questions. Since our mother's death, which she had announced to me over the phone, I braced myself for the worst every time she called. I knew she did, too. Strangely, our father's death hadn't changed a thing. If I worried about my girls, it was somewhat at a remove, a muted feeling. It was a relief not to deal with their messes, not to worry about meals, not to listen to their bickering. Not to have to negotiate with their father about who would empty the dishwasher. Dispense with the wretched mediocrity of daily life, Papa would have said. Its boredom! I heard Maman sigh. Except I missed my girls horribly. I missed their cuddles in my bones. Never mind. I would learn to live without them. One had to make sacrifices. I was just fine where I was, alone, with my twin beds turned into a barricade. I shouldn't have had children, I told myself again, as I scrolled through pictures of them on my phone. I had been a devoted daughter, yet I was a flawed mother. I hoped my daughters wouldn't worry about me the way I had worried about my mother.

Late one night in Paris—it must have been before the girls were born—I got into a cab whose driver started making conversation. Perhaps he was trying to stay awake; I remember it was very late. He launched into an elaborate story about how his daughter had recently had surgery for an ingrown toenail. It was a simple medical procedure but very painful—well, still less painful, he added, than the agony the poor girl was subjected to daily. Even with shoes two sizes above her own, her poor toe was constantly sore and swollen. We were passing the statue of La Fayette along the cours La Reine.

Unfortunately, he continued, the surgery was pretty invasive, aesthetically speaking, and she just won't have very pretty feet, he said; she may never wear open-toed sandals. The surgery consisted of cutting down the big toenail—the hallux, maybe you've heard of hallux valgus? he interjected—or nearly amputating it, so that it's down to a tiny piece of nail, the size of a little fingernail. "The size of a baby tooth?" I asked. "Yes, sure, about that size." A few hours later, I was meeting my father for lunch at a restaurant. I asked him if he had ever had an ingrown toenail, if that explained his deformed big toe. What a bizarre question, he commented, and not the best topic for working up an appetite, but yes, he went on, indeed he had. He had undergone a similar surgery to the one I had just heard about, when he was ten years old. "You mean during the war?" I asked. "Ah maybe, yes, you must be right, it must have happened during the war," he replied casually. "I had many more serious illnesses in my life; I had peritonitis, and a hernia, and stents put into my arteries after my heart attack . . ." I reminded him I'd been there for that one. "Remember, Papa, it was Christmas, and we could see the Eiffel Tower shimmering like a Christmas tree from your hospital room." "Nothing as painful as that damn ingrown toenail," Papa continued. "How is it possible for such a tiny little piece of flesh to be so horribly painful? Incomprehensible. I was always deeply ashamed of my feet. They're so ugly, my my, abominable, just abominably ugly! Thankfully, my beloved darling, you didn't take after me. Your feet are lovely, little angel." String of kisses. "Speaking of which, those are nice shoes you're wearing! Did I buy them for you?"

I was brushing my teeth in my lime-green bathroom in Marseille, horrified at the number of lines on my forehead, when my phone rang. I didn't take the time to spit out my toothpaste. It was

Bruno. "Your girls are well? How's your work going?" His jocular tone settled my panic. I muted myself to rinse my mouth. "Everything okay?" I asked. "Yes, more than okay," Bruno replied. "In fact, I have great news! So you know that Valmondois is officially partnered with a village in Casamance, in Senegal? You didn't? Well, now you do. In any case, that's not why I'm calling, that's just the backstory, I can tell you about it some other time. Listen, the other day I had a meeting with the Senegalese woman in charge of the partnership. I mentioned Papa's library, our wish to donate it. She was fascinated by the quantity of books, amazed, really, and immediately thought it might be of interest to her cousin, who happens to be president of the Cheikh Anta Diop University in Dakar. You've heard of it? Very well. To make a long story short, the president wrote to me the same day. He told me that he had been introduced to philosophy through the *Vergez & Huisman*, that he thought of the name *Huisman* as that of a personal hero, the person to whom he owed his vocation, his whole career, really. He couldn't imagine a higher or more appropriate honor than to create a home for Papa's library in Dakar. We still have a few practical details to look over, like shipping, etc., but he promised to establish a reading room in Papa's name, with the kind of pomp that Papa would have certainly approved of. He added that this donation could allow him and his colleagues to create one of the most important philosophy libraries on the African continent. Hello? What's that? I couldn't hear you anymore. Well, no, that's all. Sensational, isn't it? I imagined you'd be moved. What did you say?"

"You think she'll be nice to him? Even just a little bit nice?" Elsa asked me in front of Papa's open coffin. "Maman, you mean?" I doubted it. "You think she's still mad at him?" my sister asked.

Wherever either of them is, I told Elsa, I hope they finally let go of their resentment. "I wish them peace, but knowing Maman . . ." As we organized the shipment of our father's library to Dakar—thirteen pallets of books, eight tons of paper—transported on a semi from Paris to Marseille and onto a cargo ship to Africa, Elsa and I wondered out loud whether Maman had something to do with it. Papa's dust-filled library was joining Maman's ashes.

In the final days of Papa's life, we took turns visiting him. Each of us would spend a few minutes or several hours, depending on what we could manage. Doctors had recommended that we interrupt all treatment. It was now a question of hospice care. Care in the absence of recovery. Waiting for death as painlessly as possible. I had taken my regional train, and the subway to Michel-Ange-Molitor, the green line. I had walked past the used bookstore on the corner of Rue Erlanger. Among the antiques on display in the window was a first edition of *Contes et légendes du Moyen Âge français* by Marcelle and Georges Huisman. I typed in the code and rang the intercom, under my maiden name, my father's name. My stepmother opened the door for me. She was taking the dog for a walk. I was relieved to see her leave us alone. My father's eyes didn't light up as I entered the room. They were half shut. He had trouble breathing. I sat on the stool next to his bed. I took his hand in mine. His weightless, shriveled hand. His breath turned to feeble, futile sips of air through his pursed lips, his toothless mouth. Late-afternoon sun filtered through the drawn curtains—that time of day again—specks of gold suspended in the room. I smoothed back his hair and kissed his temple, his cheek. "I love you, Papa *chéri*," I whispered in his neck. "I love you so much. May your journey be peaceful."

Acknowledgments

My gratitude goes to my editor, John Burnham Schwartz; to my agent, Susanna Lea, for her enduring faith in my work; to Hélène Serre de Talhouët for allowing me to fictionalize her research on my grandfather Georges Huisman; to Frédéric Maria for his constant encouragements; to Ben Lerner for our ongoing conversation.

Tatyana Franck, President of L'Alliance New York, has been a steadfast ally in my creative pursuits since I have joined her team. I am thankful to her personally, and to all of our colleagues, especially Louise Bertin, Chloé Dheu, Clémentine Guinchat, Anastassia Perfilieva, and Jake Perlin.

Tom, George, and Sissi: *Je vous aime.*